Life's What You Make It

Theresa Troutman

Lynette,
Make your life
an adventure!
Theresa Troutman

ACKNOWLEDGMENTS

Special thanks to my amazing editor, Amy Jackson.
Cover: Cover Designs by James, GoOnWrite.com

This book is dedicated to Rebecca Maxwell and Judy
Kopperman, who read this book in its many formats.
Your critiques and support is very appreciated.

Give Me Women, Wine and Snuff by John Keats – 1815

Part 1 - England 1985

Chapter 1 - The Boy Wonders

The bright sunlight peeked through the heavy burgundy curtains of the great room. Sebastian Irons felt the warmth of the sun on his face and squinted as he opened his eyes. For a moment, he wasn't even sure where he was. A quick glance around the room told him he was in Alistair's flat. He looked down at himself sprawled across the horsehair paisley sofa, wedged between Jemma and Astrid, the two leggy beauties he had picked up at the club last night. Jemma's messy blonde mane tickled his neck as she lay nuzzled in the nook of his shoulder. Astrid's legs were intertwined with his and her right arm was draped across his stomach. Sebastian's suit coat was crumpled up in a ball on the floor and his white shirt was unbuttoned and rumpled. He had no idea what had happened to his silk tie.

Across the room, he spied Colin Harris and his girl asleep on the chaise. Oliver Harris looked uncomfortable sleeping with his girl on his lap in the straight-backed chair, his feet propped on an Oriental chest. Sebastian was able to maneuver his wrist to read the time on his Rolex. It was noon. *Oh well*, he thought; he didn't feel like going to class today anyway.

He untangled himself from the girls and slowly stood up. A yawn escaped his lips as he stretched his arms above his head. Then he made his way to the breakfast room, where the smell of freshly brewed coffee beckoned.

Upon entering the room, he found Holmes, wearing a simple black suit and round spectacles, hovering over a tray of fresh fruit and warm croissants. "Ah, Lord Sebastian, good morning to you," Holmes greeted him.

"Good morning, how are you?" Sebastian asked while snagging a croissant.

"Very well, indeed," Holmes replied, handing Sebastian his coffee in a china cup along with two aspirin.

Sebastian sat down at the table. A copy of *News of the World* lay open to page two. "Quite a night you had there," Holmes commented, gesturing to the paper.

"Yes," Sebastian agreed, glancing at the photo of Colin, Oliver, Alistair, and himself stumbling out of The Chinaman Club with the girls draped on their arms. He closed the paper and downed his coffee.

"I laid out your clothes in Prince Alistair's dressing room when you are ready to freshen up." Sebastian spent most of his time at Alastair's flat, so Holmes made sure to keep a few of Sebastian's items on hand when he slept overnight.

"Thank you, Holmes. You take very good care of me. I don't deserve it."

"Nonsense!" he retorted. "You always were my favorite," he whispered with a wink.

Sebastian laughed. "You're a good man." He grabbed the silver coffee carafe and headed for the bathroom.

Sebastian stripped off his smoke-laden clothes and turned on the double-headed spa shower. He took one last sip of coffee before stepping into the marble enclosure. The hot water washed over him. It felt good and seemed to help the headache he was nursing from another heavy night of drinking.

When he finished showering, he dressed in a pair of starched khakis, a striped woven shirt and a lightweight, navy cashmere sweater. Sitting down at the dressing table, Sebastian picked up the ivory handled brush and tamed his damp brown hair. The image of the young man in the mirror, with his fair skin and pink blushed cheeks, was handsome. But something seemed foreign to him, almost as if he didn't recognize himself at all. He sat there for a long while staring back at his reflection. How many other seventeen-year-old men would sell their soul to the devil to live the life he led? He shook his head in disgust and pushed away from the table.

It was fun to kick back and blow off steam. That seemed to be all Sebastian had done this year. As the school year came to a close and the impending threat of Oxford University stood in the near future, all Sebastian wanted to do was forget—forget that his life was already planned out for him by his domineering mother, with little regard for his feelings; forget that he was destined to be the future president of Irons Electronics, whether he wanted a career in electronics or not.

The ticking clock brought him back to reality. He glanced at it and realized an hour had passed. It was time to get the rest of the group up and ready.

Holmes was still puttering about in the breakfast room. Everyone sat around the table poring over the gossip paper and generally ignoring the butler.

"Sebastian, what are we doing today?" Oliver inquired. Somehow the task of entertaining the group always fell upon Sebastian's shoulders.

"Patience, Oliver, patience," he chided. "Has Alistair made an appearance yet?"

"Not yet," Jemma answered.

He kissed her on the cheek. "Well, I shall have to wake him then." He grabbed the coffee carafe and two china cups. "Lads, go home and make yourselves presentable," he commanded. "Holmes, please take the girls back to their flats so they can pack."

"Where are we going?" Astrid asked, on the edge of her seat.

"I'm not telling." Sebastian flashed a knowing grin as he walked toward Alistair's room. "And don't over-pack. You won't need much clothing," he warned as he vanished from sight.

The heavy mahogany doors proved a challenge for Sebastian to open while holding the carafe and china. Once inside, he placed the items on the bedside table and walked over to the floor-length curtains. As suspected, Alistair and Penny were still asleep, dead to the world. Only Alistair could sleep through the clamor coming from the group, he mused, giving a great pull on the drapes to open them up. The bright afternoon sun streamed through the room like beams of light from a torch.

"Blue blood, get your arse out of bed. It's a beautiful day and I have a plan," he announced with a grand gesture of his right arm.

Penelope opened her eyes and sat up in bed, trying to pull the ivory silk sheet around her chest. Sebastian noted the delicate rise and fall of her breasts. Being a gentleman,

6

he handed her a cup of coffee and purposefully diverted his eyes.

"Thank you," she smiled up at him from the tangled sheets.

"You're welcome, Pen," he smiled back, kissing her on the cheek as his face brushed up against her silky straight, blonde mane.

Alistair rubbed his eyes as he sat up in bed, propping his back against the padded leather headboard. He put his hand through his floppy blond fringe to get the hair out of his eyes. "Why do you have to be so bloody charming?" he grumbled as he grabbed his own cup.

"I'm not royalty. I can't get by on my birthright," he responded. "All I have is my charm."

Alistair rolled his eyes. "Then why do you have to be so damned cheerful in the morning after a heavy night of drinking?"

"I'll have you know it's one o'clock in the afternoon," Sebastian corrected him, pointing to the ornate French clock on the mantel.

Alistair quickly grabbed his watch from the nightstand. "Bollocks! I'm supposed to be taking my English final," he groaned.

"Yes, I know. I'm missing the same exam, remember? We can buy them a library or something and I'm sure we'll get good marks," Sebastian reasoned.

Alistair laughed. "Irons, you are incorrigible. So what is this great plan of yours?"

"I think some fresh country air is in order—a place where the paparazzi can't find us."

Alistair took another sip of coffee. "What page?" It was a game they played to see who could garner the best gossip coverage in the London tabloid papers.

"Two."

"Only two?" Penny inquired with disappointment.

"I should think a picture of the four of us would warrant front page coverage," Alistair agreed.

Changing the subject, Sebastian said, "I'm driving Colin and Oliver. Holmes will bring the girls. I assume I'll see you there once you've gotten ready?"

"Yes, it will be nice to get away from the royal abode for the weekend." Windsor Castle was just around the corner from Eton campus.

Sebastian nodded. "I saw the flag." The flag flying over Windsor Castle signaled the Queen was in residence—in other words, party-free zone. "It's settled then. I'll see you there. Dinner is at eight o'clock sharp."

Sebastian stepped out into the glorious spring afternoon. He was glad he'd ditched school. The weather was perfect. The sky was an amazing shade of blue. The air was crisp and clear in his lungs. He decided to walk the two blocks back to his flat to collect his car so he could head to his family's country estate to prepare for his guests.

Sebastian planned out the weekend in his mind and made mental notes of the things he would need to phone ahead for. A few of his fellow Eton classmates, dressed in the traditional gray striped trousers, black vest and morning coat, waved hello from across the quad. Sebastian waved back. It was true: charm and wealth made him popular on campus and afforded him many acquaintances—many indeed—but few real friends, he ruminated. Alistair and Penelope were the only ones. The trio called themselves the Libertines. Colin and Oliver seemed to be incidental companions, who were more interested in partying and drugs than building a friendship. They always had a good supply of alcohol and cannabis, which Sebastian did enjoy.

He unlocked the front door of his flat and entered, throwing the keys on the vestibule table where they skidded to a halt just short of falling on the marble floor. Thumbing through the mail, he found nothing of great importance and tossed it next to his keys. Sebastian strolled into the lounge, grabbed the phone, and rang home. The butler dryly answered on the second ring.

"Monroe, I take it everyone will be away this weekend?"

"Yes, Lady Irons is in Paris. Your brother and sister are remaining in London," he replied.

"Brilliant." He smiled to himself. "I'm bringing a group of friends up for the weekend. Will you please tell Cook so he can prepare dinner for seven people and have three guest rooms made up?"

"Certainly, sir," Monroe replied.

"Thank you. I'll see you in a few hours."

Chapter 2 - This Charming Man

Sebastian collected Colin and Oliver an hour later. The twins threw their overnight bags into the boot of the silver Aston Martin and then hopped in the car. Colin took the front passenger seat; Oliver sat in the back. Turning sideways with his back to the door and his feet up on the seat, Oliver asked, "Anyone want a fag?"

They talked and smoked cigarettes on their hour-long drive into the countryside to the Irons' family home. When they pulled onto the long winding driveway, Colin and Oliver spied the large estate in the distance. "Not bad," they agreed in unison. It was their first time to the house and they seemed genuinely impressed—for it wasn't a mere house, it was a castle. It had been in the Irons' family for over two hundred years. To Sebastian, it was simply the place he was raised. But on days like this, he relished having the place to himself.

Sebastian laughed. "It's not mine. It's my mother's. So behave yourselves and do your best to keep me out of trouble."

"Oh, Sebastian, trouble is our middle name," Oliver reminded him.

"Yes," Sebastian sighed, "and the best birthday present you could give me is to stay out of trouble this weekend so I may avoid a long lecture from my mother next week."

"It's your birthday. Why didn't you tell us? We didn't get you anything!" Oliver exclaimed.

"I didn't invite you to get presents," Sebastian replied.

"No worries," Colin jumped in, "I have something right here for later." He grinned, patted the left breast pocket of his jacket.

Sebastian turned off the car engine. One of the uniformed servants met him at the door of the car, opening it for him before he had the chance to grasp the handle. He looked at the man and said, "Good afternoon. Please take Colin and Oliver's bags to their rooms." The servant bowed and went about his work.

Sebastian turned to the brothers. "Lads, make yourselves at home. I need to check in on someone special. I'll meet you in the drawing room in an hour."

Oliver raised an eyebrow. "Don't tell us you have another girl stashed here?"

Sebastian flashed a smile as he ascended the old stone stairs. He opened the brass handled wooden door and entered the castle without answering Oliver's question.

Sebastian bounded up the back spiral staircase, taking the steps two at a time until he reached the third floor. He found the door he was looking for from a lifetime of practice and gently knocked.

"Come in," a female voice beckoned from inside. He opened the door and stepped into the room. "Sebastian, what a lovely surprise!"

"Hello, Nanny," Sebastian greeted her with a kiss on both of her lightly creased cheeks.

She was a wonderful woman, seventy years young. Her delicate gray hair was pinned up in a chignon. The small wire frame glasses she wore helped her see the knitting pattern she was diligently working on in her lap.

Sebastian adored her. She was the only one who truly cared for him. She raised him, taught him. To Sebastian, she was his real mother.

"Get us some tea, love," she said, nodding her head toward the tea trolley near the fireplace. Although it was a warm day outside, she kept a small fire going. He followed her request and handed her the first cup. "What are you doing here? I thought you had an exam today."

"I decided not to take it," he replied, awaiting her motherly chiding.

"Sebastian, you cannot get by on just your good looks and charm. One day they will fade and you need something up here to fall back upon," she reminded him, pointing to her temple with her long, thin index finger.

"I know you're right, Nanny, but it's such a beautiful day," he reasoned, hurt from the scolding he knew he deserved.

"My dear boy, you'll have many more beautiful days in your lifetime. If you slack off too much, there will be consequences to be paid." She paused for a moment; Nanny could never stay angry with him for long. "Well, I am happy to see you. How long will you be staying?"

"Until Sunday. I've brought some friends up for the weekend."

"Will the Prince be here?" she inquired, letting the subject of Eton fall to the wayside.

"Yes,"

"Oh, good, I do like him. You must tell him to stop in and say hello."

"Absolutely," replied Sebastian, glad for the change in tone of the conversation.

They talked for a half hour. Sebastian regaled her with stories of his time at Eton. Nanny talked about the books she was reading and *EastEnders*, her favorite TV show. The time went by so quickly whenever he was with her. The clock on the mantel rung the hour and he realized he had to get back to his friends. "I must be going, Nanny. Sorry to cut this short, but we'll have more time this weekend for visiting."

"Of course. You have guests to attend to."

When Sebastian was young he would inadvertently call her 'Mummy.' Nanny made sure to nip that habit in the bud and reminded him his mother was Lady Lily Irons. Sebastian disagreed; however, arguing the point with Nanny got him nowhere. So he devised a secret phrase just for her. Of course, she could not refuse. He leaned over and gave her a hug, whispering, "I love you more than anyone in the world."

"And I you," she would always reply.

Oliver and Colin were in the in the drawing room playing chess and drinking Guinness. Sebastian found chess an odd choice to turn into a drinking game. It wasn't the quickest game to play if the goal was to get inebriated. "Have the girls arrived yet?" he asked.

"Yes, they did, while you were mysteriously gone. They're freshening up," Colin replied.

"Which will undoubtedly take an hour or more," Oliver interjected.

The girls—Jemma, Astrid, Claire, and Jade—eventually joined the lads in the drawing room, casually dressed in skirts and polo shirts. Sebastian would never understand why it took so long for a woman to primp. He laid his magazine on the coffee table, announcing, "How about a game of croquet?"

"Oh, yes, that will be splendid," Jemma agreed.

"Especially if there is champagne," Claire chimed in.

"Because playing when you're sober just isn't any fun," Colin teased his girl before kissing her hard on the lips.

"Then it's settled," Sebastian announced, leading the troupe to the vast back garden.

Sebastian watched his friends having a better time drinking than actually playing croquet. As the drinking progressed, the game became wilder. It was clear there would be no winner. They were having too much fun laughing at one another's attempts to get the wooden balls through the wickets, as they tended to go in the wrong direction with each successive swing—at one point becoming aloft and glancing off a window in the gardener's shed.

Astrid was failing miserably, too tipsy to effectively hit the ball. She threw her mallet at the ball instead and kicked her white tennis shoes off in frustration. She watched the projectiles fly over the bushes and the perfectly manicured grass, finally landing in a fountain, much to the amusement of the others.

Sebastian ignored the shoes, picked up her mallet, and came up behind her. He enveloped her in his arms and placed his hands lightly on top of hers to guide the shot evenly through the wicket where it gently tapped the ball sitting on the other side. "I don't think the shoes are your problem, Astrid," he whispered in her ear.

"Hmm, probably not," she replied, turning her head to look at him, "but I like this." She made sure to press her body closer into his.

"You're a very naughty girl," he whispered.

"Oh, you have no idea," she replied with a wicked grin.

Sebastian laughed, sweeping her up in his arms. "I think we need to get your shoes out of the fountain." He walked over to the fountain and dropped Astrid into the chilly water.

She sat there in shock, soaked head to toe, her wet hair matted against her head. The others laughed hysterically at her misfortune. Sebastian tried to walk away, but Astrid quickly gathered her senses and grabbed at his wrist, managing to dig her perfectly polished red nails into his skin just far enough to hold him, and she pulled him into the water with her. They embraced, both cold and wet, and laughed at themselves.

"All in!" Oliver delivered the battle cry. At once, shoes were shed and landed haphazardly in the general direction of the fountain as bodies ran at full tilt to the beckoning mêlée. It was instant mayhem; they were splashing and laughing, unaware Alistair and Penelope were watching from the patio.

"You've ruined my jumper," Sebastian proclaimed.

"I'll buy you another," Astrid replied.

"That's not necessary."

"I'm sure I can think of some way to repay—" Sebastian cut her off with a passionate kiss before she could finish her sentence. They were oblivious to the horseplay around them, locked in an embrace and their own thoughts.

Alistair and Penny walked down to the fountain holding a stack of folded towels. Alistair stepped up on the short stone wall of the fountain and cleared his throat. "Ahem. Ladies and gentlemen, dinner shall be served in precisely one hour. I expect you will all be presentable at that time and properly dressed for the meal." Oliver reached for his arm to pull him into the fountain, but Alistair was too quick and jumped down to the ground, throwing a plush white cotton towel in Oliver's direction.

"You certainly know how to throw a party," Alistair complimented, handing the last towel to Sebastian.

"All in a day's work, blue blood." He patted Alistair on the back, trying not to dampen his friend's dry shirt.

Sebastian and his friends gathered in the formal dining room at eight o'clock. During the course of the meal, Sebastian enjoyed listening in on bits of conversation between his guests. He joined in when a topic interested him, but mostly sat back and ate the scrumptious meal that the cook had prepared.

After dinner they retired to the great room, where they smoked Dunhills and drank smooth brandy in large crystal snifters. The relaxing meal energized them. It appeared the night was still young as the clock on the mantel chimed eleven. Oliver pulled a clear plastic bag out of his jacket pocket. A white powder was nestled in the bottom corner of the bag. "Any takers?" he asked, waving the bag of cocaine in the air. Immediately several people gathered around him. "Do you have something to cut it on, Sebastian?"

"Use the decanter tray," he replied, extinguishing his cigarette in the ashtray.

Claire—after removing the decanter—placed the large rectangular tray, with its reflective bottom, in front of Colin. He cleaned it off with his sleeve and gently poured the drug on the tray. It flowed out of the bag into a neat pile. He took to task and cut and lined it for his friends and himself. "Sebastian, as you're the birthday boy—you first." Sebastian, already standing next to Colin by this point, knelt on the floor in front of the tray. He took the proffered twenty pound note, neatly rolled it into a straw shape, and snorted the first line. Leaning his head back, he closed his eyes and smiled. Then he turned and passed the note on to Astrid, who was eagerly awaiting her turn. Sebastian sat back onto the couch, waiting to let the drug's effect to overwhelm him.

Soon his temperature rose and his heart began to race as he entered the euphoric stage. He watched them take turns snorting the coke and felt oddly detached from the whole scene. It wouldn't be long before the full effect of the drug kicked in and he would feel energized, as if he could do anything.

The next morning Sebastian awakened to find himself naked in his own bed with Astrid and Jemma. His brain was slow to recall the details of his sexual escapade the night before, but from the looks of his crumpled bed linens and strewn pillows, it must have been intense. Sebastian didn't like the effects of coming down from the cocaine—the fatigue, headaches, the gaps in time. He really needed to learn to say no when it was offered.

Careful not to wake the girls, Sebastian quietly got out of bed and padded to the en suite bathroom. He relieved himself with a sigh, hoping to stay accurate with his aim, given his physical and mental condition. He then made his way to the sink to wash his hands. Sebastian forced himself to look at the mirror and the image was appalling: his sapphire blue eyes were bloodshot and his brown hair was standing on end. Sebastian didn't feel any better than he looked. He reached in the medicine cabinet for aspirin, turned on the brass cold water tap, and filled a glass with water.

Sebastian stepped in the shower, the hot stream of water beading down his bare skin. It felt invigorating. When he closed his eyes he could imagine he was in a far-off land, maybe under a waterfall in Hawaii or on a cruise down the Amazon River. Daydreaming was a waste of time. He was stuck in England, living this crazy lifestyle, because it was easier to go along with his friends than say no to them.

Today, Sebastian would act as ringmaster to the circus they lived, and entertain his friends again. Sometimes he wondered what it would be like if life had handed him something different. What would it be like to have two parents who worked nine-to-five mundane jobs? What would it be like to have a family meal every night because they could not afford to eat out—and more so, they enjoyed each other's company? Would he be happier with two parents who loved each other raising him? Sebastian led a privileged life and had the good fortune to be raised by the most wonderful woman in the world: his nanny. Things could certainly be worse.

"Stop thinking so much, Irons," he muttered to himself. "You have guests to tend to. The circus awaits."

They spent a leisurely day frolicking in the pool, playing tennis, and lounging about reading and drinking cocktails. At one point, Sebastian became so engrossed reading Evelyn Waugh's *Brideshead Revisited* that he didn't realize he was alone. Just as well; he enjoyed silence from time to time.

Penelope popped her head in the room, calling Sebastian's name to get his attention. She was dressed in a perfectly pressed short sleeved white blouse and navy pencil skirt, looking as if she had walked out of one of her fashion magazines. Her blonde hair was pulled back in a slick ponytail, every hair in its place. "Sebastian, I need your help," she requested as he looked up from his novel.

"Where's Alistair?" he questioned, almost annoyed at the interruption.

"I don't know, and besides, it's you I need," she replied, taking his arm and pulling him away from the sofa.

"I'm at a really good part in this book!" he protested to no avail as she dragged him out of the room.

She led him down the long, red carpeted hall toward the dining room. Its large double doors were shut. "Pen, what you are doing?" he asked.

She leaned in to give him a quick, friendly kiss on the lips before she swung open the doors to loud, boisterous shouts of "Surprise!"

Everyone stood surrounding the antique sideboard, which held a birthday cake ablaze with eighteen candles. There were blue and white balloons and streamers decorating the room. The girls wore paper party hats. The boys blew into plastic noisemaker horns and threw handfuls of confetti at Sebastian. He was taken aback. Penny eased her arm through his and escorted him to his birthday cake. "Make a wish," she whispered.

He took a moment and stared at the candles flickering above the buttercream icing. With one deep breath, he leaned over the cake and blew out the candles. Everyone clapped as they broke into a chorus of *For He's A Jolly Good Fellow*.

"Time for presents," Alistair announced, handing Sebastian a very large white box with a black satin ribbon. "This is from me," he said, pushing Sebastian onto the sofa and taking the seat next to him. Sebastian untied the ribbon and lifted the lid. Inside he found a beautiful black wool Paul Smith suit complete with a white shirt, perfectly coordinated tie, and gleaming lace-up shoes.

Sebastian admired the tailoring as he gently touched the soft lightweight fabric. "This is amazing, Alistair. Thank you."

His friend smiled, patting him on the back.

"Me, next!" Penny exclaimed, handing him a small box wrapped in silver paper. He opened the box to find a book of poetry by Keats. "It's a first edition. I know he's your favorite," she chimed in.

Sebastian was overcome by her thoughtfulness. He stood up and gave her a hug. "It's brilliant. Thank you."

Oliver and Colin were next and handed Sebastian a black velvet bag. Sebastian chuckled. "I wonder what this could be?"

"Oh, go on then," Colin prodded, with a devious smile crossing his lips. Sebastian pulled the drawstring to reveal a rather large amount of cannabis. The aroma swirled out of the bag and teased his senses. He closed his eyes for a second, drew in a breath of it, and smiled.

"The best money can buy, mate," Oliver informed him.

Sebastian secured the drawstring on the bag and stuffed it in his pants pocket. He crossed the room and opened the doors of an armoire to reveal the stereo system.

"Any requests?" Sebastian inquired as he browsed the cardboard sleeves lining the shelf.

"Bananarama!" Jemma shouted.

"David Bowie," Alistair chimed in.

Penny sighed. "Play whatever you like, Sebastian. But if you put on another Smiths record, I swear I'll slit my wrists."

He turned to Penny, holding up a copy of their new album, *Meat is Murder*. "Morrissey is a god," he explained.

"So is Eric Clapton, and you never play any of his records," she announced, giving him a quick peck on his cheek.

"I don't have any Clapton records. Maybe you should choose what I play next," Sebastian suggested, enjoying their banter.

Alistair came up behind Penny and placed his arms around her waist. "No flirting with my best mate," he playfully warned.

Penny turned around and kissed Alistair full on the lips. "Your jealousy is adorable," she remarked, tapping the tip of his nose with her finger.

The girls started dancing as the sound of Duran Duran's *Girls on Film* filled the room. Sebastian popped open another bottle of champagne. It was a wonderful surprise birthday party. He looked at his friends, laughing, dancing, and having a good time. Everything was perfect.

Suddenly, he heard Colin gasp for air. When Sebastian turned to face him, Colin had dropped to his knees, clutching his chest. The crystal champagne flute shattered on the hardwood floor as it slipped from his grasp. Claire and Jade began to laugh, thinking it was part of the fun. They quickly realized that Colin was not playing a joke and something was terribly wrong. Claire screamed.

"Penny, get the girls out of here now!" Alistair ordered. "Sebastian, phone for an ambulance!"

Alistair dropped to his knees next to Colin and grasped his wrist to check for a pulse.

Oliver knelt down next to his brother. "Come on, Colin. This isn't funny." He put his hand over Colin's mouth to feel for his breath. "He's not breathing," he said in a panic. Oliver began shaking his brother by the shoulders.

"Oliver, stand back! You're not helping the situation," Alistair yelled as he loosened Colin's tie and unbuttoned his shirt.

Sebastian joined Alistair on the floor and together they began to administer CPR. Breathe in, pump chest, count *one, two, three, four.* Alistair and Sebastian continued their rhythmic undertaking.

"You have to save my brother!" Oliver cried, pacing back and forth.

"What is he on, Oliver?" Alistair demanded.

"He was doing coke earlier. Maybe some pills."

"How much?"

"I don't know—a lot!" he responded in a frantic tone.

Penny ran back into the room and knelt next to Colin. "What can I do to help?"

Alistair continued to work on Colin. Without looking up, he said, "Penny, get my wallet. Locate John Covington's card. It should be in the front. Call him now. I want an attorney here. And turn off that music."

Penny accomplished her tasks and then touched Sebastian's shoulder to get his attention. "Let me take over. You should wait outside for the ambulance."

He looked up at her, nodded, then left the room. The fifteen minutes it took for the ambulance to arrive seemed like an eternity to Sebastian. Finally, medics pulled up to the house and Sebastian escorted them to Colin.

They ran into the room, laden with bags and monitors. The lads moved out of their way and the medics took over the resuscitation attempts. They radioed the hospital as they administered oxygen from a tank, and they pushed needles under Colin's skin and set up an IV line. They placed his limp body on the gurney and rushed out of the room to transport him to the hospital, but he still didn't have a heartbeat.

Sebastian was standing in the doorway, his back against the doorframe, trying to will Colin back to life. The others were scattered around the room with looks of horror and disbelief. One of the emergency medical crew approached Sebastian. "We'll need to call the authorities," he said.

Sebastian nodded. "We're doing everything we can," they reassured.

The room was silent. They couldn't look at one another. Sebastian knew Colin was dead. He didn't want it to be true, but his gut feeling was telling him differently. He glanced at the confetti and streamers, half eaten birthday cake, and discarded champagne flutes. How could such a perfect day go so wrong?

Chapter 3 - Blue Monday

After meeting with the lawyer and police, the group disbanded and headed back to Eton Sunday evening. When Sebastian arrived back at his flat well after midnight, he couldn't sleep, so he sat in the darkened lounge with yesterday's events on a continuous loop in his brain.

The phone rang. He picked up the receiver. "Hello," he managed in a groggy voice.

"Mr. Irons, this is Alice Merriwether from the headmaster's office. He would like to see you in his office at eight o'clock this morning."

It was already seven o'clock. A hot shower was definitely in order. The past twenty-four hours had not been kind to him. Somehow, he found the strength to pull himself together. He was knocking on the heavy wooden door to the headmaster's office precisely one hour later.

"Enter," the commanding voice ordered from inside the room.

Sebastian took a deep breath and slowly turned the doorknob. He was not looking forward to this.

"Mr. Irons, take a seat."

Sebastian did as he was told and sat quietly until spoken to.

"You are aware that you missed your English final on Friday?"

"Yes, Headmaster," he replied, avoiding the man's stare.

"What is your excuse?"

"I was out late the night before and overslept."

"Yes, that was Prince Alistair's excuse as well," the headmaster responded, making notes in the file in front of him. "May I remind you of your chemistry final at nine o'clock this morning?"

"Yes, sir."

"Make it a point to be there and to be prepared to pass the exam." The headmaster closed his file, then stood up. He loomed over Sebastian, which only added to Sebastian's insecurity and unease.

"Yes, sir," he muttered.

"And as a favor to Lady Irons, I have rescheduled your English exam this afternoon for both you and the Prince. You are a very lucky man, Mr. Irons, but your luck will eventually run out. Your marks this term have been deplorable." He paused for effect. "If you do not improve your final scores, you can be assured your chances of attending Oxford will be slim to none."

Wonderful, he thought. Now his mother was involved. Could this day get any worse? Sebastian stood up and extended his hand to the headmaster. "Thank you for the opportunity, Headmaster."

"Do not disappoint me again, Mr. Irons. You are dismissed."

Sebastian gave a slight bow of his head and quickly left the room. He moped through the quad toward his chemistry final, which he would undoubtedly fail. Sebastian certainly was not looking forward to the lecture from his mother. He wondered what she would be the most upset about: Colin dying in the house or Sebastian getting expelled from Eton. Either way, the meeting with his mother would be far worse than what had just transpired in the headmaster's office. The only bright spot was the news about Oxford. If it was true, he would not have to attend Oxford. He secretly smiled at the thought of breaking his mother's heart. It had always been her plan to send him there; Sebastian was never offered a choice.

He had a thought to dash it all. Colin was dead. Obviously, news of the event had not reached the headmaster. How the hell was he supposed to sit for an exam after he watched Colin die yesterday? Sebastian was so engrossed in his own thoughts that he walked straight into Alistair.

Alistair looked about the same as he did: as if he had not slept in days and that the weight of the world was pressing down on his shoulders. "Did you have your meeting with the headmaster yet?" Alistair inquired.

"Yes," he sighed, "I've just come from there. Now I'm supposed to take a chemistry exam. Could you please explain to me how the hell I'm going to do that, Alistair? The headmaster doesn't even know Colin is dead, does he?"

Alistair grabbed Sebastian by his jacket lapel and pulled him back into a deserted stone archway. "Irons, pull yourself together. You need to act as if nothing has happened. Sit for the exams and pass them. I told you, none of this will get out."

"What if one of the girls talks to the bloody press?"

"It's been taken care of," Alistair repeated in a slow, intense voice.

"But how can you act as if nothing has happened?" Sebastian raged back, pushing Alistair brusquely into the wall.

"Because I have to, and it would behoove you to learn that lesson, too," he glared at Sebastian, the warning sounding like a threat. "Now keep a stiff upper lip and go about your day as planned." Alistair brushed the dirt off his jacket and heaved a heavy sigh, unable to stay angry at his best friend. "Come on, we'll be late for chemistry."

They walked together in silence, never to utter the name Colin Harris again. They were the last to arrive in the exam hall and ended up having to sit in the front row of the room. It was a gray, gloomy day, perfectly matching Sebastian's mood. Rain was approaching. The proctor stood at the front of the room and cleared his throat, making a deep, disgusting sound. It snapped Sebastian back to the present.

"You will have two hours to complete your exam. You may open your booklets and begin now," the teacher announced, noting the time on the large wall clock.

The sound of rustling paper echoed through the large hall. Students were hunched over their test papers, feverishly writing their answers in a race against the clock. Sebastian stared at his paper. It might as well have been written in a foreign language. He couldn't focus. He was feeling lightheaded, sick to his stomach, and couldn't breathe. The image of Colin collapsed on the floor and their futile attempts to save him burned in his brain. Beads of perspiration formed on his forehead. The pencil he was holding snapped between his fingers. Sebastian stood up and quickly walked out of the room without asking permission. The teacher called after him, but he closed the door and made a sprint down the corridor leading to the quad. The cool, misty air smacked his face as he flung open the glass door. He turned, fell to his knees, and vomited in the bushes. His mind was racing. Sebastian didn't know what to do. All he knew was that he needed to get away from this place.

Sebastian made his way back to his flat just as a loud clap of thunder shook the heavens and produced a heavy deluge of cold rain. He slammed the heavy front door closed behind him. Sebastian peeled off his black suit jacket and frantically tore at the buttons of his purple satin vest, throwing them both on the floor. Tugging at his matching purple tie, he loosened the Windsor knot so it hung loosely and finally he could breathe a little easier.

He poured a tumbler of scotch and downed it in one gulp, shaking off the sharp bite it left as it slid down his throat. Closing his eyes, he focused on his breathing in an attempt to calm his nerves. *Inhale, exhale*, he told himself. Unsure if it was the alcohol or the breathing, his mind suddenly became very clear and focused. He remembered an evening, a few months back, when Alistair rang him begging Sebastian to take Penny to dinner.

"I have this function I need to attend tonight and I promised Penny I'd take her to The Ivy for dinner. Can you take her for me?"

"You realize you're asking me to take your girl on a date? Why don't you just take her another time?" Sebastian questioned.

"I've already been photographed with her too many times. The only saving grace is that you are always with us. They don't know who she's with, me or you. And besides, I hate to disappoint her. She likes you, Sebastian. Please?"

"Fine," Sebastian surrendered. "You're lucky I enjoy Penny's company or otherwise you would owe me hugely."

"Brilliant! I've made reservations for eight. Holmes will you pick up," he instructed as he rung off.

Holmes chauffeured Sebastian and Penny to the restaurant.

"Are you ready for this?" Sebastian inquired.

She nodded. Sebastian opened the car door and walked around to assist Penny, holding out his hand. Lights flashed from the gathered paparazzi as the couple was snapped on the sidewalk before they walked into The Ivy.

They were seated promptly at a prominent table and handed embossed leather menus. The sommelier arrived and a bottle of French wine was ordered. Turning her attention back to Sebastian, Penny said, "They got a good photo. Alistair should be pleased." She began to peruse the main courses. "That should take the heat off. I hope you don't mind being my faux boyfriend?" she asked with grave concern, her voice taking on a serious tone.

It was apparent to him that Alistair and Penny were falling for each other. How sad that they had to play these games to keep their relationship a secret. "You shouldn't have to hide, Pen. But I'm very happy to be your faux boyfriend," he whispered, leaning closer to her.

"It's quite all right. I knew what I was getting myself into. It's hard enough to maintain a relationship, let alone try to grow one under the scrutiny of the press and the royal family. I'm perfectly happy keeping it quiet and doing whatever it is to avoid suspicions.

I'm extremely grateful Alistair asked you to take me out, and not Colin or Oliver," she admitted.

Sebastian appreciated the change of pace. He didn't have to be the group leader and entertain when he was alone with Penny. He didn't have to drink to excess or take drugs. With Penny, he could just be himself. How nice it would be if he could find someone like her with whom he could fall in love.

They left The Ivy around ten o'clock and made their way back to Penny's flat. Sebastian opened the car door and walked her to the front door. He stared at her face for a long moment.

"What is it?" she asked, fearing something was stuck in her teeth.

"I'm very lucky to have you as a friend," he complimented.

"I've had a fantastic evening. Thank you for being my escort."

"It was my pleasure. Have a goodnight, Pen." He leaned in and kissed her softly on one cheek and then the other. He turned to leave and headed down the short stone stairs. He was halfway to the car when she called out to him. "Sebastian, I would love it if you could join me at the Tate next week for the Pre-Raphaelite exhibit."

He stopped mid-stride and turned to face her with a huge grin on his lips. "I would like that very much. Wednesday?"

"Perfect. It's a date. I'll ring you later." She turned the key in the door knob, opened the red door, and disappeared inside the old stone building.

Sebastian grabbed his car keys. Soon he was on the M3, speeding toward London in the torrential rain. The teeming water made it difficult to see through the windscreen as the wipers frantically swished back and forth, unable to keep up with the rain. The wheels slipped as he took a sharp turn, Sebastian instinctively tightening his grip on the leather-wrapped steering wheel.

It wasn't long before he found himself in Kensington, parking along South Hampton Mews. He walked to number 52 and hesitated on the doorstep. Finally, he reached out and rang the doorbell. The red door opened to reveal Penelope. The storm had plastered his brown hair flat onto his face. His white shirt clung to his bare chest, accentuating his well defined abs. The leather shoes on his feet were surely ruined. Sebastian held out a bottle of vodka as if it were a peace offering.

"Sebastian, get in here!" she exclaimed, pulling him by the arm. "What in heaven's name are you doing?"

He couldn't answer. He stood there in the foyer dripping water on the marble floor, looking dejected and painfully alone. Penny took the bottle and placed it on the foyer table. She gently took his hand. "Come on, I'll get you some dry clothes."

They walked the length of the hallway and into her bedroom, and then she led him straight through to the bathroom. Penny took a few Egyptian cotton towels from the linen closet and handed them to Sebastian. "Get out of those wet clothes. Put them on the towel warmer to dry them out."

Penny rummaged through her dresser drawer until she came across a white T-shirt and navy plaid boxers. She knocked on the bathroom door. It slowly opened to reveal Sebastian with a white towel wrapped around his waist. She handed him the boxers and shirt. "These are Alistair's."

He joined her a few minutes later, clad in clean, dry clothes. His hair was spiked in all different directions from his attempt to towel-dry it. Penny gave him a cup of tea with a shot of whiskey. "Drink this. You'll warm up."

Sebastian attempted to smile. It dawned on him that Penny and Alistair handled stressful situations in the same manner: there was always a calm, in-control method to it. He thought maybe that was one reason they seemed so well suited for each other.

They sat together on a floral Laura Ashley love seat. Sebastian slowly sipped the tea, breathing in the warmth and aroma, until the cup was empty. He placed the cup and saucer on the small coffee table at their feet.

"Please tell me what's happening?" she pleaded, a look of concern crossing her face. "You should be with Alistair taking exams."

"That's a little difficult to do when you're vomiting in the bushes," he told her.

She quickly touched his forehead with the palm of her hand to see if he had a fever. "You don't feel warm," she observed.

"Why do you do that?" he questioned.

"Do what?"

"Act as if everything is perfectly normal in the face of tragedy. How do you do it?" he repeated.

"Oh, Sebastian," she sighed, laying her head on his shoulder, "it's not that easy. I can't get that image of Colin collapsing on the floor out of my mind. You tried to save him, it just didn't work."

"Alistair gave me the 'stiff upper lip' speech this morning," he informed her.

"Don't be angry with him. It's how he's wired. It's royal protocol. Show no emotion. Keep calm and carry on. Alistair doesn't know any other way," Penny explained.

Sebastian focused on the rose-colored wallpaper. His head touched the top of Penny's head. Neither one spoke for at least half an hour. Sebastian was slowly calming down. It was comforting to be with Penny. He knew he made the right choice to come here today. She never judged him.

Penny took his hand. "Feeling better?" she asked, as if reading his mind.

"A little," he admitted. "You seem to be the only one who will allow me to grieve."

"We're all grieving, just in different ways."

Sebastian closed his eyes and winced at those words. Penny was trying to be a good friend, yet he found himself whisper, "I can't stop thinking it's my fault. If I hadn't invited everyone to the castle, maybe he'd still be alive."

Penny sat straight up and turned to face him with alarm. "Do not say that. There was absolutely nothing you could have done to save him. Colin had a major drug problem."

"We certainly didn't help him."

"You're right," she agreed, "but you can't save someone with an addiction unless they want to be saved. Sebastian, you did *not* kill Colin Harris." Penny stared into his eyes with great intensity as she spoke those words.

"Pen—" Sebastian was unable to finish his sentence because she cut him off with an eager kiss on the mouth. They had kissed several times before, but this time was different.

He quickly pulled away, caught off guard by her sudden move. Then the most amazing thing happened; his mind went completely blank. There was no pain, no anxiety—just calm. He reached out and touched her face and kissed her back.

The kissing became more urgent and passionate. Penny straddled his lap, pushing him back against the sofa. They were pulling at each other's undergarments, channeling all their pent-up energy and grief into sex. All Sebastian could think of was comfort. It was comforting to be here with his friend. It was comforting to have sex with Penny. He knew in his mind it was wrong, but he didn't care.

They collapsed in each other's arms, sweaty and breathing heavily. Sebastian's T-shirt was damp with perspiration. Penny's pale gray linen dress was a mess of wrinkles. "Pen—" he uttered before she placed her soft finger tips against his lips to quiet him.

"People deal with grief in different ways," she reiterated.

"I'm not sorry this happened," he confessed.

She gave a melancholy smile. "Nor am I."

"We can't tell Alistair."

"No," she agreed. "He wouldn't understand." Penny stood up and attempted to smooth out the wrinkles in her skirt. "Draw us a bath. I'll get us some drinks." She turned to leave the room and Sebastian simply watched her walk away.

Sebastian lifted himself from the sofa and padded back to the bathroom. He stripped off Alistair's shirt and boxers as the hot water poured from the faucet into the large Victorian claw-foot tub. He examined the bottles of oils and bubble bath Penny had neatly arranged on the teakwood tray that sat on the tub's edge. He unscrewed the black lid to the lavender-scented bottle. It was the same aroma he often associated with Penny, floral and calming. He tipped the bottle under the running water and let the two mix together as a myriad of tiny bubbles began to appear. The overhead incandescent bulb gave off a harsh light, so he switched it off and lit the many candles that were placed around the bathroom. His eyes scanned the room. When he determined that he had made it as inviting as possible, Sebastian stepped into the tub, leaning his back against one of the broad curved ends. He closed his eyes and cleared his mind of everything. His only focus was the heat of the water and the smell of the lavender.

Penny walked into the room carrying a tray filled with an assortment of juices; glasses filled with ice, and Sebastian's bottle of vodka. She placed the tray on the long, flat window ledge. Penny poured a healthy measure of vodka over ice and added a splash of orange juice, stirred briefly with her finger, and handed it to Sebastian. She made herself a cranberry-and-vodka. She stripped off her dress and placed it on the hook on the back of the door as Sebastian watched. Penny lit a cigarette and then lit another off the glowing end. She handed Sebastian both and slipped into the tub with him, retrieved her cigarette, and leaned against the opposite end.

They smoked and drank their vodka in silence. Sebastian extinguished the butt of his Dunhill in the glass ashtray on the bath's ledge, letting the last puff of smoke trail above him. "You know how they say there are moments in your life that you'll never forget?" he finally spoke aloud.

"Hmm," she acknowledged wordlessly.

"This is one of those moments for me. Penny, you have no idea how grateful I am to you."

She reached over and touched his left hand, which was gripping the cool porcelain side of the tub. "You helped me, too. Just because I seem cool, calm, and collected doesn't mean I really am. We all hide behind facades, don't we?"

"I'm getting sent down from Eton," he said, unconsciously changing the subject.

"Yes, well, considering you just walked out on your final, that is sort of a foregone conclusion."

"I need to get out of England."

"Where shall we go?" she asked nonchalantly.

His mood brightened. "You'll come with me?"

"Absolutely. How about Paris?" she suggested.

Sebastian frowned. "No, it's awful this time of year. Too many people. Too hot."

"Agreed." She thought for a moment then offered, "How about Alicante? We have a villa there. We could hide away from the world. My mother and father are in Cape Town. No one will bother us."

"Spain? That sounds perfect. When can we leave?"

Penny chuckled. "You sound like a fugitive."

"When the headmaster rings my mother to let her know I've been chucked out of Eton and she finds out about Colin…" He trailed off in thought. "Let's just say I'm better off running."

The bath water had become cold. Sebastian stood first and wrapped a towel around his waist after drying his chest and shoulders. He opened another for Penny to step into as she placed her feet back on the floor.

He allowed her some privacy to dress and wandered over to her stereo cabinet to look at her record collection. He flipped through the LPs until he came across Aztec

Camera's *Stray*. He slipped the vinyl out of the shinny cover, put the record over the spindle of the turntable, gently lifted the needle, and placed it on track one. The sounds of a melancholy piano filled the room and Roddy Frame began to sing.

Penny walked up behind him and gently touched his shoulder. Sebastian turned around to face her, taking her in his arms. They danced.

"Did you have to pick the saddest album?" she asked.

"It suits my mood," he responded, slowly twirling her under his arm and then pulling her even closer into his embrace. The ivory silk robe she wore felt nice against his skin.

The song ended, yet they remained in each other's arms, eyes closed. The incessant ring of the telephone brought them back to reality. Penny walked over and picked up the receiver. "Hello?"

"Penelope, have you spoken to Sebastian? I can't find him anywhere," Alistair asked her in an almost frantic tone.

"Yes, I've spoken to him, Alistair. What's going on?" she asked while gazing at Sebastian, who was vehemently shaking his head, imploring her with his eyes to not let on that he was standing right next to her in nothing but a bath towel.

"He ran out of his chemistry exam without a word. I've looked all over campus for him. I even went to his flat and found Lady Irons there."

Penny cut him off. "Oh, no. What happened next?"

"We talked about Colin's death. She is none too pleased to have the police in her home. I convinced her everything would be taken care of. She was very grateful, but she was not happy. She's put Sebastian's flat up for let and was having the servants pack up his things. He's been sent down, Penny. I need to find him and tell him what's going on."

She held out the phone to Sebastian and silently pleaded for him to take the receiver and talk to Alistair. Sebastian turned his back on her and walked across the room to look out the window.

"Penny, are you still there?" Alistair asked from the other end of the line.

"Yes, I'm here. I talked to Sebastian earlier today. He's taking Colin's death really hard. He said he needed to get out of England for a while," she confessed.

"Well, where is he going? He needs to know what's happening."

"I think he's pretty much sorted that all out. It won't be a surprise to him. He mentioned Paris, but he didn't say for sure."

"Bollocks," Alistair cursed under his breath. "Well, if you hear anything else, please let him know what's happening. If you talk to him, please tell him to call me."

"Alistair, how are you holding up? Are you okay?"

"Of course," he quickly replied. "I'm just concerned about Sebastian. How are you?"

"As well as can be expected," she wearily replied.

"You could come over tonight, if you wanted."

"I think it is best we just lay low for a week. Let Colin have his funeral. Is that all right?"

"You're quite right," Alistair agreed.

"Thanks for calling, Alistair. Take care," Penny said before placing the receiver back on the phone base. She continued to stare at the phone until Sebastian spoke.

"Thanks for covering for me."

"Alistair was just trying to warn you. Your mother knows and has already cleared out your flat. You'll have to go home."

He sighed, slowly sitting down on the bed next to her. "Not this week." He handed her his Barclays credit card. "Please call the airline and make the reservation. Get the first flight out. I can't handle this."

Chapter 4 - Stray

Sebastian and Penny were on the 10:00 p.m. British Airways flight 23 to Alicante, Spain. Exhaustion had finally taken its toll. Sebastian fell asleep straight away, his head resting on Penny's left shoulder. She didn't disturb him and quietly read a book through the two-and-a-half-hour flight.

Upon landing, they collected Penny's luggage and hailed a cab to take them to the villa. There was no time to fetch Sebastian fresh clothes, so he was forced to wear his Eton trousers and white shirt.

"It shouldn't take long to get to the villa at this time in the morning," Penny said, looking at her watch.

The house was a small but beautiful villa overlooking the sea. There was nothing ostentatious about it. It looked like any other terra cotta roofed house along the coastline, furnished with traditional Spanish decor and colors.

"You can take any room you like, Sebastian."

Sebastian dropped Penny's bags in the front hall and headed directly for the patio. The best feature of the house was the tiled patio with a sweeping view of the sea below.

The still water in the pool glowed in the moonlight. They crashed onto some red lounge chairs, not bothering to turn on any lights. Sebastian listened to the soothing sounds of the lapping waves. He stared up at the twinkling stars. There were a thousand of them. Being away from the bright lights of the city allowed you to see so many more stars.

"I think I'd like to sleep out here tonight," he told Penny, his eyes still transfixed by the constellations.

"Whatever you'd like," Penny agreed.

She left him alone with his thoughts while she headed inside the house to change. She returned, dressed in red Chinese silk pajamas, carrying a cotton blanket and feather pillow. Penny gently placed the blanket on top of him and propped the pillow behind his head. "Goodnight, Sebastian." She leaned in and kissed him on the forehead. "Sleep well."

The early morning sun woke him just before 6:00 a.m. Sleeping outside was a grand plan; however, it did not do any favors for his aching back. He slowly stood and made his way inside the villa. Penny had told him that he could take any room he wanted; but all he wanted—all he needed—was to be with Penny.

Sebastian found her in the third room he searched, and the sight of her peacefully sleeping stopped him in his tracks. She was beautiful. He quietly took off the wrinkled pants and shirt he'd slept in last night before slowly crawling into her bed, attempting not to wake her. Penny deserved a peaceful night's rest after she so selflessly took care of him. He was a handful, he knew. Nanny had never let him forget it and loved him all the same. Penny was like that, too.

She stirred, rolling over on her side, spooning herself around his body. It didn't take very long until Sebastian drifted back to sleep.

When Penny awoke, she raised her head from the pillow and squinted at the alarm clock. It was noon.

Sebastian stretched his arms overhead while yawning.

"Sorry to wake you. You can go back to sleep if you want," she offered.

Sebastian's stomach let off a low growl. "I'm famished," he announced suddenly, realizing he hadn't eaten in forty-eight hours.

"So am I. There's a great little café down the road."

"Excellent. We should shower first," he declared seductively.

"Your shower is down the hall," Penny informed him, tousling his messy bed head.

"But we could save water if we shower together."

"Yes, but then we'll never leave the house and you'll starve, so get your arse out of bed and be ready in half an hour. You can borrow some clothes out of my brother's closet."

"Yes, Miss Stanton."

As promised, he was ready and waiting thirty minutes later. Sebastian had raided her brother's closet and found a pair of navy shorts, flip-flops, and a white polo shirt.

"You look almost human," she announced, strolling into the room in a pale blue halter dress. Her hair was pulled up back in a ponytail. Her makeup was perfect.

"You look stunning."

She laughed before she kissed him on the cheek. "Your charms won't work on me, Irons." She grabbed her purse and they set off, walking hand in hand, to the café at the end of the lane. Upon arrival, they were greeted by the owner, a sweet, little round man with a thick, black head of hair and a welcoming smile.

"Señorita Penelope! It is so good to see you again."

"Señor Salvador, it is good to see you too," she replied, sitting down in the chair Salvador graciously pulled out for her. She introduced Sebastian and went on to tell the owner that they were famished.

Without haste, their luncheon was served. Salvador provided an amazing feast with a Spanish frittata, fresh local fruit, warm homemade bread, juice and rich, robust coffee. The conversation was minimal as they concentrated on their meal and devoured the food. When the meal was fully consumed, Penny sat back in her chair and held her stomach. "I didn't realize how hungry I was. How are you feeling, Sebastian?"

"Much better now," he admitted, wiping the corner of his mouth with the linen napkin. "So what shall we do today?" He gazed up at the cloudless, sky above the canvas umbrella that covered their outdoor table.

"We should hit the market for food and some clothing for you. Then I think we relax by the pool."

"Sounds perfect." It was so nice for someone else to take charge for a change.

Sebastian relished being pulled here and there as Penny escorted him among the various street vendors. He dutifully held the accumulating bags as they shopped. "Penny, what are we going to do with all this food?"

"I'm going to cook," she replied with great satisfaction.
"Really?"

Penny stopped short and faced him. "I'll have you know I have several talents you know nothing about."

"I bet you do," he flirted.

Penny picked up a pair of knockoff Ray-Bans from a vendor's stall. She opened them up and placed them on Sebastian's face. "That's better," she announced and handed the vendor a few pestea. "Now we better get home to get these groceries into the refrigerator."

Back in the kitchen, they unpacked the groceries and put them away, except for those things Penny would need to prepare dinner. She sorted the fresh vegetables and began to marinate the fish with olive oil, fresh herbs, and a splash of freshly squeezed lemon juice.

"So where did you acquire this amazing cooking skill?" Sebastian inquired with strange fascination.

"My mother thought I should go to cooking school. She said it was an excellent way to win a good husband," she informed him matter-of-factly.

"So how's that husband hunt going for you?"

Penny rolled her eyes and threw a tomato in his direction. Sebastian gently caught it and laid it back down on the cutting board. "I think I'll leave you to your culinary foray. I'll see you by the pool when you're finished." He turned on his heel and headed out the door before any more vegetables were launched at him.

Sebastian lounged on top of a clear plastic inflatable raft with his left hand dangling in the water. His wet brown hair was slicked back, while his faux Ray-Bans shielded his eyes from the intense sunlight. It was so peaceful here. Wouldn't it be wonderful if he could spend the rest of his life in this place?

"It's about time," he called out, sensing Penny joining him on the patio.

"Patience, Irons, or you'll go hungry tonight," Penny warned. With that she dove into the pool and swam underwater until she came up under his raft and toppled it, sending Sebastian into the water.

He caught his breath and immediately lunged after her, grabbing her shoulders and playfully pushing her under. He quickly pulled her up for air and she instinctively wrapped her legs around his waist to avoid being dunked again. In the tussle, Sebastian's sunglasses slipped off and slowly sank to the bottom of the pool. He squinted through the sunlight at her face; it was full of wet, messy, blonde hair. Gently, he tried to comb it back with his fingers. Then he leaned in and kissed Penny with abandon.

There was no turning back from this. He longed to really make love to her—wanted more than quick, grief-ridden sex. Maybe Sebastian longed for her too much, yet she was kissing him in return. Sebastian walked through the water to the shallow end of the pool with Penny still wrapped around his waist. He stepped out of the pool and carried her into her bedroom, both of them dripping wet.

The cool cotton sheets felt good against their warm, sun-drenched bodies. They continued kissing. Penny reached behind her neck and untied the string of her white bikini top. He worried no longer: this was going to happen for them here and now. He smiled with great delight while planting little kisses along her slender neck, trailing down to her abdomen until he reached the Libertine tattoo that was written in cursive on her right hip bone.

Their afternoon of lovemaking was sensual and unabashed. For the first time, all Sebastian wanted to do was pleasure her and make her happy. This thought had never before occurred to him with his other sexual partners. Did this mean he was in love with her?

Wrapped in each other's arms, naked on top of the sheets, they felt the cool breeze as it fluttered the white sheer curtains of the open window. Penny studied his face. "You're genuinely smiling," she observed.

"So."

"It's nice to see. You always seem sad."

"Am I that transparent?"

"I didn't know those smiles back in London were a facade until I got to spend this time alone with you," she tried to explain.

"Oh, please don't psychoanalyze me," he pleaded.

"I'm not. I'm just trying to tell you that I love seeing you so happy."

He leaned in and kissed her. "Run away with me, Penny."

"I already have, Sebastian."

"Permanently."

She laughed aloud. "Where will we go? How would we support ourselves?"

"If you're as good a cook as you say you are, we'll open a café and give Señor Salvador a run for his money."

Penny gently traced the matching Libertine tattoo scrolled across his left upper arm with her forefinger. "It's a beautiful dream, but if we ran away our families would cut us off." She sighed. "Sebastian, we have this week. It will be our secret, something we can remember with great fondness when we're old and gray."

"I need a drink," he announced, eager to change the subject. Sebastian was trying not to allow his feelings to be hurt after his idea was shot down. "Can I get you something?"

"Ice cold water, please."

Sebastian leaned over and kissed her bare shoulder before leaving for refreshments. He found a wooden tray in the kitchen and prepared a pitcher of ice water with fresh sliced lemons, and added it to the bottle of scotch he found in an overhead cabinet. Sebastian snatched the packet of Dunhills that was lying on the counter and added it to the tray. Before he returned to the bedroom, he made a detour to her brother's room to collect something he'd found earlier in the day.

Sebastian quietly crept down the tiled hall and stopped in her doorway. Penny was lying on her side, her head propped up in her hand, waiting for his return. The silky skin of her waif-like frame glistened in the sunlight filtering through the curtains. Sebastian raised the Polaroid camera, placed his eye against the viewfinder, and pressed the button with a loud click.

Penny was caught off guard. She grabbed a pillow and threw it at him. "Sebastian Irons, what are you doing!"

He ducked out of the pillow's flight path, roaring with laughter as she grabbed another to take aim. The photo shot out of the camera. He pulled it out completely, holding it by the large white strip on the bottom, and waved it in the air in an attempt to hasten its development. He padded back over to her and bounced down on the bed as they watched the picture slowly develop, holding it just out of her reach.

"I can't believe you just took a naked photo of me!"

"Since when did you get modest? Anyway, I need something to look back on with fondness when I'm old and gray," he teased.

"Fine," she sighed with exasperation. "But tuck it away safely. I don't need the tabloids getting hold of it. You won't sell me out with the headline, *'My wild night with Penelope Stanton?'*"

"Never," he promised.

Penny playfully pushed him off the bed. "Go get my water."

Sebastian and Penny spent the remainder of the week lounging about the villa, taking midnight swims, eating good food, and making love. It truly was a perfect week. Sebastian wished they could stay like this forever.

Penny was right—it wasn't Sebastian's fault that Colin had died. It was a tragic accident. But Sebastian realized that it could have easily been him instead of Colin, and Sebastian didn't want to die. This week with Penny gave him the incentive to start making some positive changes in his life.

As the week drew to a close, they found themselves together in bed again. Only this time there was an unspoken sadness between them.

"Are you in love with Alistair?" Sebastian asked out of the blue. It was an odd question to ask, he realized, while lying naked next to her. He'd never actually heard Penny say it.

"I care about him," she replied, not answered his question. "I care about you, too."

He kissed her, not sure how to translate her reply. "I'm sorry for all of this. I really fucked things up." He let out a heavy sigh as he rolled over on his back, staring at the ceiling in frustration.

"Don't ever say that," she reprimanded, turning to face him, propping her head up on her hand. "We did this together. We're adults and we have to deal with it."

Sebastian laughed—not at Penny, but at what he felt was his own pathetic self. "I won't be treated like an adult when I go home tomorrow," he mused aloud.

"What do you think will happen?"

He shrugged his shoulders. "Don't know, but it will surely be extreme. She'll most likely send me off to boarding school in France or Switzerland."

"But if you passed your sixth form, you don't have to go to school anymore."

He gave her a feeble smile. "That's sweet, Pen, but we both know I didn't pass—not with the way I've acted this year. I've been so desperate to thwart my mother's plans, I rebelled."

"But what did you hope to accomplish?"

"I don't know. I wasn't consciously thinking about it. I just wanted to push her over the edge, just like she pushed me. I feel so trapped. I don't know what to do."

Penny took his hand in hers. "We don't have to worry about that tonight."

"I'm so glad you came with me this week. Deep down I wanted to know what it was like to have you all to myself." His voice became softer. "I didn't plan on falling for you, Penny," he quietly confessed.

"I know."

"You know what the worst part of all is? Tomorrow I have to take you back to London; back to Alistair. I only hope he can forgive me."

"Alistair will never know about this. It will be our secret. Can you live with that?"

"I'll have to, won't I?"

"Sebastian, make love to me one last time."

He couldn't refuse her. She was right—it would be the last time. He tried to force that thought out of his mind and concentrated on the fact that today, she was his. Things would be very different when they were back in London. Sebastian didn't know what his future held, but he was sure he would always cherish this moment in time. Even though she would never utter the words 'I love you,' Sebastian knew the week he'd spent with her meant just as much to Penny as it had to him. He silently hoped his intuition was correct. He actually hoped his mother would send him off to a boarding school in some remote country, because he had no idea how he could ever be 'just friends' with Penelope Stanton again.

Chapter 5 - How Soon Is Now?

It was raining when the plane touched down at Heathrow Airport. "Welcome home," Sebastian announced with a tinge of sarcasm as they collected Penny's bags and loaded them onto a trolley. The bad weather slowed down the drive back to Kensington. Neither spoke a word for the duration of the trip; they had been jolted back to an unwanted reality and the future was unclear.

With the car unpacked and Penelope's belongings neatly stacked in the hallway of her flat, Sebastian took one last look at Penny. They didn't touch, kiss, or speak. Instead, Sebastian simply smiled a beautiful and genuine smile that let her know how happy and grateful he was for their time together.

His mother's house was unusually quiet when he arrived home that afternoon. He was only a few steps up the grand marble staircase when he heard his mother's domineering footsteps enter the foyer. "Sebastian, I want to see you in the study," she said with an eerie calm. There was no inclination of his pending doom.

He dolefully followed her into the study. She was wearing a black-and-white plaid Chanel suit and modest black pumps. Her brown hair was neatly fixed in an updo. Lady Irons sat behind the large cherry desk with great authority. The chill in the air was palpable as Sebastian took a seat opposite her.

"You've disappointed me more than I could ever have imagined. You are a lazy and irresponsible embarrassment to this family," Lady Irons declared, her steel gray eyes boring a hole straight through him.

There it was: that was the woman he knew. "You've forgotten drunken fornicator," he reminded her, trying to push her over the edge.

She ignored him, continuing, "You brought illegal drugs into this house. Your friend overdoses and there is a police investigation. Did you honestly think I would not find out?"

"Alistair said it won't hit the press," Sebastian attempted to reassure her as much as himself.

"Yes, well, how fortunate for you to have a Windsor as a close personal friend," she said with great disdain. She opened the top desk drawer and pulled out a folder, her eyes never leaving his. Lady Irons slid the folder across the desk and it fell into Sebastian's lap.

Gathering strength, he picked up the folder and slowly opened it to see what lay in his future. It was a paper airline ticket from London to … "Philadelphia?" he questioned, with equal parts disgust and horror.

"Pack your things. You're leaving in two days time. I've enrolled you in St. Alexander's Catholic School, where you will repeat the year…"

"We're not Catholic," Sebastian interrupted. "You really think I can get a better education there than at Eton?"

"Have you forgotten Eton is longer an option for you? Has your drunken debauchery affected your memory?"

"I'm not an imbecile!"

"Then stop acting like one," she said, devoid of emotion. "St. Alexander's is one the top schools in the state. I've arranged a tutor, the brightest student they have. Maybe the strict environment will make an impression on you."

Sebastian shook his head in disbelief. "Why don't you just send me to a home for juvenile delinquents?"

"It was one of my considerations," she replied with an evil smile. "You'll be accompanied by Mrs. Jones, who, in conjunction with the small staff I've hired, will report back to me on your progress."

"Where will I be living?"

"I have an investment property in the suburbs of Philadelphia. You'll stay there."

Lady Irons stood and straightened her jacket. "You have one year to fall in line. If you refuse to shape up, you will endure my wrath and wish you'd never been born."

"You've been an absentee mother my entire life. What gives you the right to dictate my future?" Sebastian spat back in anger as he watched her walking toward the double doors to leave the room.

"My money."

He watched her open the doors and quietly close them behind her. "What the bloody hell just happened?" he wondered aloud to himself. Never in his wildest dreams would he have imagined she'd send him to America. He felt like a convict being put on a ship to Australia. The punishment was harsh. He shoved the ticket into the breast pocket of his khaki linen jacket and tore off for Nanny's room.

He burst into her room without knocking. Caught off guard, she jumped. "Sebastian, you know you should never barge into a room unannounced."

"Sorry, Nanny," he apologized, slumping onto the sofa.

"Don't slouch, dear. Now tell me what's going on. You've been missing in action for a week."

Sebastian corrected his posture. "I've been sent down from Eton and Mother has banished me to America," he gloomily responded. "But you know that already, since she's shipping you off to watch over me."

"Sebastian, this couldn't have come as a great surprise. I tried to warn you."

"If she wants to treat me like delinquent, then I'll bloody well act like one!"

"Stop it, Sebastian. It's about time you take responsibility for your actions," she scolded. "I love you, but I am tired of this destructive attitude. Grow up and do the right thing."

Sebastian was taken aback by her stern words. It wasn't like Nanny to treat him this way. "Please don't, Nanny," he pleaded. "You're right. You're always right. Now I just need your help to get myself out of this chaos."

Nanny left her knitting behind in her chair to join him on the sofa. She took his hand, saying, "My dear, you are an intelligent young man who has *not* made intelligent decisions."

"What do you want me to do?" he asked in despair.

"I want you to be happy. To do that, you have to make a conscious choice to change your life. The world is far from perfect, Sebastian. There is conflict and heartache, but there is also contentedness and joy. It's yours for the taking if you just change the way you live your life."

"And just how do I change my life?"

"Buckle down. Take your education seriously. Have you given any thought to what you want to do with the rest of your life?"

"I was never given a choice, Nanny—you know that. Mother has me graduating Oxford and taking over the reins of Irons Electronics. What's the point of pondering anything different?"

Nanny took his chin in her hand and turned his head so she could look him straight in the eye. "Sebastian Irons, I raised you better than this. Never, never, never give up."

"You can quote Winston Churchill, but that still isn't going to help me."

"I want you to go back to your room and allow yourself to dream. What do you love? How do you want to spend the rest of your life? What would you do if you knew you couldn't fail? You always have a choice, Sebastian." She patted his knee. "Go on. When you find some clarity, come back here and we'll come up with a plan to make your dreams a reality."

Sebastian hugged her. "I love you more than anyone in the world."

"And I you."

Sebastian walked into his bedroom and threw his linen jacket on the sofa. Flopping on the bed, he grabbed his Walkman from the bedside table, pushed the play button, and adjusted his headphones as he lay back on the feather pillow. Nik Kershaw's *Wouldn't It Be Good* began to play.

He reflected as the music swirled around his subconscious. Nanny challenged him to come up with a list of things he loved. It wasn't a very long list. He could count them all on one hand: Nanny, Penny, art, and poetry. Penny could never belong to him. Artists and poets usually had to die to achieve any type of wealth or fame. Although he was as miserable as a poet and painter, he wasn't ready to die yet.

Sebastian grabbed the battered golden brown teddy bear that sat next to him and plopped it on his stomach. "I don't suppose you have any brilliant ideas, Charles?" The bear didn't respond. It simply stared back at Sebastian with its crooked black felt smile. He pulled the bear in to his chest and closed his eyes. Soon he drifted off to sleep.

The clicking of the Walkman shutting off woke Sebastian. He took off the headphones and looked at the clock. It was seven in the evening, but he had no appetite. Might as well start packing. But before he would do that, he picked up the phone to make a call.

Sebastian dialed the number, the familiar tones beeping in his ear, and waited patiently. Eventually a click signified that someone had picked up the receiver on the other end of the line. "Alistair?"

"Sebastian, where the bloody hell have you been? I've been trying to find you for a week."

"I needed to get out of England. I'm sorry I didn't call sooner," he apologized—not so much for the lack of communication, but for sleeping with Alistair's girlfriend.

"Are you okay? Penny said you were out of sorts."

Sebastian really didn't want to answer the question, and hearing Penny's name felt like a small knife stabbing his heart. "Look, I rang you to let you know that I'm being sent to America. I leave in two days. I won't have the chance to see you before I go. I just wanted to say goodbye."

"You must be joking!"

"I wish I were."

"What will Penny and I do without you? We're the Libertines."

"Alistair, do me a favor? Break the news to Pen, will you?"

"Of course," the Prince agreed. "You'll keep in touch?"

"Absolutely. Goodnight, blue blood." He set the receiver down in its cradle with a heavy sigh, poured himself a scotch, and hauled the largest suitcase out of the closet to start packing.

Sebastian had all his clothes packed by morning. He decided to visit Nanny to see if he could assist her in any way before they departed. He gently knocked on her partially opened door and entered. "Hello, Nanny. I've come to see if you needed any help packing."

"Good morning, dear. I'm prepared to leave. I don't require all the bits and bobs you young people need."

"Are you going to make me feel guilty already?"

"Oh, no, not at all. I just don't need all these modern gadgets like Walkmen and CDs. All I need is my small wardrobe and my knitting needles."

"It's a Walkman," Sebastian corrected as he sat next to her on the sofa.

"So have you given thought to the questions I posed yesterday?"

"Yes," he responded in all seriousness. "I know that I love art and poetry. I guess it wouldn't be a bad thing to attend university and study art history or perhaps English literature, even if it is at Oxford."

"Who said you had to go to Oxford?"

"Nanny, you know Mother won't hear of any other place," he responded in exasperation.

"What if you worked diligently this upcoming year to correct your marks? If you would show vast improvement, I believe you will look very appealing to some universities in America." She planted the seed in his mind with one simple sentence. Now all it had to do was take root and sprout.

For as long as Sebastian could remember, it was instilled in his brain that he would attend Oxford. The thought had never occurred to him that there was a vast array of choices out there. He never let himself contemplate those choices. He loved her for putting forth the idea, but frowned. "Mother would never go for it. She pays the tuition, after all."

"Take your mother out of the equation," Nanny insisted.

"And how will I pay for this fantasy education?"

"I'll pay for it," she replied. "Your mother has paid me handsomely throughout my years of service to her family. With her burgeoning career after she divorced your father, I was the one who raised you because she was not around. She provided me room and meals and all of my essentials, so I really had no need for a salary." Nanny winked at him. "Seventeen years of saving and sound investments add up, young man. I think this is a lesson you need to learn now if you wish to make your own way in life."

He looked upon her with all the love and affection he could muster before he quietly said, "I can't take your money. I don't deserve it."

Nanny took his hand, smiling sweetly upon him. "That's why I need to you promise me you'll take every advantage of the opportunities that await you in America. You are a smart young man with a great capacity to love. I expect you to make an extraordinary life for yourself. I will be pleased with nothing less."

He hugged her tightly. "I promise I won't let you down."

Nanny gave him a stern look as Sebastian pulled away. "Now, this won't be easy. Nothing worth having ever is. I expect you to use this summer to research universities and decide which ones you wish to attend. Your mother has informed me that she has hired the best student at St. Alexander's to tutor you. You must take full advantage of your tutor's guidance to help you achieve your goals. Will you do that for me?"

"Absolutely," he swore. He still wanted to stick it to his mother, but now Nanny was involved. For her, he would do anything. So now he had no choice but to become the model student Nanny wanted.

"We have a big day ahead of us tomorrow. I think I'll have a nap now."

"Of course," Sebastian agreed. He kissed her on the cheek and left her in silence, softly closing the door behind him.

There was an optimistic pep to his step as he bounded down the hallway. Maybe he really did have a shot at making his own way in life and escaping his mother's vice-like grip. He rounded the corner with a smile on his face and started down the marble staircase, two steps at a time.

Just then, the doorbell rang. Lady Irons was crossing the foyer as the butler answered the door. There, in the broad doorway, stood Alistair and Penny. Sebastian stopped in his tracks, grasping the banister for support.

"Prince Alistair, please come in," Lady Irons welcomed with a curtsey.

"Thank you, Lady Irons. We are sorry to arrive unannounced. We're hoping we could visit with Sebastian before he leaves for America."

"By all means. One of the servants will summon him."

"I'm right here," Sebastian announced. It was unexpected to see them both. Happy to have a proper goodbye, he continued down the stairs and met them at the bottom.

"I'll leave you to say your goodbyes," his mother announced, excusing herself from the trio.

They made their way into the drawing room. Sebastian poured them each a glass of scotch. Alistair raised his glass to make a toast. "To the Libertines."

They all raised their glasses in unison and repeated, "To the Libertines."

Sebastian studied his friends. Penny looked lovely as ever in a pale pink silk sheath dress. Alistair was wearing one of his Savile Row suits. It hurt Sebastian to see how perfect they looked together. "I'm glad you came to see me off," he said.

"What will you do in America?" Penny asked.

"I have a plan. Well, the beginnings of a plan anyway. I think it will be a good trip for me. I can sort out some things. Get my life on track. We can't continue to party and drink forever, can we? We have to be adults." He directed the last line at Penny, remembering their last night in Alicante.

Penny nodded solemnly. "You'll write us, won't you? I don't want to miss a moment of your great American adventure."

"And I promise that Penny and I will come visit you once you've settled in," Alistair added.

"Yes, I would like that."

Alistair gave Sebastian a hug while slapping him on the back. "Take care, Irons."

"You too, blue blood."

He turned to Penny and gently hugged her goodbye.

Sebastian escorted them to the front door and watched as they descended the stone steps to Alistair's Range Rover. He turned away, closed the door, and started back to his bedroom.

As Alistair opened the passenger door of the vehicle, Penny stopped in her tracks and put her hand over her mouth in distress. "Oh! I forgot my silk scarf. I must have left it in the drawing room." She glanced over her shoulder toward the front door.

"I'll fetch it for you," Alistair offered.

"No, I can get it. Just start the car. It will only take a minute," she told him.

Penny returned to the house, opened the door, and ran down the foyer calling out Sebastian's name. He turned, halfway up the stairs, and rushed back down to meet her.

She threw her arms around him and passionately kissed him goodbye. She pulled away, wiping a single tear from her eye. "Be happy, Sebastian."

"You too, Pen," he whispered back.

She smiled at him, then quickly turned on her heel and rushed out the door, back to Alistair. She artfully pulled the hidden silk scarf out of her handbag and held it aloft for Alistair to see.

Part 2 - America 1985

Chapter 6 - Cruel Summer

"Well, here we are," Sebastian muttered as they deplaned at Philadelphia International Airport.

"Cheer up. You look as if you're going in front of a firing squad," Nanny said.

"I may very well be." They followed the signs that lead to customs. "I hope this doesn't take long," he sighed, looking at the line of travelers queued to have their passports stamped. Sebastian put the palm of his hand on his lower back, wincing as he stretched.

After they cleared customs, Sebastian escorted Nanny down the escalator in search of the hired help, Henry Cummings. Soon he spied a man holding up a white sign with 'S. Irons' printed on it. Henry was a fit, middle-aged man with thinning blond hair and pale blue eyes. He was simply dressed in khakis and a white, short-sleeved, button-down collared shirt. Sebastian noticed he wasn't wearing a tie.

"I'm Sebastian Irons and this is Mrs. Martha Jones," he introduced.

Henry took Sebastian's hand and shook it firmly. "Welcome to America. I hope you had a relaxing flight."

"It was fine, thank you. I'd like to get Nanny Jones home, wherever that may be, as soon as possible. She doesn't travel well."

"Yes, of course, sir. I'll collect your luggage and take you to the car."

They waited in silence for the carousel to begin its revolution. Bags slipped down the ramp and dropped onto the belt. Sebastian pointed out their luggage as it crested the top of the ramp and Henry removed each as it reached the bottom. Once all the bags were stacked neatly on the metal trolley, Henry escorted the pair to the Lincoln Town Car in the nearby parking garage.

The hot and humid air smacked Sebastian in the face. "Is it always this oppressive, Henry?"

"Sorry, sir. We do have humid summers here on the East Coast."

Sebastian helped Nanny into the back of the air conditioned car while Henry loaded the trunk with their luggage. Before long they were on their way to their new home. Sebastian tried to relax as he stared out the window. Various cars, trucks, and greenery were passing by at a rapid clip. The Americans drove on the wrong side of the road and it unsettled him. Everything seemed off in this foreign land.

Thirty minutes later, the driver signaled to make a right hand turn. Tall, wide bushes protected the land and Sebastian could not tell what lay behind them. As they turned into the drive, he noticed a small white plaque with the words 'Edgewood Estate' engraved on it. The house loomed in the distance. It was a large, stone mansion, three stories tall, with a balcony extending from the center of the second story.

"This is Edgewood," Henry announced with pride, looking over his shoulder at Sebastian.

"It's rather small," Sebastian complained.

"Don't be petulant," Nanny scolded. "You can't always live in a castle."

He sighed aloud. "I suppose you are right."

"Now, Sebastian, be mindful of your attitude. If you expect the worst, that's what you shall receive."

The car came to a halt in front of the house just as a woman came walking down the stone stairs to greet them. She seemed to be in her forties, with mousy brown hair that was neatly pulled back into an unflattering bun. "That's Alice, my wife," Henry announced as he turned off the ignition.

Sebastian helped Nanny out of the car. Alice welcomed them with a warm smile. "Sir, I'll be happy to take you on a tour of the house and answer any questions you might have. Henry and I are here to make your stay as comfortable as possible."

Sebastian smiled back. "Thank you very much. Right now, I'd like you to show me Nanny's room."

"Please, follow me." Alice led them up the stone stairs and into the foyer. Sebastian thought it large and forgettable, with nothing but a round table in the center, which currently held an oversized bouquet of lilies. They reminded Sebastian of his mother, so of course he detested them. A set of stairs began at both the left and right sides of the table and joined at the top into one staircase. Sebastian felt like he had just walked into an episode of *Dynasty*.

After Nanny was situated in her room, he joined Alice, who was waiting for him in the hall.

"I'll take you to your room now. Henry will bring your belongings up to you shortly. We'll leave Mrs. Jones' things in the hall until she is ready for them."

"Thank you. She is very special to me. Whatever she needs, see that she receives it."

They walked together down the long, navy-carpeted hallway. At the end, Alice stopped and opened a large oak door. She motioned for him to enter first. "This is the master bedroom. Your mother instructed me to see that you are settled in and comfortable. Dinner will be ready at six o'clock," Alice informed him. Her voice was formal, but caring. "Let me know if you need anything." She turned to leave the room.

"Alice, please remove the hideous lily bouquet in the foyer. Nanny is partial to roses."

"As you wish, sir," she said, and left him alone in his new bedroom.

Sebastian took a good look around the generously sized room. A king sleigh bed, adorned in maroon and navy paisley Ralph Lauren linens, dominated the main wall—not really his style, but he didn't particularly care. There was a small sitting area with a sofa placed on a hand-knotted rug fronting the stone fireplace. On the far right side of the room, glass French doors led to the same balcony he had observed when they drove up. The en suite bathroom was on the left side of the room.

He reached into his jacket pocket and grasped his cigarettes. Sebastian had not smoked since leaving Heathrow and was desperate for a calming hit of nicotine. He quickly lit up and slowly inhaled, enjoying the strong smell of tobacco and the sensation of smoke filling his lungs. Pulling the brass handles of the French doors, Sebastian opened them wide and stepped outside. *The property seemed nice enough*, he thought, flicking the excess ash onto the pavement two stories below. He wanted to explore the rest of it.

Sebastian pulled open the bedroom door just as Henry was poised to knock. "Ah, Henry, thank you for bringing my things. You can place them right inside. I will unpack later. I want to look at the grounds."

"Of course, sir."

"Can you find me an ashtray and bring a decanter of scotch up to my room when you have a moment?"

After a brief hesitation, Henry responded, "Your mother has requested there be no alcohol in the house during your stay."

"Of course she did." Sebastian smiled politely. "Then why don't we just keep that a little secret between you and me?"

"Sir, I know the legal age for drinking in your country is sixteen, but here in Pennsylvania, you must be twenty-one."

"I'm not an alcoholic. I just want a bloody scotch. Can you do that one simple thing for me?" Sebastian snarled. "And for God's sake, stop calling me sir."

"Sebastian, while I'm in charge here, there will be no alcohol," Henry informed him. "Please don't put me in the position to have to report your misdeeds back to you mother."

Sebastian lit another cigarette and walked away, fuming. How dare Henry stand up to him like that!

Entering the foyer, he noticed the lilies had been whisked away as ordered. At least Alice was efficient. Sebastian would have to be more cunning if he wanted to survive this wretched place. If Henry and Alice were reporting back to his mother, he would have to appear to be a model citizen. The only problem was, he had no idea how to do that.

Walking through the front door, he followed a brick path around to the back of the house. There were several acres of verdant, hilly land. Sebastian admired the immaculate landscaping. In the distance, he noticed a three-car garage and slightly past that was what appeared to be a stable.

Sebastian went to the garage first and opened the door. It was empty. Where was his car? Was his mother going to deprive him of this, too? She might as well just put iron bars on the doors and windows to make it look like an authentic prison.

Thankfully, in the stables, there were two horses. He approached the Arabian and patted its nose. "Hey, boy, how are you?" The horse rubbed his head against Sebastian's hand, enjoying the attention. "Don't worry. We'll get you out for a ride very soon." The smell of the stable reminded Sebastian of England, and for a moment he did not feel so lost and alone. Sitting on a wooden bench, he watched the horses for the longest time. There was much to ponder. What were Henry and Alice's intentions? Alice seemed nice enough, but could Sebastian sway her to his side? His mother had already gotten her claws into Henry, who was acting more like his minder than his servant. So far America had not impressed him.

He rose and bade farewell to the horses and wandered out of the stable toward the rose garden. *This will make Nanny very happy*, he thought. Sebastian could not wait to take her for a walk through the garden. It was small by comparison to the one back home in England, but it contained many roses that he did not recognize and assumed they were American varieties. This would certainly excite Nanny and give them both a way to spend their summer afternoons if he were forced to remain on the grounds.

Sebastian opened the door to the greenhouse. It had been there for many years and a few of the glass panels were cracked, but it was charming nonetheless. The wrought iron holding the glass panels in place were corroded, and the paint was peeling. Inside there was a cobweb-covered garden table with various rusted planting tools, a utility sink, and a dusty café table and chair set. Apparently, the greenhouse had not been used for ages. Sebastian wondered what restoring it would entail. The only dilemma was not having the slightest idea on how to go about the repairs. Maybe this project could be the means for Sebastian to win Henry over to his side.

Reentering the house through a rear door, Sebastian ended up in the kitchen, where he found Henry and Alice preparing dinner. They looked up as he entered. "Henry, I'd like to repair the greenhouse as a surprise for Nanny. Do you think you could help me make a list of the items we would need to make the repairs?"

"Yes, I would be more than happy to help."

"Good."

Alice stepped forward and handed Sebastian of glass of iced tea. "It's homemade. It will quench your thirst on a hot day like this."

Sebastian took the glass. He really wanted a scotch, but knew not to ask again. The tea was unsweetened and tasted refreshing, as Alice had promised. He thanked her with a small nod of his head.

"Sebastian, I took the liberty of picking up this driver's education booklet for you. You will have to take a written test and driving test to get your American license. When you obtain that, your mother will have a car delivered for you before school starts."

"Mother isn't going to make you drive me?"

"I can if you like."

Sebastian put his hand up. "No, that's quite all right. I want the car." He tucked the booklet under his arm, thanked them both, and retreated to his room.

The next morning, Henry knocked on Nanny's door. It was slightly ajar, so he stuck his head inside her room. "I've come to collect your tray, if you've finished with breakfast."

"Please, come in."

Henry walked into her room and picked up the tray. "Do you have a moment to sit and talk?" Nanny asked him.

"Yes," Henry responded, taking a seat in the chair opposite Nanny. "What can I do for you, Mrs. Jones?"

"I'm concerned about Sebastian. How do you think his transition is going?'

Henry contemplated the question for a moment and then replied. "As well as can be expected. He tried to get a bottle of scotch out of me yesterday. I sense a lot of anger in Sebastian. I'd even say he's a spoiled brat."

"Sebastian is a good boy. He just needs guidance."

"He's eighteen years old. Haven't you given him enough guidance?"

"Sebastian was sent to boarding school when he was eight years old. I only had the opportunity to spend time with him during summer vacations," Nanny answered. "His mother has been absent from his life, only stepping in when Sebastian gets in trouble."

"He excels at that, from what Lady Irons has told me," Henry interrupted.

"Sebastian feels as if he is in a no-win situation. His mother makes demands, so he rebels." She took a sip of tea and continued. "Sebastian never had a father, and that complicates the situation even further."

"Mrs. Jones, it's clear that you love Sebastian. I hope I have a chance to get to know the boy like you do. But for now, I've been hired to keep tabs on him and report back to Lady Irons."

"I understand, Henry. I just ask that you try to sympathize with what Sebastian is going through. Try to get to know him better. I promise I'll do my best to make him realize he's heading down a path that will only bring him harm." Nanny looked into Henry's eyes and implored, "Sebastian needs support. He needs to feel safe here. Can you and Alice help me do that?"

Before Henry could respond, Sebastian entered the room. He was unsure of what he walked in on, but it seemed to be a serious conversation. "Good morning, Nanny," he greeted, bending down to kiss her on the cheek.

"Good morning, dear."

Henry stood up and collected the breakfast tray. "I'll leave."

"Henry, I've studied the driver's education book you gave me. Can you take me to DMV to take the test today?"

"You just got the book yesterday," Henry reasoned.

"I'm ready to take the test."

"Okay, I can take you in an hour."

Sebastian joined Nanny in the library for tea upon returning from his outing with Henry.

"How was your day, Sebastian?"

"Fine," he replied, sitting on the sofa next to her. "I passed my written test, but I have to wait to take the driver's test, so it looks like my prison sentence continues."

"Oh, don't be so dramatic."

"I'm not used to being stuck in one place, Nanny. I'm trying to behave. I've just been shopping with the hired help for construction materials."

"Construction materials?"

"I thought it would be a good idea to repair the greenhouse in the garden."

"I'm sure Henry will be happy to help you with that project."

"Maybe. I just can't seem to figure Henry out. One minute he's the house warden and the next we're going shopping together." Sebastian took an empty tea cup from the tray and poured the steaming contents of the china tea pot into the cup.

"Henry's in a tough position. Your mother has made demands on him, and at the same time he wants to get to know you better."

"He wouldn't give me a bottle of scotch. Said mother told him no alcohol should be kept in the house."

"I'm happy about that," Nanny admitted. "I think you drink too much."

Sebastian groaned in frustration. "Not you, too."

"You've made too many mistakes, Sebastian. Your mother has to crack down if you have any hope of righting your path. Unfortunately, that now falls on Henry's shoulders. He's a good man. Give him a chance."

"Nanny, I promised you I'd turn things around. I will not let the money you're spending on my education to go to waste," he reassured her.

"I'm glad to hear it."

The next day, Sebastian found himself surrounded by glass panels, utility knives, and paint brushes. Various other tools where laid out and he wasn't quite sure of their purpose.

"I'll leave you to it," Henry said.

Sebastian began to laugh aloud. "Henry, you can't expect me to repair the greenhouse on my own."

"I left you a do-it-yourself manual. I'm sure you can figure it out. " He turned and began to walk back to the house.

"Henry, please," Sebastian swallowed his pride. "I need your help. I've never done anything like this before. I don't even know what half these tools are called."

Henry slowly turned and smiled. "You'd like my help?"

"No, I desperately *need* your help." Sebastian sighed. "Look, I know I can be a prick, but I am trying to be on my best behavior. I want to repair the greenhouse for Nanny. She'll be so pleased if we can restore it. If you won't do it for me, will you at least do it for her?"

Henry pondered the request for a long moment. "Okay, we'll do this together." He reached out his hand as a peace offering. Sebastian grasped it in a firm handshake.

A few hours later, Sebastian was nursing a bloody thumb, smashed under his own inept attempts with a hammer. Henry bandaged the wound. Alice supplied the iced tea.

"I think we should call it a day. We can pick up again tomorrow," Henry said.

"Thank you. I really do appreciate your help."

Henry sat back in the chair and studied Sebastian. "You're an enigma. One minute I want to send you to your room for being a brat; the next minute you show me a glimpse of vulnerability and I'm amazed at the lengths you'll go to for Mrs. Jones—the unconditional love you have for her."

Sebastian shrugged. "I never claimed to be perfect. I'm just trying to figure out how to live my life under very difficult circumstances."

When the restoration of the greenhouse was at last complete, Sebastian proudly escorted Nanny through the rose garden to see the finished product, holding a parasol over her head to protect her from the sun. "What do you think?" he asked.

Nanny observed Sebastian and Henry's workmanship: the glass was sparking clean and the wrought iron was freshly painted a crisp, bright white; the inside was swept and tidy; the planting tools were cleaned and neatly arranged on the work table; and the little café tabletop was decorated with a linen cloth and a simple yet elegant floral arrangement. She smiled, patting his hand. "I think it's beautiful, Sebastian."

He beamed. "I did it for you, Nanny."

"You should do it for yourself, not me."

"I have to confess—I really enjoyed spending time with Henry. I never could have pictured myself using a hammer or paint brush. Now I look at the finished product and see that I helped make this happen. Could you ever believe it?"

"Henry is good for you. You need a positive male figure in your life."

Her comment reminded him the subject he was never allowed to broach—but he would try again, anyway. "Why won't you talk to me about my father?"

"You know I can't, Sebastian. Please don't bring this up again."

"She's not here. How would she know?" Sebastian reasoned.

"Lady Irons has an uncanny ability to know everything, no matter what continent she may be on."

"I appreciate your discretion, Nanny, but I'm eighteen years old. I think I deserve to know, and Mother won't tell me." He turned sideways to face her. "There must be something you can tell me. Why did he leave?"

Nanny pondered the questions for a long time. Sebastian waited patiently. Finally she said, "Your father didn't leave on his own accord. Your mother found him in her bed with another woman. She sent him away that very day and quickly divorced him."

"Seems a bit extreme. Why not just send him to another wing of the house?"

"Your father was quite the ladies' man. I think finding him in her bed was the last straw. Now we mustn't speak of such unpleasant things."

Sebastian wasn't surprised by Nanny's story. He knew how strict his mother could be and the lengths she would go to rectify an unpleasant situation. Sebastian imagined he'd be driven to have affairs, too, if he were married to Lady Lily Irons. "I have no memories of him, Nanny."

"Sebastian, your mother found out she was pregnant after she sent your father away." She tried to smile as she reached for his hand. "I'm so sorry, my dear boy."

Sebastian shrugged. There was no point in grieving over someone he never knew. "It doesn't matter. I've had you to raise me. I couldn't ask for anyone better." And with that, he dropped the subject all together.

Friday morning, Sebastian escorted Nanny to breakfast. "Let's eat in the kitchen with Henry and Alice," she suggested. "There is no sense in using the formal dining room when it's only the two of us. I like Henry and Alice's company."

Sebastian didn't argue. Since his exile had begun two months before, he and Henry seemed to be forging a relationship, despite the bumpy start. In a way, Henry had become a surrogate father—teaching Sebastian to drive, showing him how to repair the greenhouse, and working in the stables with the horses. Suddenly Sebastian found that life at Edgewood Estate was not all bad. It seemed as if he had found an unconventional 'family' with Nanny, Henry, and Alice.

Alice smiled as Nanny and Sebastian entered the kitchen. "Good morning, I'll have breakfast ready in a moment."

"We'd like to eat in here this morning, Alice."

"Okay, I'll get the dishes from the dining room." Alice stopped in the doorway. "Oh, Sebastian, there's a letter for you that's just arrived today from England—it's on the table."

"Thank you, Alice." He picked up the letter and looked at the return address. It was from Penny. He stared at it for a long time, not sure if he wanted to open it. Curiosity eventually won out and he ripped the flap of the envelope, pulling out its contents. Inside, on crème-colored Symthson stationary, Penny had written in beautiful cursive.

Dearest Sebastian,

I hope you are well and making your way in America. I'm sure the culture shock has been difficult, so I did not want to disturb you while you settled in. Things are progressing with Alistair. He's taking me to the Live Aid concert next week. It will be our first public outing as a couple. I'm more than a little nervous. I wanted to let you know that I think of you often and miss you terribly. I cannot seem to shake the memories of our secret week, nor do I want to. I hope you are on the way to finding the peace and happiness you so deserve.

With much love,
Penny

After reading the letter, three things entered Sebastian's mind: he didn't know if he should crumple the letter in his fist, tear it into a million little pieces, or carefully tuck it away.

"Are you all right?" Nanny asked in a concerned tone. "Was it bad news?"

Sebastian shook his head. "It's nothing, Nanny. I'm fine." He slipped the letter in his pants pocket.

A few minutes later, the four of them were sitting together eating eggs Benedict. "What are your plans for today?" Nanny asked Sebastian.

"I don't know. I groomed the horses yesterday and visited the library the day before that." He tried to be pleasant, but the news from Penny had left him with little appetite.

"Have you talked to your sister lately?"

Before Sebastian could respond, Alice jumped into the conversation. "You have a sister?"

"I have two older sisters and a brother."

"Sigourney lives in New York City," Nanny explained to Henry and Alice. "You should go visit her, Sebastian. I know she would love it."

"I don't have a car, Nanny."

Henry glanced at Nanny, who nodded her approval. "You could take the train," Henry suggested.

Sebastian had often thought of visiting Sigourney, but assumed his 'house arrest' would prevent him from leaving the grounds of Edgewood. What were they thinking encouraging Sebastian to take a trip to New York? The city was brimming with temptation at every turn. Maybe that was exactly what he needed after two months of perfect behavior—a little fun in the city and a means to forget about Penny, who again entered his thoughts. "Can we leave after breakfast?"

The Amtrak train sped along the tracks of the Northeast Corridor toward Penn Station. Sebastian stared out the window watching the scenery pass by, a book sitting unread in his lap. He couldn't shut his brain off. Images of Penny invaded his mind and he couldn't tune them out. Why did he miss her so much? It was no use: she belonged to Alistair. He hoped that New York would banish her from his consciousness.

Sebastian knocked on the front door of his sister's house, a beautiful old brownstone on the Upper East Side. A minute later, a maid opened the door. "I'm here to see Sigourney," he announced. Stepping into the foyer, he observed a flurry of activity inside. Men were moving furniture in the sitting room. Women were arranging flowers and setting up cocktail glasses.

His sister entered the foyer. "Sebastian!" she exclaimed with delight, rushing to hug her brother. "What are you doing here?" She was dressed in a khaki skirt and Lacoste polo, her long brown hair pulled back in a ponytail.

"Visiting. I was sprung from prison with time off for good behavior." Motioning around with his arm, he asked, "What are you doing?"

"Throwing a party. What good timing you have. How long are you staying?" she asked, pointing to his overnight bag.

"Don't know. I just needed to get out of Philadelphia for a while."

She leaned in and kissed him on the cheek. "Well, make yourself at home. The party starts at eight. I've got a ton to accomplish before then." And with that, Sigourney was gone.

Wandering into the sitting room, Sebastian found the bar stocked for the party. He grabbed a crystal glass and the bottle of scotch and made his way over to an oversized chair in the corner of the room. Ignoring the frenzied activities surrounding him, he poured the scotch and took a sip. The wonderful flavor of oak, leather, and apricot swirled over his taste buds. Leaning back in the chair with a grin on his lips, he thought, *This is heaven.*

Once showered and dressed for the party, Sebastian walked to Sigourney's room. Inside, she was sitting at the vanity table, brushing her long brown hair. "Come sit," she instructed. "I want to catch up with you."

Sebastian lay on the bed, propping his head with his right hand. "What kind of party is this?" She was wearing designer jeans and a silver silk halter top. Sebastian was conservatively dressed in a suit.

"Oh, I'm just having a few chums over from school. It's nothing formal."

Sebastian groaned. "Please don't subject me to boring musos who like impromptu Beethoven jams."

"Nothing about Beethoven is impromptu," she admonished.

"Fine, then tell me you'll have beautiful women that I can flirt with at this party."

Sigourney turned to face him and threw her hairbrush at Sebastian.

"What? I've been celibate for two months!"

"You must be in a great deal of pain, darling," she teased.

"Excruciating."

"Enough about your sex life. Tell me about Henry and Alice. Are they terrible to you?"

"How do you know about them?"

"Mummy, of course."

Of course Lily would have filled her in on the whole sordid affair. "They're not so bad. Alice is an amazing cook. Henry has been teaching me to drive and we repaired the greenhouse together," Sebastian explained.

"Interesting."

"Yes, I've been reduced to manual labor to stave off boredom. I've no car, drugs, or sex, and I'm almost out of cigarettes. Which reminds me—please tell me there's a shop in town where I can pick up some Dunhills?"

"There's a British shop on Fifty-Second and Lex."

"Brilliant."

Sigourney stood, surveyed herself in the full length mirror, and smiled. "Time to party."

Sebastian observed the party guests' arrivals from the chair in the corner of the sitting room. Sigourney greeted every guest—a mix of wealthy, educated, and bohemian people.

One woman in particular caught his eye. She was tall and exotic looking with short black hair, high cheekbones, and glowing dark brown skin. Sebastian had a strong urge to touch her and see if her skin was as soft and luxurious as it looked. He stood and made a beeline in her direction. Sigourney was standing close to the woman. They seemed to share a private joke, laughing as he approached.

"Sebastian, this is my friend Ashia," Sigourney introduced.

Sebastian took Ashia's hand and kissed it. Her skin was as soft as silk against his lips. "Pleased to meet you. That's a lovely name."

"Thank you," she replied in a South African accent.

"What brings you to America?"

"I'm studying economics at NYU."

Sebastian slid her arm through his and steered her to the bar, winking at Sigourney as they left his sister's company.

"NYU? And here I thought I'd be surrounded by stuffy Juilliard types all evening."

Ashia laughed. "I assure you, I'm not stuffy. What university are you attending? Wait, let me guess." She studied him for a moment, looking up and down at his body. "Columbia, right?"

Sebastian grinned. "You are both beautiful and perceptive." He let her believe whatever truth she wanted to impose on him. "What would you like to drink?

"Cosmopolitan."

The bartender nodded and looked at Sebastian. "Scotch—neat."

Ashia stayed by his side the entire evening. Sebastian enjoyed talking, dancing, and drinking with her. He was very glad he had taken Nanny's advice and made the trip.

"Would you like a tour of the house?" Sebastian inquired, eager to leave the crowd and get her alone.

"Let's start with your bedroom," she purred, taking his hand.

They made their way upstairs to his room. As soon as the door was opened, Ashia grabbed Sebastian's jacket and pulled him into a kiss. He backed her up against the wall and greedily accepted the kiss, opening her mouth with his tongue to taste her. He was buzzed from the alcohol and so turned on he wasn't thinking straight. This wasn't slow and sensual lovemaking. He just had a strong urge to fuck her, so that's exactly what he did, up against the wall. They were sweaty, grinding and moaning in unison. When the deed was done, Ashia pulled down her skirt and softly kissed him on the lips. "Thanks for a good time," she murmured in a sexy voice.

"My pleasure."

She left him alone in his room. Sebastian was drunk and sated, but still very lonely.

The next morning he woke with a throbbing headache and parched throat. Why did he always give in to the temptation, he wondered, slowly making his way to the bathroom.

Sebastian sat on the closed toilet lid and attempted to open the childproof aspirin cap, with no luck. He threw it across the bathroom in frustration. It hit the far wall and the top popped off, sending dozens of little white pills bouncing off the floor. "Brilliant," he muttered, getting down on his knees to pick them up.

Turning on the shower to its hottest setting, he stripped off his clothes and stepped into the stall. The warm water seemed to sober him up and lessen the headache. *I can't do this anymore*, he thought to himself, attempting to let the flow of water wash the indiscretions of the previous day down the drain. Sebastian stayed in the shower until the water ran cold.

Come Monday he would get back on track. Nanny, Henry, and Alice would be none the wiser of his New York encounter with the beautiful South African. He would go back to Pennsylvania where Henry would take him to the DMV for his driving test. Once he had his license, Sebastian would go to the library and do research on universities that he might like to attend. If Nanny was going to pay for his college education, he had to prove to her and himself that he was taking it seriously. He definitely wanted to do some research on NYU.

Chapter 7 - The Kids in America

Sebastian took a deep breath before he grabbed the metal handle of the glass door. *You can do this*, he thought to himself. He stepped inside St. Alexander's High School to the sounds of a multitude of footfalls walking along the highly polished floor. Some students laughed and hugged one another, happy to reconnect after summer vacation; others looked downright depressed to be back. Sebastian was definitely siding with the latter group.

He studied the other young men in their navy blazers and starched white shirts adorned with red striped ties. The young ladies were wearing navy pleated skirts and white oxford blouses. He certainly looked the part, he thought, but Sebastian still felt ill at ease.

After receiving his class schedule and a map of the building from the dean's office, Sebastian made his way to room 102 for English class. He kept a low profile and tried to avoid any attention. It seemed easy enough through the first two classes of the morning, but then homeroom occurred. This concept was very foreign to Sebastian, who was used to coming and going as he pleased without having to account for his whereabouts between classes at Eton.

Mrs. Royer was this year's homeroom teacher. She started the period with roll call. There were whispers in the back of the room about him, the new student that had come to St. Alexander's. Sebastian tried to ignore it, but sat uneasily, the stares of twenty-seven students bearing down on him.

Mrs. Royer looked down at her seating chart and called, "Sebastian Irons."

"Present," he replied in a perfect American accent.

It took no more than a mere moment until laughter broke out from the far corner of the room. "The Bradley F. Walters Prep School is down the block," Sean Moore, quarterback of the football team, muttered under his breath.

Mrs. Royer shot an angry look to the back of the room. "Sean, I will not put up with this behavior in my homeroom. I think you owe Mr. Irons an apology."

"Yes, Mrs. Royer. Sorry," he said unconvincingly. He turned back to his friends and continued talking, ignoring the reprimand.

The girl who had been sitting quietly next to Sebastian leaned toward him and softly said, "Don't let them get you down. Since you're new around here, you're not going to get much respect. You might as well be a freshman to them. Sean's a jerk anyway."

Sebastian turned to look at her. She was a plain-looking girl. He had to admit that if he passed her on the street he would not have looked twice in her direction. She had wavy, brown, shoulder-length hair, a fair complexion, and wasn't wearing any makeup. Her smile was warm and inviting, but when he looked into her eyes, he was struck by their kindness. "Thank you," Sebastian whispered. "I would have called him a daft prick, but thought it might be best to stay out of trouble my first day of school."

He gauged her reaction; the corners of her mouth turned up slightly. She was trying to suppress a laugh. "Now that's one I haven't heard before." She extended her hand. "I'm Tess Hamilton. Welcome to Alexander's."

He returned the handshake. "Sebastian Irons—but you already know that."

The announcements blared over the PA system and the room quieted. All attention was off Sebastian for a few minutes. The homeroom period was finished with the sound of the ringing bell, and everyone began to rise from their seats. Tess stood and collected her books.

"I'll be seeing you around, Sebastian," she said with a knowing smile.

"I hope so," he replied.

Sebastian followed Tess into the maze of hallways. "Where is your next class?" Tess asked as the sea of students flowed past them like the rushing tide.

"Biology—room 302."

"Go down the hall and take the stairs to the third floor."

Sebastian was about to thank her, but Tess was already making her way down the hall in the opposite direction. She'd been nice to him with seemingly no ulterior motive. It caught him off guard. This transition to ordinary American teenager was going to require far more patience and perhaps more skill than he had estimated. He wondered if he could pull it off.

Sebastian had been dreading lunch, but was relieved when he spied Tess Hamilton in the corner of the cafeteria seated with a few girls. The cafeteria was brimming with loud students catching up with each others' summer adventures and already complaining about their new teachers and homework.

Sebastian found a table near Tess and her friends and took a seat alone. They were engrossed in conversation and didn't notice him as he approached. He opened one of his textbooks and pretended to read, but in reality he wanted to eavesdrop on the girls' conversation—especially to find out more about Tess, the only friendly face in this cold school.

Jordan asked, "Did you guys see the Jag out in the parking lot this morning?"

"No," Courtney replied as she took a bite out of her hamburger, "but I bet it belongs to the mystery man over there." She motioned in Sebastian's direction. Apparently they weren't too engrossed and had noticed his presence after all.

Jordan looked over her shoulder to see Sebastian sitting at the end of the table alone. "He's rich and good looking, but he seems weird."

"Not weird, Jordan, eccentric," Courtney corrected.

Tess, who had purposely stayed out of the conversation to this point, interrupted. "He's new here. Can you imagine how hard it must be to start a new school in your senior year?"

"Well, maybe you should go invite him to sit with us?" Jordan suggested.

"He's studying. I don't want to interrupt," Tess reasoned.

"He's not a gorgeous as Jeff," Jordan announced, changing the subject.

"Jeff who?" Courtney inquired with a raised eyebrow.

"Jeff Phillips: Kramer High, popular, extremely attractive, six-foot one, gorgeous blond hair, athletic, just an average student—but then we can't have everything," Tess informed Courtney.

"Yeah, well at least I like boys," Jordan challenged.

Tess sighed and turned her attention to Courtney. "She always does this to me. It's not that I don't like boys—I simply choose not to have a boyfriend. There is a difference. High school boys are immature and stupid. When I find one that has some intelligence and good manners, I might change my mind."

"Whatever," Jordan replied, focusing on her salad.

Having heard the whole conversation, Sebastian couldn't help but chuckle. Maybe this school year would have some entertaining moments after all.

The rest of the day dragged on as Sebastian made his way through his class schedule. There were sideways glances, stares, and muttered comments since his arrival at school, but he ignored them the best he could and went about his business. When the last bell chimed at 2:45, signaling the end of the school day, Sebastian navigated his way to the study hall. He was there to meet the genius tutor his mother had arranged for him. He wasn't in the mood to study and all he really wanted was a cigarette, but he was mindful of Nanny's instruction to blend in and buckle down, so he dutifully awaited the arrival of his savior.

Tess Hamilton promptly entered the study hall at 2:50 and walked up to him, laying her textbooks on his table.

"You?" Sebastian blurted out, slightly startled, but with a broad grin on his face.

"They didn't tell you I was your tutor?"

"No."

"Well, at least you look pleased—that's half the battle. Why didn't you ask who your tutor was in the dean's office? Weren't you curious?"

"I don't care who is doing the tutoring. My job is to listen and learn. I'm not interested in your body, just your mind."

Tess did have a nice body, he observed, finally able to get a full view of her standing next to him. She was petite, about five-feet two inches, with an hourglass figure.

"Gee, way to make a girl feel wanted," she teased.

"If you're looking for sex, I'd be happy to oblige. This table looks sturdy, and I like a girl who doesn't have an aversion to public displays of attraction."

"Public displays of affection," Tess corrected, not missing a beat.

"I hardly think carnal desire has anything to do with affection," Sebastian countered.

"Then it's a good thing you're not interested in my body." She placed her hands on her hips and shook her head. "What did I get myself into?"

Sebastian didn't reply, but stood up and pulled out a chair for Tess to sit.

"You're charming," she commented.

"Yes," he merely agreed, with no sense of false modesty.

"And arrogant."

"I prefer aloof," he corrected her.

"Well, with a vocabulary like that, you should have no problem with the English portion of your SATs."

He smiled to himself. He liked her straightforward attitude. Tess was not one of those polite socialite types he was so used to, who smiled demurely then quickly gossiped behind your back. She was a breath of fresh air.

"I printed out a schedule for you. We'll meet on Tuesdays and Fridays. I have yearbook and the school paper on Mondays and Wednesdays. I can probably squeeze you in if you need a few SAT prep sessions before you take the exam in October. What was your last score?"

"What score are you referring to?"

"Your SAT score."

"I haven't taken it yet."

She didn't hide the surprise from her face. "What universities are you planning to apply to?"

At least he could answer this question. "NYU and Princeton."

"Hmm."

"Why did you just 'hmm?' It is absurd to think that I could attend either one of these schools?" Sebastian spat back, slightly annoyed.

"I didn't say that. I just find it curious that I'm tutoring you this late in the game and you have such lofty aspirations. You'll have to work hard to get into these schools. What type of extracurricular activities have you been involved in?"

Again, she was speaking a different language he didn't quite understand. He was sure she was not talking about parties, drugs, and sex. These were the only extracurricular activities he knew. "I'm sorry," he apologized. "I don't quite understand."

She gave him a mystified glance. "You need activities to put on your application. You know—student council, honor society, school paper."

"Yes, well, I can't really say I've done any of those things."

"Okay, it's your lucky day," she replied. "Since I'm editor of both the school paper and yearbook, I can get you on the staff."

"I would appreciate that."

"Let's get started. We have a lot of work to do," she instructed him, opening her calculus book to chapter one.

Sebastian buckled down, as he'd promised Nanny, and survived the first week of school. He honestly liked Tess, so studying alongside her wasn't so bad. Even when he tried to give her a hard time, she gave it right back, unfazed and resilient.

He walked Tess to her car after they finished his Friday afternoon tutoring session. "Do you think you could spend some time with me tomorrow to help with the SAT prep?" he asked her as they stopped in front of Tess' brown Chevy Chevette. It was well used, with a few scratches here and there, but clean and tidy inside and out. She kept it in good condition, which did not surprise him in the least.

"I'm working with Habitat for Humanity tomorrow afternoon, but I could squeeze you in during the morning."

"What's Habitat for Humanity?"

She looked at him as if he were from another planet. "They build and rehab houses for those who can't afford to do it themselves."

"I could do that," Sebastian offered.

"Sorry, you don't look like you've ever touched a hammer or paint brush in your entire life," Tess said, looking at his perfectly manicured hands.

"Well, there's a lot you don't know about me, Tess," he responded, putting his hands in his pockets. "What time should I come over?"

"Ten o'clock." She neatly printed her address on a piece of notebook paper and pulled it out of the tablet, tearing it smoothly along the perforation. "Here's my number and address."

He took the piece of paper and slipped it inside his blazer pocket. "I'll see you tomorrow then."

She unlocked her car, got inside, fastened her seat belt, backed out of her space, and drove away. Sebastian was left behind, watching her car disappear around the bend.

Sebastian woke early the next morning and lay in bed reflecting on the past week, his new tutor and the prospect of the work required to be accepted into the two universities that he had picked. He couldn't charm his way out of this one. Tess was single-minded in her goal to make him an excellent student. It was unlike him to work so hard for something. There was a new focus to life that he didn't particularly mind. The thought of this made him laugh aloud. He had managed to make a complete hundred and eighty degree turn from the life he led five months ago.

Tess lived in Spring City. Sebastian enjoyed the drive through the quaint little town. The main street was lined with mom and pop stores and family restaurants. He checked the notebook paper and glanced at addresses on the mailboxes as he slowly rolled down the far end of the street. He found Tess' house with little problem and arrived promptly at ten o'clock. It was a small, cute Cape Cod situated on a tree-lined street. It looked like something out of a Norman Rockwell painting. He parked on the street in front of her house. Sebastian bounded up the front lawn and knocked on the door. Her mother, Kate, answered almost immediately.

"Hello, you must be Sebastian. Please come in." She had the sweetest smile. Tess looked just like her, he observed. She was dressed in white nurse scrubs with little teddy bears on them. She seemed too young to be a mother to someone Tess' age. He extended his hand and shook hers. She had a soft grip.

Sebastian looked up as Tess came down the stairs clutching SAT prep books, pens, and notepads. She was wearing a navy St. Alexander's hooded sweatshirt and jeans. Her hair was pulled back in a ponytail, not as a fashion statement but as a matter of practicality. "Right on time," she said, walking past him and waving for him to follow. "Ready to get started? We'll sit at the kitchen table."

"Lead the way," Sebastian replied, already following behind.

They sat at the table and opened their books. Tess started explaining the type of exam questions Sebastian would be asked during the test. Tess' mother found a pause in the lesson and interrupted briefly. "There's some homemade soup in the crock pot and sandwiches in the fridge for lunch." She turned to Sebastian. "Make yourself at home and don't let Tess make you work too hard. It is Saturday, after all."

Sebastian stood up. "Thank you for your hospitality, Mrs. Hamilton."

Mrs. Hamilton patted him gently on the back. "Tess was right, you are a charmer."

"Please don't hold that against me."

She simply smiled at him and then turned to Tess. "I'll be home around eight o'clock." She grabbed her coat and keys and headed out of the house to go to work.

"Your mother is a nurse?" Sebastian inquired.

"Yeah, she works in the pediatric division. All sorts of crazy hours. She does it so I can go to Alexander's and get into a good college."

"What does your father do for a living?"

Her voice dropped a notch. "He died when I was fourteen."

"I'm so sorry. I didn't know," Sebastian apologized.

"It's okay. I've had three years to get used to it. But you never really do get used to it, do you? I still don't understand it to this day. He was thirty-nine years old. He went to work in the morning just like any other day. In the afternoon, a police officer showed up at our door to inform us he had died of a heart attack."

"I never knew my father," Sebastian suddenly found himself confessing softly. He would never have done this with any other new acquaintance. Somehow, Tess was different. He felt an easy connection with her that he couldn't explain.

Now Tess was apologizing. "I'm sorry. That's terrible. I can't ever imagine not knowing my dad. Did your father die, too?"

"No, he was banished from the kingdom," he replied without emotion. "He had fidelity issues. I don't even think he ever knew I existed." He tried to explain, but it just sounded awful.

"Did you ever think of looking for him?"

"Yes, but from the little I know about him, he wasn't a very nice man. I'd rather live with the image I've created in my imagination. There's less disappointment that way." He tried to laugh it off. "I sound very morose and pathetic. We should study."

On that suggestion, they put all thoughts of their fathers away and dug into the books. She quizzed him. He scribbled notes and paged through books, finding the correct references and explanations for his errors.

"Okay, time for lunch," Tess said, closing her workbook after they had studied for an hour and a half. Sebastian piled the books and papers together and made room for their plates and bowls. Tess served up the sandwiches and hot beef barley soup.

Sebastian breathed in deeply. It smelled fabulous. He picked up his spoon and tasted the soup. Tess watched in silence. He could feel her eyes on him. Sebastian could not take it any longer; he put down his spoon and said, "What's wrong? Why are you staring at me?"

"You're not like the other boys at St. Alexander's," she replied. "You hold yourself differently. Your vocabulary and diction is different. You have intelligence and manners. It's like you stepped out of an episode of *Masterpiece Theatre*."

"What if I did? Would that change our friendship?"

"Are we friends?" Tess asked with raised eyebrows.

"I consider you my friend."

Sebastian stood up and pulled the billfold out of his perfectly fitting khaki pants, and opened it to locate his dog-eared passport. He handed it to Tess. She looked at the gold embossed lion and unicorn crest on the red cover. *European Community of United Kingdom and Northern Ireland* was stamped across the top. Tess opened the passport to find a photo of a much younger Sebastian, perfectly groomed and looking straight ahead, without expression. She read the information next to the photo.

> Irons, Sebastian Andrew. D.O.B. 31 May 1967
> Place of Birth - London, England

He could see the mix of shock, disbelief, and maybe a little bit of anger in her expression. He hoped he had not blown any chance of friendship he might have with her by revealing his identity. "But you don't have an accent. Were you raised in America?"

"No, I just had the foresight to hire a very good dialect coach. Are you angry with me?"

"How could I be angry? I really don't know you. Why keep it a secret?" she asked, handing back the passport.

"Come on, Tess. You saw how I was treated on my first day at Alexander's. It's bad enough that I had to start my senior year at a brand new school where everyone already knows everyone else. I'm ridiculed for my social status. I didn't need an accent to bring even more attention to myself," he explained.

"I do understand, Sebastian. But you shouldn't have to pretend to be someone else. When we're alone, just be yourself. I want to hear your real voice."

Sebastian closed his eyes and took a minute to compose himself. He was so happy she had accepted him so readily. Finally he said, "It's not an easy thing to switch on and off. I really have to concentrate when I speak to get the accent right. It's just easier to stay with the American voice," he explained in his own British accent.

"You never have to worry about that again, not around me," she reassured. "I have so many questions."

Sebastian looked at his watch. "Well, you will have to save them for later. We have a house to build."

They headed for the foyer, grabbed their coats, and locked the door of the house behind them as they stepped outside. Sebastian pulled out his car keys from his coat pocket. Tess spoke up and said, "I think you had better let me drive. We're going to a pretty poor neighborhood."

"I'm not worried," he said reassuringly, thinking she was concerned that his car would be stolen.

Tess stopped in her tracks. He had misunderstood her. "Sebastian, your car is a little too ostentatious. Think of what we're going to do today. I don't think we should pull up in a brand new Jaguar."

"Okay, you drive."

They got into the Chevette and Tess started the engine. Level 42's *Something About You* blared from the stereo speakers. "Oops, sorry. When I drive alone I like to turn up the stereo and sing," she admitted with a hint of embarrassment.

"Well, go on then," he quipped in an outright challenge.

"No, I only sing alone." She quickly changed the subject. "Why did you decide to come to Alexander's?"

"It wasn't my choice. It was my mother's. My turn," he countered. "Why do you work so hard?"

She stared straight ahead as she drove, her eyes checking the mirrors at regular intervals. "I don't have a choice, either. Since my dad died, my mom has been working extra shifts to pay my tuition to Alexander's and save for my college education. I can't let her down. I figure the best way I could help is work my ass off, graduate as valedictorian, and get a scholarship to NYU so she can take it easy for a change."

"Hmm."

"What's the 'hmm' for?"

"Wouldn't that be a coincidence if we both ended up at the same university?" Sebastian queried. "And what would you be studying?"

"Journalism," she replied matter-of-factly, as if this had been her goal for her entire existence. "Now since you just asked me two questions, I get to do the same," Tess informed him. "You said you got the feeling your father wasn't a nice man. Why?"

"I swear, you are the most confident and aggressive girl I've ever met," he stated in amazement as a smile crossed his lips. These were qualities in a girl he was not used to encountering. It intrigued him and he wanted to learn more about her, not tell her his life story.

"You didn't answer my question." She stole a glance at him as the car came to a complete stop at a four-way intersection. "Stop stalling."

He sighed and tried to formulate his thoughts into a coherent explanation. "My father had several mistresses. One day my mother came home and found him in her bed with one of them. She divorced him and paid him to disappear. I can't really blame him—I'd do the same if I had to be married to her. Evidently, after he was gone, she found out she was pregnant with me."

"You don't like her very much, do you?"

"No, I don't like her at all," he replied without emotion.

"How can you possibly say that?"

"She's an evil woman."

"But she raised you!"

"No, she didn't." He began to fidget in the passenger seat. "I've had enough of this game for today. Can we please stop?" He reached for the car stereo without waiting for an answer and turned up the volume.

Sebastian and Tess spent the afternoon rehabbing a house in North Philadelphia. The neighborhood may have been very depressed, but there was a feeling of happy togetherness from everyone around. He had never experienced a sense of community like this before. Sebastian and Tess' job was installing wallboard. He was happy to help, and being selfless felt good. It wasn't a quality he was known for, but he was determined to try it more often. Of course, spending the afternoon with Tess was a bonus.

They were dirty and a little sweaty, with flecks of drywall clinging to their hair and clothing. A few neighbors waved goodbye and the future homeowners patted Sebastian on the back and gave Tess heartfelt hugs as they were leaving the home.

"That was a good day," Sebastian announced, walking back to Tess' car. "You worked hard today—I'll drive."

"Are you sure? It's doesn't ride like a Jaguar," Tess reminded him.

"Yes," he reassured her, opening the passenger door for Tess. "Let me take you to dinner. Your mother won't be home until eight. You should have a decent meal. We can get her some takeaway so she won't have to cook when she gets home."

"Where did you have in mind?"

"There are several restaurants I've read about here in the city that I'd like to try. What are you in the mood for?"

"McDonald's."

Sebastian laughed until he realized she was serious. "I've never eaten at McDonald's," he admitted.

"Never?" she asked in disbelief. "They must have McDonald's in England."

"Oh, they do. I've just never been to one."

"Well, that's where I would like to go, please."

Sebastian leaned in to touch a few loose strands of hair on her head. Tess instinctively pulled away from him. "You have some dried paint in your hair," he said, trying to explain his sudden action.

She laughed nervously. "See, I'm an absolute disaster. McDonald's is the only place I'm dressed for."

They walked into the restaurant and looked at the lighted menu board above the cashier. Sebastian was not enthused. Tess turned to him. "It's only a hamburger. It won't kill you. It's one of the simple pleasures in life."

"A simple pleasure is a fifteen-year-old single malt scotch," he shot back instantly, without thinking.

"I said simple pleasure, not expensive pleasure," Tess chided before stepping up to the teenaged cashier and ordering. "We'll have two number three meals with Diet Cokes." She didn't give Sebastian a choice. He was in her territory now.

The cashier pushed a few buttons. "That will be seven fifty."

Sebastian reached around and handed the bored employee a twenty dollar bill. He had the change in his pocket before she could complain. "You're a cheap date," he joked as their drinks were poured and their cheeseburgers and fries placed on a small plastic tray and slid across the counter to them.

"I'm not your date," she reminded him, picking up the tray of food before Sebastian had a chance.

They grabbed some napkins and packets of ketchup from the condiment counter and sat in a corner booth. "So why don't you want a boyfriend?" He was curious in general, not just for personal reasons.

"Who said that?" Tess asked.

"You did at the lunch table with your friends the other day," he reminded her.

"You were eavesdropping!"

"Yes, I was," he admitted without shame. "I was sitting alone. What did you expect I do?"

"So what do you think about the cheeseburger?" she asked, changing the subject.

"It's nice."

"Nice?"

"Well, it's not a filet mignon. I suppose it's okay for a simple pleasure," he reasoned.

Now she would have to answer his question. "I don't have time for a boyfriend. Studying and getting into NYU is my priority right now."

He pondered this for a moment. If her father had passed away when she was only fourteen, she must have missed out on so many things a normal teenage girl experiences. "So you've never been on a date, never had a first kiss, never had your heart broken—what a tragedy." He looked upon her with concern in his eyes. He had experienced so much in his short life. He was cultured and well-traveled. He had partied, had many lovers, yet somehow he had never managed to fall in love. Given time, he could have fallen in love with Penny. Even so, it hurt like hell when he had to leave her. For some reason he could not explain, he was attracted to Tess Hamilton. It made no sense. They were from completely different backgrounds and upbringings. Sebastian only knew he wanted to learn more about the girl sitting across from him, who had paint in her hair and a dot of ketchup on her upper lip.

"I don't need your pity," she lashed back. "It's my choice." She dabbed the ketchup away with a napkin.

"I don't have time for love, either," he told her, trying to defuse the situation. "I have to graduate with honors and I can only do that with the help of my serious and motivated tutor."

Chapter 8 - Come Dancing

Monday at lunch period, Sebastian made his way to the table where Tess Hamilton and her friends were seated. "May I sit with you?" he inquired.

Courtney looked up with a wide smile. "Have a seat," she said before Tess could reply.

"I'm Courtney Summers."

Sebastian shook her hand and took the empty seat next to Courtney. "It's a little awkward sitting alone. Thank you for letting me join you."

"So how is St. Alexander's treating you?" Jordan started the inquisition.

"Fine. I'm still getting used to it."

"Where did you go to school before this? It's unusual to start your senior year in a new school."

"Eton," he replied.

"Where's that?" Courtney jumped in.

"England."

"Like the country?"

He looked to Tess for help, but she sat across from him with an amused grin on her face. She wasn't about to come to his rescue. "That would be the one," he whispered in his English accent.

"Why the fake American accent?" Jordan asked.

"Trying to stay under the radar, as you say. I'd appreciate if you kept my secret."

"Do you have a girlfriend?" Courtney asked, leaning into him.

"Courtney!" Tess was mortified.

"What? You're not interested, Tess."

Sebastian simply chuckled. "No, I don't have a girlfriend."

"I'm very available," Courtney flirted. "What do you say we go out sometime?"

Sebastian glanced at Tess, who looked as if she wanted to strangle Courtney. He thought very carefully before answering. "I'm afraid I don't have time for dating right now. I'm very busy with all the tutoring and I really need to improve my grades if I have any chance of getting into a good university."

"God, you sound just like Tess. You two are perfect for each other," Jordan deadpanned. Then she changed the subject. "Do you guys want to go to Jersey on Friday night? Adam and the Ants are playing at The Jug Handle Inn."

"I love Adam!" Courtney replied. "I'm in."

"Tess?"

"You know I don't drink and I don't have a fake ID."

"Party pooper." Jordan turned to Sebastian. "What about you?"

"I'd like to go, but I don't have a fake ID either," he admitted.

"How old are you?"

"Eighteen."

"Well, then you don't need one. Are you in?" Jordan asked again.

"I thought you had to be twenty-one to legally drink," Sebastian said in confusion.

"You do in Pennsylvania. But in New Jersey, you only have to be eighteen," Tess explained.

"I'm in," Sebastian agreed. He was curious to see how American teenagers partied. Would it really resemble a John Hughes movie? "Come on, Tess. You don't have to drink. Just come to see the band," Sebastian prodded her.

"I don't want to spend any money."

"I'll pay, if that's what you're worried about."

"Thanks, but I don't want to go." Tess was adamant and Sebastian wasn't sure he could change her mind, but he was going to do his best to convince her. He really wanted to see her in a social setting—one where she wasn't tutoring or doing charity work.

After school, chemistry books spread out over the library table, Tess tutored Sebastian. He wasn't paying much attention, however, and Tess gave him an annoyed look. "If you aren't going to take this seriously, I really do have better things to do with my time."

"I've been a model student."

"I've only been tutoring you for a week!"

"Why don't you want to go out on Friday?"

"I told you I'm not interesting in dating."

"I'm not asking you on a date. It's a group of your friends going out together," he explained. "I just want to see you have some fun, Tess."

"I know how to have fun," she defended.

"Then come dancing with Courtney, Jordan, and me on Friday night."

"I'll tell you what: you get a perfect score on your chemistry quiz tomorrow and I'll go with you guys on Friday."

Sebastian held out his hand for Tess to shake. "Deal!"

"Okay, back to work," Tess instructed.

"Can I ask you one more thing?"

"What?" she asked in exasperation.

"How much is my mother paying you to tutor me?"

"I really don't think that's any of your business."

"Of course it is. I'm the reason you got this job."

"The standard pay rate is seven fifty an hour. Your mother offered fifteen, so I jumped at it," she explained.

"You should have held out. I'm worth at least twenty," he admonished.

Tess laughed. "Well, I took the fifteen before I knew what I was getting myself into."

"Did she contact you personally?" He wondered how much interaction the two women had so far.

"No, she arranged it through the dean's office. Are you afraid of me meeting her?"

"You won't have the chance, unless you happen upon her in Tokyo or London."

"Since I won't be traveling to those places, you're safe. Can we please go back to work?"

"I'm ready," he replied, pulling the chemistry book toward him.

The next day, Sebastian joined the girls at lunch. He slipped a paper in front of Tess with a smug grin. Tess looked down to see *100%* written in red ink across the top of Sebastian's chemistry quiz. She stuck her tongue out at him.

"Jordan, Tess is going to need a fake ID after all."

"How did you get her to agree?" Jordan asked, amazed.

"Perfect score on my chemistry quiz."

Jordan rolled her eyes. "You two are weird."

Sebastian anxiously watched the clock in the library. Tess tapped the table to get his attention. "The sooner we finish, the sooner we can go." It was finally Friday and he was looking forward to seeing Adam and the Ants. He hadn't stepped foot in a bar since he'd left London.

"Can you please explain when I will ever use the Pythagorean theorem in real life?"

"You won't," she replied.

He was gobsmacked at her simple, honest answer. "You don't lie."

"No, I don't need to."

"Tess, everyone lies."

"Well, I'm not everyone, Sebastian."

This was certainly true, he thought to himself, but remained silent. Instead he gave her a sad, pathetic grin until she giggled. "You're unbelievable! Come on, I could use the extra time to go home and get changed before we head to Jersey."

He slammed his math book shut with great satisfaction. "I'll pick you up at seven."

Sebastian selected the plainest items he had in his wardrobe: a pair of khakis and a long-sleeved navy polo shirt. He sensed a suit would not be appropriate apparel for The Jug Handle Inn. Taking a few drags on a cigarette before extinguishing it in the ashtray, he popped a couple Tic Tacs into his mouth. After dressing quickly with anticipation, he bounded down the stairs.

"I'll be home late," Sebastian informed Henry.

"Could you be a little more specific?"

"The band goes on at nine o'clock. I'll have to take Tess and Courtney back home after the show. I'll probably be back around one o'clock. Henry, you don't have to worry. I would never put the girls in danger by drinking and driving."

"I was just going to wish you goodnight. Have fun."

"Thanks, Henry."

Sebastian pulled up in front of Tess' house at seven o'clock, sprinted to the front door, and rang the doorbell. Mrs. Hamilton opened the door and greeted him warmly. "Sebastian, come in. How are you?"

"Fantastic, thank you for asking."

Tess walked into the room. She was dressed jeans that fit her perfectly, showing off the curve of her hips and her slim waist. She sported a black tank top and had covered it with a women's cut denim jacket. Her hair was pulled back with a headband to show off her gold hoop earrings. She frowned when she saw Sebastian. "You're overdressed."

"I'm wearing khakis," he said defending himself. "I normally wear a suit. I feel extremely underdressed at the moment."

Tess' mom pushed them both out the front door. "You kids have a goodnight."

Sebastian opened the passenger door of the car for Tess, who slid into the comfortable leather seat. They drove to

Courtney's house to pick her up on their way to New Jersey. Jordan and Jeff were meeting them at The Jug. They soon picked up the Schuylkill Expressway, exited at Roosevelt Boulevard, and headed through Northeast Philadelphia and over the Tacony Palmyra Bridge into New Jersey. Five miles down Route 73 into Pennsauken, they reached their destination.

The bar was certainly unlike any club or pub Sebastian had experienced in England. He believed this was what the Americans called a 'dive bar.' The door person checked IDs as everyone entered the building. Sebastian took it all in. The place was cramped, with the bar situated in the center of the room. People were vying for the bartender's attention to fill their drink orders. To the right was a small stage. To the left were a few scattered round tables and a bank of booths along the wall. The bar was dark and filled with the smell of cigarette smoke and stale beer. The place was crowded beyond capacity.

Sebastian leaned toward the girls and asked, "What can I get you both to drink?"

"Beer," Courtney replied.

"Diet Coke," Tess chimed in.

"Do you want a shot of vodka in that?" Sebastian questioned.

"No, just a soda. Thank you."

He left the girls and fought his way to the bar. The piped-in music over the PA was loud. "Do you see Jordan and Jeff?" Tess shouted, scanning the room.

"Over there!" Courtney responded, seeing Jordan waving her hand from a corner booth.

Sebastian came back from the bar with drinks in hand, doing his best not to spill them as he navigated the current of people. The trio made their way to the corner booth. There were already several empty beer bottles on the round table.

"How long have you guys been here?" Courtney questioned, sliding into the circular booth.

"About an hour," Jordan answered. "It was the only way to get a table and a little breathing room."

"Are you trying to get alcohol poisoning?" Tess muttered, pointing to the row of empty bottles.

Jordan laughed. "Will you please slip her something to loosen her up, Sebastian?"

Sebastian didn't reply. He just sat back and enjoyed his mediocre scotch. There was at least an hour before the band went on, and there was probably some local band up first who would be boring and out of pitch. *No matter*, Sebastian thought; it was nice to be out somewhere—even it if was New Jersey. Jeff and Jordan set down their beers, backed into the relative darkness of the corner, and started kissing. Tess sipped her soda, looking as if she would rather be anywhere else. Courtney chugged her beer in a few gulps. Frankie Goes to Hollywood's *Relax* started thumping through the speakers.

"Oh, I love this song! Somebody dance with me," Courtney pleaded.

Jeff and Jordan were paying no attention. Tess shook her head, dismissing the idea. Sebastian stood up, "I'll dance with you, Courtney." He took her hand and helped her onto the small dance floor. It was teeming with dancing couples crushed together in the slight space. Sebastian ended up a little closer to Courtney than he wanted to be. Tess took notice and looked even more miserable, if that was possible. This made him happy. Was she jealous? Courtney began gyrating up against Sebastian, misconstruing his smile as sexual attraction. The quick beer didn't help matters. Sebastian politely pushed her away by spinning her under his arm.

"How about another drink?" Sebastian offered as the song came to an end.

"Okay." She leaned in and kissed him on the lips.

Sebastian headed back to the bar while Courtney joined the others back in the booth. Tess grabbed one of the open Miller bottles and took a small sip. She grimaced at the awful taste. "Did you see us out there? He's a great dancer!" Courtney exclaimed, plopping down next to Tess.

Sebastian walked back with another round of drinks. He handed the Miller to Courtney and gave Tess another Diet Coke, while he switched to Guinness. Sebastian noticed the beer in Tess' hand. "I thought you said you didn't drink?"

Tess, clearly angry with Sebastian, refused to look him in the eye, refused to speak to him. She took another swallow of beer, shaking her head as the alcohol slid down her throat. Jordan and Jeff stopped their make-out session long enough for Jeff to light up a joint. The smell of marijuana clouded the table but was lost to the smell of cigarette smoke permeating the room. Obviously no one paid attention to the signs posted throughout the bar stating USE OF ILLEGAL SUBSTANCES PROHIBITED. Tess stood up and stormed outside.

Sebastian quickly followed. "Tess, where are you going?" he shouted after her, trying hard to be heard over the sound of Bon Jovi playing on the juke box and the drunken patrons shouting at the top of their lungs as they sang along.

She stepped outside and pushed past the line of people still waiting to get into the bar. "I'd like to go home, please," she pleaded, still refusing to look him in the eye and on the verge of crying.

"We can't leave Courtney," he explained.

"Just drive me home and you can come back for her later."

She was in a great deal of distress and looked as if she were about to hyperventilate. He gently touched her forearms, and in a very soothing voice, kept repeating, "Just breathe, nice and slow." He walked her to the car and placed her in the front seat. "I'm going back inside to tell Courtney we're leaving. I'm sure Jordan can drive her home. Just keep breathing."

He returned five minutes later and then they were on Route 73 heading back to Pennsylvania. "Why were you drinking that beer? You were adamant that you don't drink. What changed your mind?"

"I wasn't comfortable in there. I wanted to see if it would calm me down. I only took a few sips."

"A few sips aren't going to loosen you up, Tess. A few bottles maybe, but not a few sips."

"Just shut up, okay," she muttered in a weary tone.

"Are you feeling better?"

"No."

"Well, then just lay back in the seat. Close your eyes and I'll get you home as soon as possible." Sebastian concentrated on his speed gauge to avoid being pulled over for drinking and driving. He didn't know what the penalties were in America, but he knew he had no family ties to get him out of trouble. He grabbed a few Tic Tacs from the center console of the car and popped them in his mouth. They drove home in silence, with only a brief stop at a convenience store for a cup a coffee. Mrs. Hamilton had been nothing but warm and welcoming to Sebastian, and he desperately needed to keep it that way.

Sebastian jumped out of the car when they pulled up in front of Tess' house. He opened the door and reached in for her hand. He helped Tess to the front door. The porch light was on. Kate was sitting on the sofa watching TV. "What are you kids doing home so early?"

"Tess wasn't feeling well. The club was overcrowded and hot. I thought it would be best to just bring her home," Sebastian explained.

"Thank you for seeing her home safely, Sebastian." She stood up and unexpectedly hugged him.

"You're welcome, Mrs. Hamilton." He was slightly taken aback by this show of affection from an adult, let alone the parent of a girl he fancied.

"I'll see you on Monday, Tess," he said softly to her.

"Okay," was all she could say before making her way up the staircase to the solace of her bedroom.

He bade farewell to Tess' mother, got in his car, and slowly drove home, all the while trying to suss out what the hell had just taken place. He must have hit a nerve with Tess by showing attention to Courtney. Why else would she start drinking? Was she angry? Nervous? Or maybe the heat and the crowd had simply overwhelmed her and she needed to get out of there. He didn't really buy into her explanation. She was so naïve. Sebastian surmised that Tess had never experienced anything like this before: the drinking, the drugs, the hookups. He was also convinced that she was starting to have feelings for him, but was ill-equipped to deal with them. Whatever it was, he would leave her alone this weekend. Hopefully, next week she would feel like talking about it. He made a mental note to send her a bouquet of flowers the following day—nothing elaborate, just a simple gesture to send his good wishes and hope she was feeling better. In his experience, flowers always got him back into a girl's good graces. On second thought, maybe he should just leave her be. She'd only get angry and misconstrue his friendly gesture as romantic.

Henry was sitting at the kitchen table reading the paper, startling Sebastian as he entered the house through the back door. "Waiting up for me?"

"Yes."

"Because you assumed I was on a bender?"

"You were in New Jersey, where it's perfectly legal for you to drink. I just wanted to make sure you got home okay," Henry explained.

Anger welled up inside Sebastian, but he could sense Henry's sincerity. It was odd encountering an adult who would stay awake to be sure of his safety. "I'm sober. Thank you for your concern," he calmly announced.

"You are home early. I expected to be sitting here till at least one o'clock."

Removing his coat, Sebastian threw it on the back of the kitchen chair and joined Henry at the table. "Tess wasn't feeling well. I took her home early. There wasn't any point in going back to the bar."

Henry's lips curled in a mischievous grin "You like this girl."

With a sigh, Sebastian placed his head in the palm of his hand. "Yes, God help me, for some reason I can't fathom, I like this girl."

"Opposites attract."

"Tess Hamilton is the polar opposite of me. I don't want to get involved with her. She certainly does *not* want to get involved with me." Sebastian said, but couldn't even convince himself.

Henry stood from the chair and patted Sebastian on the back. "You keep telling yourself that. I'm turning in. Goodnight."

Chapter 9 - If Paradise Is Half As Nice

Sebastian stood next to Tess, flipping through the card catalog in search of books they could use for their English term paper. They had to analyze and compare selected poets from the Romantic and Realist periods. "Finally, a subject I enjoy. This project will be a breeze to complete," Sebastian said, excited about the project.

"You seem pretty confident about this topic."

"Well, I am English."

"So that makes you predisposed to be an expert on the subject?"

"Something like that."

Tess shook her head and continued thumbing through the cards.

After twenty minutes of searching, Sebastian closed the file with a heavy sigh. "This is no use. I have better poetry books at home. We can go there now. What do you say?"

"You want to show me your house?"

"No, I want to show you my books." He hesitated for a moment. "God, I never thought that sentence would come out of my mouth."

Tess looked at her watch. "Okay, I guess I could do that. I just have to call my mom and let her know."

He patiently waited while she used the pay phone in the gym; then he escorted her to the hunter green Jaguar. He opened the passenger door and Tess got inside. She sank into the tan leather interior as she buckled her seatbelt.

Sebastian got in the driver's side, started the engine, and drove off.

"You didn't have to drive me. I could have followed in my car," Tess said as they drove along and entered the main street.

"I know, but Edgewood is secluded and I wanted to drive so we could talk."

"Because I engage you with my sparkling conversation?"

"Absolutely," he grinned.

"Will I get to meet any of your family?"

"I don't live with my family."

"So you live alone?"

"No, I live with the servants and my guardian."

If Tess was going to take her questions down this path, maybe it wasn't a good idea for him to bring her to the house. He'd only known her for a week when Tess had invited him into her home, so four weeks later Sebastian wanted to show her his world. He didn't understand why he felt so compelled to do this—let her into his inner sanctum. He just had a gut feeling the time was right.

"Do you have any brothers or sisters?"

"I have two older sisters and a brother."

"Ah, that explains a lot."

"What do you mean?"

"You're the baby of the family. It explains why you act so …"

"Yes?"

"Pampered and petulant."

Sebastian laughed. "You're not the first person to accuse me of that."

"You have a sense of humor after all."

"If you were trying to insult me, I've been called far worse. I know deep down you think I'm fascinating. I wager you've never met anyone like me before," he challenged.

"You got me there."

They pulled into a private drive and Sebastian parked the car in the garage. Walking toward the house, through the rose garden, Tess said, "It's so beautiful."

"It's all right, I suppose."

"Why would you take living here for granted? Does the money make you that jaded?"

Sebastian felt like saying, *This is nothing compared to the castle back in England,* but then he would come off as an arrogant arse. He was trying to impress Tess, not alienate her.

Tess whispered, "This seems like utopia."

"In my experience, utopia doesn't exist." He opened the front door and ushered her into the mansion. "The library is just down the hall."

"Why didn't you just tell me you lived in a mansion?"

"I thought you would have sussed that out on your own. I was also hoping to avoid the look of sheer awe you have on your face right now. I'm not here to flaunt my privilege. I just want to write a bloody term paper."

"I'm fine. See?" Tess was standing perfectly still, but the sparkle of excitement in her eyes gave her away.

"No, you're not," he sighed. "You're dying to freak out. Go ahead."

She twirled around, taking in everything. "This is amazing! It's like living in a museum."

All he could do was laugh. "You want to see the rest of the house?"

"Yes!"

"Follow me. There's someone I want you to meet first." He put his hand on the small of her back and escorted her up the grand staircase to Nanny's room. He quietly knocked, then entered.

"Sebastian, come in. Who is your friend?" Nanny asked.

"Nanny Jones, this is Tess Hamilton," he beamed.

"Tess, Sebastian has told me so much about you. Sit down." She patted the seat next to her.

"What did he say?"

"Only good things, dear. How is the tutoring coming along?"

"He's a good student."

"I always knew he was intelligent. He just needed to apply himself."

Sebastian sat back and watched Nanny and Tess talk, getting to know each other. The conversation was easy and comfortable. When they finished their visit, Sebastian gave Nanny a hug and whispered in her ear. Nanny smiled back at him. Sebastian walked across the room, opened the door, and motioned for Tess to join him in the hall.

"She is the one who raised you," Tess realized aloud as they walked down the hall.

"Yes, to me, she is my mother."

"I like her. What did you whisper to her?"

He gave her a sly smile. "A gentleman doesn't give away his secrets. I thought you wanted to see the rest of the house."

"Fine, but I still don't understand why you can't tell me. Whatever it was, you made her smile."

"What would you like to see next?"

"Show me your bedroom."

Sebastian arched his brow. "My bedroom? I don't think you should go in there without a chaperone."

Tess nudged him in the side with her elbow. "Oh please, It's 1985, not 1885. I'm sure I'll be perfectly safe. You did just say you were a gentleman, after all."

"But what if I lose all senses and try to ravish you?" he asked in low, sensual voice. The thought certainly was appealing.

"Than I'll just have to knee you in the balls," she replied with a demure smile.

He swallowed hard, opened the bedroom door, and allowed her to enter first. Sebastian noticed her mouth drop open ever so slightly to form a little O shape. *Her silence is a welcome change of pace*, Sebastian thought to himself, but he knew better than to voice it. He could tell it was all too much for her to absorb. Tess made her way over to his record collection and casually flipped through the albums. Then she turned and eyed a delightful old teddy bear sitting amidst the mound of pillows on his bed. She walked to the bed and picked it up.

"I didn't peg you as the stuffed animal type."

"This is Charles. Nanny gave him to me on my first birthday. I like him very much. He never talks back—unlike some people I know."

Tess ignored him and examined the bear. Charles was worn and obviously well loved. His head was slightly crooked and she felt a chamois patch on his foot. "What happened here?"

"Ah, that was his riding incident."

"What?"

"We were out riding Dr. Manson…"

"Dr. Manson?" she questioned.

"My horse's name was Dr. Manson."

"That's a peculiar name for a horse."

"Do you want to hear the story or do you plan to keep interrupting?"

"Go on," she said sitting on the edge of the bed.

"Well, anyway, we were riding along, enjoying the sun and the warm weather—Charles has always loved the springtime, you know—and he lost his grip and fell off the horse. Dr. Manson stepped right on top of him, the poor thing. Charles was hurt, of course, and Dr. Manson was very distraught. So we quickly got him into surgery and Nanny mended his foot quite nicely. Don't you agree?"

"How old were you when this happened?"

"Seven."

Tess shook her head with a chuckle. "You are not only aloof, you're eccentric."

"Thank you," he replied, happy with the compliment.

She placed the bear back on the bed, and then headed for the French doors. "What's out here?"

Sebastian turned the brass handles and flung them open with a swooshing gesture. Tess stepped out onto the balcony and looked out over the grounds. The trees on the property were just beginning to turn with the autumn weather; the leaves were glorious shades of red and gold.

She seemed lost in thought when Sebastian quietly stepped up behind her and whispered in her ear. "I told her I loved her more than anyone in the world."

Tess slowly turned to face him. They were standing quite close to one another. Her hair smelled like honeysuckle, and he could feel her gentle breath on his neck. He had caught her off guard.

"What?"

"You asked me what I whispered to Nanny."

"Oh," she replied softly, her breath shallow.

"I think we need to get started on that term paper." Sebastian slowly stepped away, reminding her of the reason they were there. If he didn't step away now, he might act on his urge to lean down and kiss her, and he didn't think she was ready for that.

Tess finally shook herself out of her daze. "Yes, we should get started," she said, pushing past him and back into the room.

He closed the doors behind them and followed her into the hall.

Alice greeted them as they reached the landing of the foyer. "Sebastian, will you be staying for dinner tonight?"

He looked over at Tess. "Is it all right if we eat in?"

"Sure, if it's not any trouble. My mom's working tonight, so I didn't have any plans."

"Thank you, Alice. We'll eat dinner in the dining room tonight. Can you bring some tea and a Diet Coke to the library? We'll be working in there until dinnertime."

"Of course." She turned and headed for the kitchen.

"She seems nice," Tess commented.

"Alice is an amazing cook. You're in for a treat tonight." He walked ahead at a quick pace, while Tess fell in line behind him. "Here we are," he announced suddenly, as they reached the closed library door. He opened the door for Tess and they entered the room together.

The library was lined with floor-to-ceiling cherry wood bookcases brimming with books. There was a wheeled brass ladder on a rail, which rolled around the room for anyone who needed to retrieve books on the top shelves. A round table sat in the center of the room. Sebastian walked to one of the cases near the door and randomly pulled poetry books off the shelves. Soon a pile had collected in the center of a book trolley: Shelley, Byron, and Shakespeare.

Tess wandered over to a photo in a sterling silver Asprey frame, which sat on the sideboard table. She picked it up and examined it. No one was smiling in the formal photo of the elegant group dressed in black tuxedos and sophisticated evening gowns. The oldest woman had her hair pulled back in an updo and was seated on a sofa with two younger women. There were two men with stiff posture standing behind the sofa. One of them was Sebastian. "Is this your family?"

Sebastian looked up from his growing pile of books. He walked over and took the photo from her hand, holding it as if it burned his fingers. "Yes," he said flatly. He pointed to the people. "Mother, Sigourney, Victoria, and Max." He placed the photograph back on the sideboard, glad to be rid of it. "I think we have all the books we need," he said, trying to turn Tess' attention back to the task at hand.

"So who is your favorite poet?" she asked, taking a seat at the table.

"Keats. And yours?"

"I don't like poetry," she admitted. "I don't understand it."

"Well, maybe it's time I tutor you for a change." He cleared his throat and launched into an off-the-cuff explanation. "You're most likely struggling with the use of Old English and symbolism. Think in modern terms. Think about music: Morrissey, Bono, Dylan. They're all modern poets. They tell a story. Sometimes the story is straightforward—there is a beginning, middle and end. Sometimes it's just about the idea or emotion the writer is trying to convey, and he does it through a series of random thoughts. Are you following me?"

She nodded her head. "Go on, Professor Irons."

Flipping through one of the books, he found the poem he wanted. "This one is Keats."

Give me women, wine, and snuff
Until I cry out "hold, enough!"
You may do so sans objection
Till the day of resurrection:
For, bless my beard, they aye shall be
My beloved Trinity.

"Pretty straightforward—the three loves of this man's life are women, wine, and tobacco. He holds these things in such high regard that they become a religious-like experience to him."

"He sounds an awful lot like you," Tess chimed in.

"I certainly share Keats' enthusiasm for those things," he agreed. Sebastian flipped through a few pages. "Now let's try something that's a little more difficult: Keats' *Bright Star*. Sebastian went on to read the poem aloud. When he finished, he leaned back on his heels, deep in thought.

"Now this is a little more esoteric. Because of its position as the last word in the poem, death carries a great deal of weight. Keats accepts the possibility of dying from pleasure. The French often compare dying to an orgasm." Sebastian stopped for effect to let what he was saying sink in for her. Then, with a coy smile, he continued: "There's also been debate that the word death was meant quite literally as Keats was dying of tuberculosis when he wrote the poem for his fiancée."

"You got all that from a fourteen-line poem?"

"Technically, it's a sonnet."

"There is so much about you that I don't know. What other strange and fascinating talents are you hiding from me?"

"I can't reveal everything all at once. I'll lose my status as 'mystery man.'"

He handed her a few books. The lesson continued as he further explained the various periods of poetry to Tess. It was so easy for him to talk about something he loved so much. He liked showing her this intelligent side of his personality. Time flew by quickly.

Alice poked her head into the library. "Dinner will be served in the dining room in five minutes."

"Come on, we've worked enough for today," he announced, closing his book. He swiftly rose and circled behind her. Sebastian pulled out her chair and helped her stand.

They exited the library and walked across the hallway into the formal dining room. There was a long dining table in the center of the room. A large Waterford chandelier dangled directly above the table. The fading light streaming in from the windows created colorful prisms of light on the walls. Two place settings were laid out at the far end of the table. He pulled out a chair for Tess and then sat down next to her.

Alice placed the china plates in front of Tess and Sebastian. Their dinner was a perfectly prepared beef Wellington, tiny new potatoes sautéed in butter and fresh herbs, and grilled asparagus spears. "This smells wonderful. Thank you, Alice," Sebastian complimented.

"Wine?" Alice inquired. It took some doing, but Nanny had agreed to allow Sebastian one glass of wine with his dinner, which he gratefully accepted.

"Not for me," Tess told her, placing her hand over the wine glass.

"Can you bring Tess a Diet Coke?"

Alice nodded as she poured the wine. When she finished, she left them and quickly returned with the Diet Coke in a crystal tumbler, the ice cubes clinking in time with her steps.

Tess thanked Alice, then took a bite of the beef Wellington.

"Well, what do you think?" Sebastian asked.

"It's not McDonald's."

"It's certainly not," he chuckled. "But do you like it?"

"Yes, it's delicious." She looked at his wine glass. "Do you always drink wine with dinner?"

"Yes," he replied. Sebastian sensed her confusion and tried to explain. "Tess, in England you are legal at the age of sixteen. You can drink, have sex, gamble, and get married. Having a glass of wine with dinner is no big deal."

"You've done all those things?"

"Well, I haven't been married," he replied.

"Do you always have dinner like this?"

"No, usually I have dinner with Nanny in her room. Sometimes we eat in the kitchen with Alice and Henry. Are you uncomfortable here?"

"A little," she admitted. "You don't have to try to impress me. I'd be perfectly happy eating in the kitchen."

"Please sit back and try to enjoy a good meal. Is my company that awful?"

"No. I'm not…It's just…your world is very different from mine," she tried to explain.

"We're both fatherless and studying our arses off to get into NYU. I don't think we're that different."

"You know what I mean," she frowned.

"So we come from different social classes—that doesn't matter to me." It wasn't helping, so he tried changing the subject. "Report cards are issued on Monday."

"How do you think you'll do?" she asked, wiping the corner of her mouth with the white linen napkin.

"I have an excellent tutor. I'm feeling very confident."

He made her laugh aloud, which was something she didn't do very often.

"I bet you'll do great," she agreed. She thought for a long moment and gingerly asked, "The grounds are so beautiful. Do you think I could come back here again to take some photos?"

Sebastian envisioned Tess walking on a tightrope, teetering on the thin wire. The only question was which way she would fall. Even though she was uncomfortable here, she was drawn to Edgewood and drawn to Sebastian, despite the litany of reasons she didn't want a boyfriend. It must have taken a great deal of courage for Tess to invite herself back. He couldn't refuse her, too curious to see how this would play out. "When do you want to come back?"

"Tomorrow is Saturday. Would that be okay?"

"Really? No charity work, school work, saving the world?" he teased.

"My schedule is completely open."

It was nearly 10 a.m. when Tess returned to Edgewood, Nikon in hand. Sebastian greeted her, ushering her into the foyer. She was wearing her usual casual attire: jeans, sneakers, and her St. Alexander's sweatshirt.

He hated that awful sweatshirt, which hid her curves. Sebastian knew she didn't have much money to spend on quality clothes. He would have gladly bought Tess proper riding attire, but didn't know her size. "Good morning. Where do you want to start?"

He watched her eye him up and down. He was dressed in his black riding pants, and brown leather boots that came up to his knees. The white turtleneck was covered with a plaid, wool, fitted blazer with a brown suede lapel. "You look every inch the upper-crust English gentleman today," she observed.

"Well, I reckon that's a good thing, since I am English, upper-crust, and sometimes a gentleman," he said with a twinkle in his eye. "I thought we could take out the horses. It will be a great way for you to see the grounds. What do you say?"

Tess hesitated. "I don't know how to ride a horse, and I don't think I'm dressed for it," she lamented, looking down at her casual attire.

"Nonsense, you're perfect! Follow me." They walked out the front door and headed for the stables. Sebastian began his instructions as they walked. "So the thing you need to remember is to let the horse do all the work. Don't tense up. Don't pull on the reins too hard. And when heading up an incline, lean forward to shift your weight so it's easier on the horse."

"Got it," she responded with apprehension.

They entered the stable and Sebastian headed toward the brown mare in the first stall. The smell of hay permeated the air. "This is Honey," he introduced, opening the gate to her stall. Honey swayed her head back and forth and Sebastian held out a treat toward the horse. She gently took it from his open hand and whinnied in thanks, looking back at his hand for seconds. He gently patted the horse on the forehead before placing the bridle in her mouth. The mare was already saddled and ready to go. She focused her eyes on Tess and whinnied again, moving her great bulk toward her.

Tess swallowed hard and walked closer to the horse while slowly putting out her hand. Honey leaned her head to the side to gently touch it.

"See? She likes you already." He handed Tess a treat to feed Honey and the horse and rider bond was formed.

Sebastian knew that Honey would take to Tess. She was a very sweet and loving horse—perfect for the first time rider. He led Honey out of the stable and stopped, standing on her left side. "Give me your right foot," he instructed, while cupping his hands. "Hold the saddle but don't pull on it. I'll hoist you and you'll want to slip your left foot into the stirrup, swing your right foot over her and put it into the other stirrup."

Tess put her foot in his hand and he hoisted her until she was able to put her foot into the stirrup. She swung her leg over the horse and sat. Sebastian put the reins in her hands. "Just sit here. Don't do anything—unless of course you want to go really fast. Then kick her with both heels, hard."

Sebastian opened another gate and coaxed a shiny black Arabian from its stall. The horse was taller and stronger than Honey. "This is Storm," Sebastian said as he mounted the horse. They sauntered out of the yard, across the back garden, and began to explore the land.

"This is so amazing," Tess uttered, relaxing as she realized Honey wasn't going to race away.

"It's a great way to clear your mind," Sebastian chimed in almost absentmindedly.

"You do this often, I guess."

"Yes."

"You look so natural on that horse, like you've been riding all your life."

"I started riding when I was four years old. I thought it would be very romantic to become a cowboy. They got to save the day and ride off into the sunset with the girl."

"I'd love to see you in a cowboy hat."

They rode for a while in silence. Sebastian would occasionally look at Tess to make sure she was okay. The Nikon, attached to a camera strap around her neck, gently bobbed up and down against her stomach. It looked expensive, and he wondered how she could afford it.

"That's a nice camera. Have you been taking photos for a long time?"

"It's really just a hobby. This was my dad's Nikon. He was a train fanatic. Dad knew the timetables, and we would always go to different train stations in the area to watch the trains pass. He would take photos. I have boxes and boxes of old train photos at home. When he died, I starting taking photos with his camera. I just prefer landscapes to trains."

"You would love Europe. It has the most amazing landscapes and train system. You could board the train in Paris in the morning and be in Vienna for dinner."

"Maybe someday I'll get there. I'm hoping to study abroad for a semester in college."

As they came up over a small hill, in the distance there stood two tall oak trees with an old wooden fence in between them, one of the wood rails split and broken. It made for an interesting photo composition. "How do I stop?" she asked Sebastian.

"Gently pull back on the reins and say 'Whoa.' Then release the reins. Don't keep them taut."

She did as she was told and Honey came to an easy stop. "Go ride over to those trees. I want to take your picture."

Sebastian broke into a grin, grabbed the reins, and kicked the horse into action. Storm galloped toward the broken fence between the trees. Sebastian felt the power of the sinewy animal move beneath him. With one quick and graceful motion, Storm jumped over the fence. Sebastian laughed with joy as he turned the horse around and repositioned him in front of the fence. He ran his fingers through his hair to smooth it and posed for the photo. As Tess pressed down on the shutter, Sebastian turned his head and looked out into the distance, an intriguing smile graced his face.

"That was fun," he announced, rejoining her.

"What were you thinking just then?" she prodded.

"I was thinking how happy I am right now," he admitted. She would never understand how rare that emotion was for him, so he didn't try to explain it in any further detail. "Does that camera of yours have a self-timer?"

"Yeah, why?"

"Follow me." They rode toward the trees together. Sebastian jumped down from his horse and helped Tess down from hers. "Set the timer for me."

She set the timer then handed the camera to Sebastian.

Taking the camera, he placed it on top of the flat wooden post of the fence. Putting his arm around Tess, he said, "Smile for the camera." The camera clicked just as Tess turned to look up at Sebastian, who was looking straight ahead, smiling.

After the lunch, Sebastian walked with Tess through the rose garden. As she would stop to photograph various roses, he would chime in with the flower's name and origin.

"Can I ask you something?" he inquired as they passed the pink Grandiflora rose bush.

"Sure."

"Why did you want to see my bedroom yesterday?"

"I was curious to see where you chill out—your domain. It should be a reflection of who you are."

"So what was your impression?"

"It's a little stuffy for my taste, but I do like the teddy bear."

"You think I'm stuffy?"

"Your furnishings are stuffy. *You* are not stuffy."

"Then what am I?" He was curious to know what she really thought of him. For his part, Sebastian was finding Tess far too interesting and it unnerved him. Could she be feeling the same?

"You're aloof and eccentric, more intelligent than you like to let on, and …"

"And what?"

"Sweet."

"Sweet? No ones ever called me sweet."

"Well, you are. The way you interact the Nanny Jones—the way you dote on her, it's sweet."

They sat on the wrought iron bench next to the greenhouse. "Would you date someone who was sweet and intelligent?" Sebastian asked looking into her eyes.

"Maybe, if I had the time." Her cheeks turned pink, just like the roses in the garden.

"If it were important to you, you would make the time."

"Right now my priority is being valedictorian and getting into NYU. I won't make time for dating," she swiftly dashed his hopes. "I find it hard to believe you would ask me on a date when I threatened to knee you if you tired to seduce me."

"I didn't try to seduce you," he protested. "And I didn't ask you on a date."

"It was implied. You were testing the waters to see how I'd react."

She was right—he was testing her, and Sebastian had never met a girl who resisted his charms so thoroughly. It was maddening. Her rejection made him want her all the more.

Monday morning, Sebastian was waiting for Tess at her locker, eager to share the good news with her: the report card he'd received said he was on the honor roll.

Tess rounded the corner with the biggest smile on her face. The next thing he knew, she was in his arms hugging him. "I am so proud of you!" she exclaimed.

"But I didn't show you my marks yet! How did you know?"

"I saw your name on the honor roll board outside the principal's office."

They stood there for a long moment. He liked having her in his arms. Her body was warm and soft. He was about to say something to her when a teacher walked by and tapped Sebastian on the shoulder. "Get to class you two," she demanded, pulling them apart.

Tess blushed and stepped back a foot. "We better get going."

She began making her way down the hall. Sebastian took a few larger steps and came up to her side as they walked toward their English class. "So where did you rank?" she asked, pushing through the bustling crowd of students. With their report cards, the students received a ranking number to show their standing in the class. Tess was always ranked number one.

"Ten," he beamed with pride.

"Nice."

"We need to celebrate. Let me take you to dinner tonight."

"I can't—I have a school paper meeting." She sounded disappointed. Maybe he could change her mind.

They took their seats just as the bell rang. The teacher instructed them to open their books to page fifty-seven. Sebastian was aware that Tess was still watching him, so he turned to her and pouted. It was childish, but totally effective.

"Oh come on, Sebastian," she whispered.

"Friday night, then? You don't have yearbook or school paper on Friday night," Sebastian reminded Tess.

"I'm not going on a date with you," she reiterated.

"It's not a date. It's a dinner celebration for me, which I happen to be inviting you to."

"You're not going to leave me alone until I say yes, are you?"

"Don't make me beg, Tess. I'll get down on my knees right now. That will get the gossip mill turning."

"No you will not!" she hissed under her breath.

"Say yes. I'll even let you pick the place—except McDonald's."

"Yes. Now will you shut up before we get in trouble?"

He nodded, breaking into a grin before turning back to his book.

They sat in a booth at Marzella's Pizza Shop sharing a large cheese pie and Diet Cokes. He enjoyed being with her, sitting and eating and not talking about school.

"Tell me more about Nanny Jones," Tess requested.

"She's the woman who raised me. She loves me unconditionally, which I suspect is not an easy thing to do."

"Do you ever see your brother and sisters?"

"Not often—Max and Victoria are ten years older than I am. We didn't grow up together, since they were already at boarding school when I was born. They work in the family business. Sigourney is only three years older. We get along quite well. She is the lucky one—doesn't have to work at Irons Electronics. She's allowed to follow her passion by studying music at Juilliard."

Tess raised her eyebrow, impressed. "It's not easy to get in there. That is quite an accomplishment. If you get into NYU, you'll be able to visit her more often."

"Yes, I suppose." He had really never given it much thought. She was only a few hours drive away, but he spent so much time studying, he hadn't had any time to visit Sigourncy since the summer. Maybe that was a good thing, considering how his last visit had ended in yet another random hookup. He picked up another slice and took a bite.

"So is that your future? Are you going to work at Irons Electronics?" she asked, sipping the last of her Diet Coke.

"Lily says it is."

"But you don't want to work there, do you?"

"No," he replied curtly. He wasn't angry with Tess. He was angry with his situation.

"So what do you want to do?"

141

"I don't know. Isn't that why you go to university—to find out what it is you want to do with your life? Everyone can't be as focused and driven as you, Tess." It came out a little too tersely. He wasn't meaning to offend Tess. Luckily, Tess was learning to differentiate between his moods and his feelings about his family, and ignored the tone of his voice.

"I don't understand why your mother would make you do something you didn't want to do if you were so strongly against it."

"Remember, we're talking about my mother, not yours."

"She can't be that bad, Sebastian."

"I hope you never have to find out," he said, a warning in his voice.

Chapter 10 - Confusion

Sebastian and Tess were sitting on the couch in his bedroom studying when the phone rang. "Aren't you going to get that?" Tess asked.

"I want to finish this thought," he responded, scribbling away in this notebook. "The machine will pick it up."

A few rings later the answering machine kicked on. The prerecorded message played over the built-in speaker. *"You've reached Sebastian. Please leave a message."* A long, mechanical beeping was followed by laughter coming from the other end of the line. "Irons, where the bloody hell are you?" a young man with a British accent demanded. "We're coming to New York this weekend. I expect you to be present and ready to party. The Libertines together again!"

"We miss you, Sebastian. Please say you'll come?" a girl chimed in after her obnoxious friend. The machine clicked off.

"Nice," Tess remarked sarcastically. "So who was that, anyway?"

"My friends—obviously, they're completely pissed." He glanced at his watch. With the time difference it was just 1:00 a.m. in London.

"What are their names?"

"Alistair Windsor and Penelope Stanton."

"Your friend is a member of the Royal Family?" she inquired. A befuddled look crossed her face.

"Yes."

"And the girl?"

"Penny's parents own a department store in London. She's dating Alistair," Sebastian explained.

"So are you going to New York this weekend?"

"No." He didn't want to get into this with Tess right now, wishing he had simply picked up the phone instead of letting the machine take the call.

"I'd like to meet your friends. I want to go to the clubs," she told him with great determination.

"No," he tersely reiterated, closing his notebook with a thud.

"Are you ashamed of me because I'm poor? Are you too embarrassed to introduce me to your wealthy and powerful friends?"

"No, it's nothing like that, Tess."

"Then why won't you take me?" Her voice was getting louder.

"You don't know what you're asking. You do not belong in a New York City club."

"Because I'm not sophisticated enough to fit in?" she fired back, her anger unabated.

He didn't want to fight with her. Reaching for her clenched hand, he was surprised when she pulled away. He calmly explained. "You're too good for a place like that.

Glamour is not all it's cracked up to be. You step foot in that club and you will be surrounded by fake people partaking in alcohol, drugs, and sex. It's all out in the open, all for the taking. The club will make The Jug Handle Inn look like nursery school."

"So you've been to clubs like this before? Something you do a lot? And how did you get in? You're only eighteen." Her voice trailed off, halfway between anger and confusion.

"I know the right people. My best friend happens to come from royal lineage. I had access to anything I wanted."

"So you did all those things: alcohol, drugs, sex?" Her voice had returned to a normal volume.

"Yes," he whispered.

"But you're only eighteen," she muttered again, trying to make sense of what he was telling her.

"And I already explained to you that in England you are a legal adult at the age of sixteen. Those things which aren't legal are easily taken care of with a bit of money." The truth was ugly and sounded even worse when spoken aloud. "Tess, I'm not that person anymore. I've painfully learned from my mistakes. It's one of the reasons I had to leave England and finish my schooling here, away from all those bad influences."

"Tell me about the mistakes."

"If you knew all the things I've done, you wouldn't ever want to see me again, and I couldn't bear that. I value our friendship too much," he admitted.

"I want to know everything," she said, looking him straight in the eye. She wasn't going to run away in fear. "Tell me about the mistakes."

Sebastian looked at her with a pained expression. His mind went back and forth. Tell her the truth, lie, or try to play it down? How do you play down death? If he really meant what he said about learning from his mistakes and taking responsibility, he had to tell her. The realization of knowing this didn't make it any easier to open up about it. He felt helpless when she cast her gaze upon him. He lit a cigarette, even though she objected to the habit.

After a long drag, he began. "I did not take my school studies very seriously. I didn't show up for class. I paid people to write my term papers. My family name and my mother's money kept me in school. That's the reason I need you to tutor me. I have one year to turn my grades around to get accepted into a university."

"But if all you need is money to get into a good school, why does it matter?"

He took another drag from his cigarette, blew the smoke behind him, away from Tess. "Before I was chucked out of Eton, I was warned that the combination of poor grades, bad behavior, and aversion to hard work was not getting me into Oxford no matter how much money my mother threw at them. I didn't care—I never wanted to go to Oxford anyway." Sebastian flicked the excess ash from his cigarette into the ashtray and continued: "Nanny convinced me the only way to go to the university of my choice was to turn my life around. She was the only one who had faith that I could do it. I wasn't even sure I could," he confessed, scratching his head.

Tess was sitting on the sofa, listening intently, seeming to believe his story thus far. *I'm doing fine*, he thought. He needed to keep going. "Alistair and I entered Eton at the same time and roomed together. Just my luck he was a Windsor. That meant he was powerful enough to have connections and get doors open, but it also meant that with no conceivable chance of actually ascending the throne, he could get into all sorts of trouble. His life was not scrutinized as much as the other more prominent royals."

"It started out simply enough: First, private parties and alcohol. Then we started going out to clubs, which led to more alcohol and the introduction of drugs—and of course the girls." Sebastian stopped, waiting for a reaction. The way he had told the story so far didn't seem that bad.

"What type of drugs?"

"Mostly cannabis, and then there was cocaine." He looked at Tess, trying to read her expression, but it was no use. She sat stone still, no emotion in her face.

"And the girls, how many were there?"

"Girls like to be bought champagne and driven in fancy cars." He tried to skirt around her question with a feeble reply.

"How many did you have sex with?" she asked directly.

"I don't know, I didn't keep track," he honestly replied, and then quickly regretted it.

"Are you serious? How the hell can you be so blasé about this!" She raised her voice again.

"You're naive to think people don't randomly hook up and fuck!" he yelled back, lashing out at her ability to hurt him.

"I don't have to take this," she spat back. Tess sprang from the couch and took a few steps toward the door.

Sebastian jumped to his feet, lunged forward, grabbed her hand, and pulled her back to him. She resisted and tried to break free, but he wasn't going to let it end this way. "I apologize for not meeting your high expectations," he seethed.

"We're not a couple. It doesn't matter."

Silence filled the room as they stared each other down, taking a moment to collect their thoughts and regain their composure. She had the most intense, furious look in her eyes, as if they were little daggers piecing his heart. He didn't know what he could do or say to make things right between them. It was his life and she would never allow him to sugarcoat it. He started to question himself as he reflected on what he had said. Perhaps this wasn't the way normal people acted. Thoughts whizzed through his mind at a blinding speed. Was Tess overreacting or was her reaction justified? The thoughts hurt his head, and looking at her face hurt his heart. "I'm sorry I lost my temper. Please don't go," he pleaded. "I'll tell you anything you want to know."

"Do you have a girlfriend back in England?"

"No, I've never had a proper girlfriend."

"A proper girlfriend?" she repeated. "But you made love with those girls!" Tess exclaimed.

"I *had sex* with those girls. It didn't mean anything other than a good time had by all. They were willing participants and they certainly weren't in love with me— my social standing, yes, but not with me." He desperately wanted her to understand. How could he possibly do that without sounding like a complete cad?

"I just don't understand how you can take something so serious and make light of it." She sounded like a broken record.

He sighed, feeling out of his depth. "I'm not making light of it. I'm trying to explain. You said you wanted the truth. I never promised it would be pretty and wouldn't offend." He shook in frustration.

"What was the final mistake that landed you here?"

They arrived at the question quicker than he was prepared to answer. Now he would have to relive that day all over. Sebastian paced back and forth in front of the fireplace, taking deep controlled breaths, willing himself to get through this. "It was my birthday weekend. I had some friends over to the house. It started out like any other party…" He trailed off, unsure of what to say next.

"But it didn't end like the other parties, did it?"

"No," he replied, sitting back down on the sofa. His left leg was bouncing uncontrollably. "There was this scream, a blood curdling scream." His mind flashed back to that Sunday afternoon. He could remember every minuscule detail: the smell of the girls' perfume; the color of the necktie Alistair had loosened around Colin's neck as they tried to revive him; the sight of Colin's lifeless body as the attendant wheeled Colin out on a gurney. "Colin overdosed on cocaine. He dropped dead of cardiac arrest. Colin was alive one minute and gone the next. He was only eighteen." Sebastian hung his head in despair. "I've told you everything. Now I need to know: what are you thinking?"

"I don't know," she confessed in shock. "I need time. I need to get out of here."

"Can I call you tomorrow?"

"Yeah, I guess," she mumbled.

"Thank you, Tess." He didn't want to let her go, but he had no choice. "Can I walk you out?"

"No, I need to be alone. I'll talk to you tomorrow, okay?" She didn't wait for an answer and bolted out the door.

Sebastian stood on the balcony watching Tess drive away, praying he hadn't messed things up for good. He hoped she could see how eagerly he wanted to change and be a better person. The waiting game had begun. Sebastian walked back inside and over to his stereo. Opening the lid to the turntable, he placed the needle on the record. It was New Order's, *Confusion* twelve-inch remix.

The hours passed as he lay on the bed listening to the music and chain smoking, flicking the ashes into the ashtray with a flair of nervous boredom. There were too many thoughts running through his mind and he wished he could just shut them out, make them go away.

The telephone rang and jolted Sebastian back to the present. He grabbed for the receiver, quickly answering it, hoping it was Tess. "Hello?"

"Sebastian, it's Courtney." He heard loud music and voices in the background. Someone beside her was giggling into the receiver.

"What do you want, Courtney?" he asked brusquely, eager to get off the phone.

"I think you better come get Tess. She's been drinking like a fish and she's the designated driver," she slurred in response.

"Where are you?" he asked as panic kicked in.

"The Jug. Can you come pick us up?"

"Stay put and please stop drinking. I'll be there in an hour," he told her, hanging up the phone before Courtney could reply.

Sebastian ran into the kitchen and grabbed his coat and car keys.

"Whoa, where's the fire?" Henry asked, looking up from his newspaper.

"New Jersey—seems Tess and the girls decided it would be fun to go and get drunk without a designated driver."

"I'll get my coat."

"No, it's getting late. I can manage," Sebastian responded.

"You're really going take on three drunk girls? You can't drive your car and Tess' car at the same time."

Sebastian looked and Henry while contemplating his words, wondering if Henry was right. "Maybe I could use your help," he conceded.

Henry nodded. "We'll take the Town Car."

"Henry, can you drive a little faster?"

"No, the speed limit is posted for a reason."

"But what if Tess is in trouble? What is someone tried to slip something into her drink? What if some lowlife tries to take advantage of her?" Sebastian knew how men behaved, and suddenly it made him very embarrassed. Not so long ago he had been one of those men. At least he'd never tricked any girl into having sex with him; the attraction was always mutual.

"You're doing a good thing for those girls." Henry looked at Sebastian. "You know, before you came to America, your mother told us some things about you and your life back in England. I have to say, I've seen none of those behaviors she warned us about. I think you are becoming a remarkable young man."

"Thank you. Lily would never say that to me," he whispered. "What do you tell her when she checks in?"

"I tell her the truth: I think you've adapted well to your new home, you've been caring and considerate of others, and you have a good friendship with Tess. You've taken her help seriously and improved your grades."

"You and Alice have been very good to me." He fidgeted in the passenger seat, avoiding Henry's occasional glance. "Why didn't you and Alice ever have any children? You would make wonderful parents."

Henry paused slightly. "We weren't able to have children."

"I'm sorry. It was inappropriate of me to ask." He didn't want to intrude on a private matter.

"Sebastian, I'm a firm believer of things happening for a reason. I don't believe in luck."

"So you think it was fate that brought us together?"

"Yes. You'll find that people come into your life for a reason. You may not understand the reason right away. Sometimes it takes years to understand the roles they play in your life, but there's always a reason."

Sebastian didn't know how to respond, so he just stared out the window, watching the headlights pass by. They turned into the parking lot of The Jug and found an empty space in the back lot.

Henry opened the car door and Sebastian put his hand on Henry's forearm. "Henry, please wait outside. Tess will be embarrassed as it is. If I need you, I promise I'm come get you."

Henry hesitated for a moment, then slowly shook his head in agreement.

Inside he found the three of them, still drinking and attempting to dance, but too wasted to do anything but bump into each other. Tess was the first to recognize him. "Sebastian, what are you doing here?" she slurred.

"You're definitely pissed," he muttered to himself, finding it hard to believe she could do so much damage in such a short amount of time.

Tess started getting very pale. "I don't feel so good," she announced to no one in particular.

"Where's the toilet?" Sebastian quickly asked.

Jordan pointed to the back corner of the bar. Sebastian pushed Tess forward, hoping they'd make it in time. The girls in the restroom gave him an odd look as he pushed through the door past them and pulled Tess into the first available stall. She fell to her knees and gripped the porcelain bowl. Sebastian held back her hair with one hand as she leaned in and threw up into the toilet. He used his free hand to gently rub her back.

"You're such a lightweight, Tess." Sebastian muttered.

They stayed there for several minutes, her kneeling on the dirty tile floor and him crouching behind her, protecting and comforting her at the same time. When it appeared that she was finished and her breathing had returned to normal, Sebastian handed her a length of toilet paper.

"Thank you," she gratefully replied, wiping her mouth. She made no attempt to rise, still looking a bit shaky.

"What were you drinking?" he gently asked, trying not to upset her any more than she already was.

"Miller and shots of Jaegermeister."

"Did you eat anything tonight?"

"No." Her voice was soft but becoming stronger. She reached for more toilet paper, wiped her mouth again, and dropped the tissue into the bowl and flushed. The paper swirled around and disappeared with the water. She placed her hands on the toilet seat and braced herself to stand.

Sebastian guided her up and helped her navigate her way to the sink. The other girls had left the room and they were alone. He watched as Tess looked up at her reflection in the mirror and bowed her head in shame. She turned on the taps, dispensed some pink liquid soap, and washed her hands. Then she swished a little water around in her mouth and spat it out. Sebastian handed her another paper towel.

"We have our work cut out for us," he grimaced. "Are you feeling well enough to go home?"

"Yes."

"Okay, let's get you out to the car."

Sebastian took Tess outside for some fresh air. He walked her over to Henry, who was standing next to the Town Car. "I'm going back to get the others."

Tess leaned against the car to steady herself, gulping in cold, fresh, night air.

"How are you feeling?" Henry asked with a concerned voice.

"Please don't say anything to my mother."

"I promise," Henry replied, opening the passenger door and helping Tess into the front seat. "I have a feeling you've learned your lesson tonight."

Sebastian returned with Jordan and Courtney. Tess was sitting the front seat. He hoped that she had completely emptied her stomach, not thrilled with the idea of her vomiting in the car. He ushered Jordan and Courtney into the backseat and buckled their seat belts for them.

"I can drive Tess' car back. You take the Town Car. I'll follow to make sure everyone gets home safely," Henry said.

"Thank you."

"No speeding."

"No speeding," Sebastian agreed.

Sebastian got behind the wheel. Turning out of the parking lot and navigating the jug handle turn, they headed back toward the Tacony Palmyra Bridge. "What the hell were you three thinking!" he finally blurted out, letting his anger take over.

"Don't yell at us. She was the designated driver," Jordan fired back. "What the hell did you do to Tess? She's really mad at you."

"Where's my car?" Tess asked out of nowhere.

"Henry's bringing it back," he clipped out. "What the three of you did was really irresponsible. You could have been hurt or killed if you tried to drive home," he admonished them.

"We can't all have a driver," Tess sarcastically chimed in.

"Well, obviously, you have one right now," he shot back, stopping at the toll plaza before the bridge. He rolled down the window and threw some change into the coin basket with disgust. "Whose house are we going to?"

"Mine." Courtney answered very quietly to avoid any further wrath from Sebastian. No one spoke another word for the rest of the drive home.

Sebastian pulled up in front of Courtney's house and turned off the engine. He opened the back door and helped both Courtney and Jordan out of the car. "Do you have your house keys?" Sebastian asked.

Courtney reached into her jacket pocket and pulled out a purple rabbit's foot keychain. He took the keys and walked the girls to the front door and unlocked it. "What about Tess? She's supposed to sleep over tonight. You can't take her home like this," Courtney said.

Sebastian looked from one girl to the other. They reeked of beer and cigarettes. Their makeup was smeared and they were unsteady on their feet. "You two are in no shape to nurse her back to health. I'll see that she gets home safely," he informed Courtney as he ushered them through the front door of the house. He handed the keys back to Courtney and turned the lock on the doorknob before he closed the door behind him.

Sebastian walked over to Henry, who rolled down the window of the Chevette. "I'm taking Tess back to Edgewood. She was supposed to stay with Courtney tonight, but she's in no shape to take care of Tess."

Henry nodded. "I'll follow you home."

Tess moaned in pain as Sebastian slammed the car door. "You can't take me home," she pleaded. "My mom will kill me."

"You're not going home. I don't intend to show up at your house and hand you over to your mother when you smell like alcohol, cigarettes, and marijuana. I'm taking you to Edgewood. You're damned lucky you have a cover story for tonight."

It was nearly 1:00 a.m. when they finally pulled into his drive. He parked the car in the garage and helped Tess out of the passenger seat. "Do you think you can walk alone?"

She shook her head no, so Sebastian gently placed his arm around her waist and guided her toward the back door of the house. They entered through the kitchen. Alice was awake, in her nightgown and robe, awaiting their return. She walked over and helped Tess to the table. "Can I make you something to eat?"

"No," Tess muttered and laid her head on the table.

Sebastian grabbed a bottle of water from the refrigerator and found some crackers in the pantry. He sat down next to Tess. "Here—drink this and eat this," Sebastian ordered, placing the items on a napkin in front of her.

"I don't want anything," she whispered, pushing it away.

"Trust me—if you don't do this, you're going to feel ten times worse in the morning." He unscrewed the cap to the water bottle and lifted it to her mouth. She must have been too tired to fight, because she let him feed her. She ate all the saltines and emptied the bottle of water.

Tess looked at Sebastian and asked, "Can I please go to sleep now?"

"Yes," he agreed.

"I can find something for Tess to sleep in and wash those clothes for her," Alice offered.

"I'll take care of her." He felt as if it were his fault that Tess was in this position; he needed to be the one to see this through.

Sebastian escorted her upstairs to his room and walked her into the bathroom. Looking through the medicine cabinet, he found a new toothbrush. He opened it and placed it in her hands. "Brush your teeth."

When he left the room, she squeezed the blue-and-white swirled toothpaste onto the brush, placed it in her mouth, and began brushing in an up and down motion. Tess spat out the toothpaste and rinsed her mouth with water. She avoided looking at herself in the mirror.

Sebastian returned with a well-worn Smiths concert T-shirt and a pair of neatly folded boxers. "You can sleep in these," he said flatly. "Can you undress yourself?"

Tess nodded. She reached for her left boot and promptly fell onto the hard tile floor, cursing under her breath. Sebastian sighed and knelt down next to her. He proceeded to remove her boots and jacket. He pulled her T-shirt over her head and began to unbutton her jeans, but Tess pushed him away.

When I make love to you, you will be a very willing participant, he thought to himself, but instead he said, "Tess, do you really think I would try to take advantage of you in this state?"

"No," she said softly, nearly in tears.

"Then please let me take these filthy jeans off."

Tess relented. With practiced hands, he removed her jeans, trying to ignore the fact that she was now sitting in front of him in only her panties and a bra. He slipped on the T-shirt. She shifted her weight so he could pull the boxers up to her waist. Then he wet a wash cloth and gently removed the smudged makeup from her face.

Sebastian lifted Tess off the floor and carried her to his bed. After tucking her under the down comforter, he placed Charles the teddy bear in her arms. "Goodnight, Tess."

She fell asleep quickly, soft snores emanating from her within minutes. Sebastian pulled up a chair and sat next to the bed, watching her sleep. The soft light of the lamp on the bedside table caressed her pale skin. A few wild curls fell over her eyes. He leaned in and gently brushed them away before kissing her on the forehead.

Henry softly knocked on the door and then opened it. "I just wanted to make sure everything is okay." He glanced at Tess, who was sleeping peacefully.

"She'll be okay. I'm going stay here and watch over her."

"Leave the bedroom door open."

Sebastian chuckled. Did everyone think he would take sexual advantage of Tess in her drunken state? He was too tired to be angry. "Yes, Henry."

"Alice wanted me to fetch Tess' dirty clothes."

"They're in the bathroom."

Henry collected the clothes and bid Sebastian goodnight.

Sebastian couldn't stop thinking about what might have happened to Tess if Courtney hadn't called him. What if a guy had tried to take advantage of her? What if she was in an accident, or killed? His body shuddered. He didn't realize until this moment how much he cared about her—until he was faced with the possibility of losing her. That terrified him even more than admitting to himself that he had fallen in love with Tess Hamilton.

Sebastian spent the night awkwardly trying to sleep on the chair with his feet propped on the bed while Tess slept soundly. When morning arrived, Sebastian decided he would let Tess sleep as long as she needed. He headed toward the kitchen to get something to eat.

"Good morning," Alice greeted him. "Can I get you some breakfast?"

"Good morning. I'll get it—you stay seated," he replied, pouring himself a cup of hot coffee. He grabbed a sesame seed bagel and smeared it with cream cheese.

"How's Tess doing?" Henry asked.

"She's still sleeping." Sebastian took a bite of his bagel and swallowed.

"You look a little worse for wear."

Sebastian looked down at himself. He was wearing the same clothes from yesterday, only now they were a rumpled mess. When his hand came up to touch his face, he could feel stubble on his chin. He realized he didn't smell particularly good either. A yawn escaped him as he placed the palm of his hand on his lower back to relive the pain. "Trying to sleep in a chair isn't very comfortable."

"I've washed Tess' clothes," Alice replied, pointing to the neatly folded pile on the edge of the kitchen table.

"Thank you. I'll take them up to her." He finished his breakfast and gathered the clean pile of clothes. With his free hand, he took a glass from the overhead cabinet and filled it with water. Alice placed a bottle of aspirin on the pile of clothing and he nodded his head in thanks.

He made his way through the foyer and up the stairs, heading to his room. Gently opening his bedroom door, he peeked inside. Tess was stirring under the covers.

"Hi," he gently greeted.

"Hey," she said, stretching her arms over her head.

"How are you feeling?"

"Like someone hit me over the head with a pipe," she groaned, holding her forehead.

"Cheap liquor will have that effect." He handed her the glass of water and dropped two aspirin into her other hand.

"Thank you for last night," she said, taking a gulp of water to wash down the aspirin. She closed her eyes and leaned her back against the wooden headboard.

"You're welcome. Just promise me you won't ever do that again."

"Believe me, I promise," she vowed, opening her eyes. "How can anyone find this fun?"

Sebastian sat down on the bed next to her. "It's not about fun, Tess. It's about forgetting. I understand why you did it. I'm sorry I was the cause," he apologized.

"Stop it. I have no one to blame but myself. I appreciate you taking care of me. My mom would have killed me if I came home drunk last night." She trembled. "You really saved my ass."

"Your mom seems so understanding. I doubt she'd kill you," Sebastian reasoned.

"When you're the perfect good girl who never does anything wrong—I don't think I could stand her disappointment in me."

"No one's perfect, Tess," he sighed. "It just comes down to whether you can forgive and move on. I really want to move on with you." He held out his hand, hoping she would be ready to reconcile after their argument. She turned to face him but remained silent. After a prolonged moment, she placed her hand in his palm.

"What is this? What are we doing?" she asked, looking at their fingers intertwined.

"It can be whatever you want it to be. There's no pressure," he responded.

"I don't want a boyfriend. I don't want a relationship."

"It's too late for that," he informed her. "Romantic or not, we have a relationship. I'll always have your back, Tess."

"I know," she admitted with a feeble smile. Tess looked down at the Smiths T-shirt she was wearing. "What happened to my clothes? Did I undress myself?"

"No, I undressed you." He sensed her horror and quickly added, "Your modesty is still intact. You had vomit on your shirt, so Alice washed your clothes for you. They are over on the chair." He pointed with a nod of his head. "She's also bringing up some food for you."

"I'm not hungry."

"You have to eat and get hydrated. Trust me—I've cured many hangovers in my time." He tried to make light of the situation to ease her embarrassment.

"I do trust you, Sebastian," Tess replied in all seriousness.

He squeezed her hand. "Thank you."

Chapter 11 - Head Over Heels

Sebastian knocked on the Hamilton's door at 8:00 a.m. sharp. Mrs. Hamilton greeted him. "Hello, Sebastian."

"Good morning," he replied, slipping into their cozy living room. He handed her a bouquet of flowers. "These are for you. Thank you for having Nanny Jones and I for Thanksgiving dinner. It was very kind of you."

"It was my pleasure. Ever since my husband passed away, Tess and I have always celebrated alone. It was wonderful to have laughter in the house again. Mrs. Jones was very lovely. Now I see where you get your good manners."

Tess' mother turned and opened the door to the hallway coat closet. She pulled out a small overnight bag and handed it to him.

"Thank you for trusting me to take Tess away for the weekend. You have my sister's number if you need to reach us."

"Yes, I called her last night. She assured me you'll take good care of Tess. I really am happy that Tess gets to take this trip. She always works so hard, and with my schedule at the hospital, we don't have any time to get away."

He dashed out of the house to place the bag in the car. How he had ever persuaded Mrs. Hamilton to let him take Tess away for the weekend, he'd never know. English charm, he supposed. When he returned to the Hamilton's front hall, Tess was at the bottom of the stairs to greet him.

She was wearing a new pair of jeans and a green crew neck sweater. Her hair was blown out straight and gently fell over her shoulders. Tess frowned when she caught sight of him. He was impeccably dressed in a bespoke navy suit with a white shirt and narrow yellow paisley tie. "I'm underdressed. Give me a few minutes to get changed." She turned on her heel to rush back up the steps, but his words stopped her before the first step.

"You look great," he retorted honestly. "Now let's get on the road."

Tess looked at her jeans and back at his suit, and then at her mother for support. "You heard him. Get going," her mother agreed, patting Tess on the shoulder.

Sebastian helped Tess put on her gray wool peacoat. He stepped forward and then opened the door for her to exit.

"Take good care of my girl, Sebastian," her mother warned him.

"You have my word, Mrs. Hamilton."

They hopped in the Jaguar and were on their way. "Will you please tell me where we're going?"

"It's a surprise," he announced.

Sebastian caught the frown on her face as she turned to stare out the window at the housing developments and strip malls they passed. They rode in a comfortable silence for nearly thirty-five minutes until Tess spoke again.

"Sebastian, against my better judgment, I agreed to your day of fun to celebrate your hard work and accomplishments. The least you can do is tell me where we are going."

"How about we test your geography skills?" he teased, knowing full well her local geography knowledge was far better than his.

"Fine," she agreed with an exasperated sigh. "What do you want to know?" As soon as she asked, she noticed they had already exited the Pennsylvania Turnpike and entered New Jersey. "What are we going to do—drive around traffic circles all day?"

"Tess, why are you so impatient?"

"I don't like surprises."

They drove over the bridge into Trenton, the large sign reading *Trenton Makes the World Takes* ushering them into the depressed city. "Where do you end up if you take I-95 north over the George Washington Bridge?"

"New York City," she replied absentmindedly. "Oh my god, we're going to New York City!" she repeated, practically jumping up in her seat.

"See, not all surprises are bad."

"What will we do when we get there?"

"You'll have to just wait and see."

"You're taking me to New York City."

Sebastian glanced over at her sheer joy and smiled. Now she was happy and relaxed. He was going to show her a weekend in New York that she would never forget.

The drive was quick for a Saturday morning. They breezed right across the George Washington Bridge and

Sebastian turned onto the Henry Hudson Parkway and headed toward midtown Manhattan. He got lucky and found a prime parking space right in front of the historic brownstone.

"We're here." Sebastian grabbed the two overnight bags from the trunk. "After you," he said as he pointed to the brownstone. "This is my sister's house."

Sebastian opened the front door and let Tess step inside first. He followed, put down the bags, and closed the door behind them. With some gentle nudging, Tess walked further inside. The foyer was narrow with a gray and white marble floor. There was a set of mahogany doors to the right of the foyer, while a straight marble staircase reached up to the second level on the left side.

Three flights above, a young woman's head peeked over the railing. "Welcome to the Upper East Side," she called out with a wave.

"Sigourney," he bellowed, "get your arse down here immediately. I have someone I want you to meet."

Sigourney glided down the stairs, smoothly and effortlessly, as if she were a skater on ice. She reached the landing and promptly gave Tess a hug and an air kiss on each cheek. "Tess, it's a pleasure to meet you." His sister was tall, about five-foot eight, with the same blue eyes and chestnut brown hair as Sebastian. She was dressed in black wide-leg trousers and a slim-fitted, ivory silk blouse. She could have been a model. Instead, she was a student at Juilliard.

Sebastian gave her a hug. "How's New York been treating you, my wonderful sister?"

"Brilliant—although I am disappointed it took you so long to come back and visit me."

"I've been hard at work. I've been hitting the books, as the Americans would say." Sigourney laughed, not believing him in the slightest.

"It's true," Tess chimed in. "He even made the honor roll this quarter."

His sister stood back with one hand on her hip, eyeing Tess with great curiosity. "You are quite the miracle worker, Tess." Then she turned to her brother. "Take whatever room you like. I suggest the master on the second floor. Mummy just had a Hastens king mattress custom made and delivered. It's like sleeping on air." She winked.

"Tess, you can take that room. I'll take another," he quickly added hoping the awkwardness of Sigourney's suggestion did not offend Tess.

"You'll have to take your own bags upstairs. This is a SFZ."

"SFZ?" Tess wondered.

"Servant-free zone," the siblings replied in unison, laughing.

"Come on," Sebastian motioned to Tess. "I'll show you your room."

Their shoes made clicking sounds as they climbed the marble stairs. They entered the second floor master bedroom. He laid her overnight bag on the bed.

"I can't believe we're here. How did you pull this off?" Tess asked, turning three hundred and sixty degrees while taking in the room.

"Thankfully, your mother not only likes me, she trusts me. I just wanted to do something to show you how grateful I am for your friendship and tutoring. I couldn't have done as well as I did this quarter without your help."

He walked up behind Tess, who was now gazing out the window onto Park Avenue. Placing his hands on her shoulders, he whispered, "We have to celebrate. It's your eighteenth birthday."

Tess turned to face him with surprise in her eyes. "You remembered?"

"Of course. I have a special dinner planned for you tonight. But first, we're going shopping."

"Shopping?"

"You need a proper dress. You can't go to Tavern on the Green in jeans."

"I wish you wouldn't spend your money on me," she said, frowning.

"Indulge me, Tess."

"I think too many people indulge you already."

"Maybe," he agreed, "but you're not one of them." He put his hands together, begging. "Please, please?"

"Fine! On one condition: I want you to buy yourself a pair of jeans and sneakers so I don't feel so underdressed all the time."

Sebastian grinned from ear to ear. "Done! Now Bergdorf's awaits."

They walked toward Central Park and turned down Fifth Avenue. It was a gorgeous day in New York City. The November air was crisp and clear. Cars and taxis inched along, horns blaring. They were making better time by walking.

"Your sister thinks we're having sex."

"And I corrected her *faux pas.*"

"How many other girls have your brought here?"

"None," he replied honestly. "You're the only one." He turned and smiled at her, wanting nothing more than to take her hand.

They crossed the street, dashing between idling cars, and landed on the doorstep of Bergdorf Goodman. The doorman looked at Sebastian in his suit then glanced at Tess in her denim jeans. He opened the door and invited them inside. She was out of her element from the first step. They entered a world of expensive perfumes and European cosmetics. Sebastian put his hand on the small of her back to guide her to the escalators. They made their way to the fourth floor, where the couture dresses were shown. He moved through the store as if it were his second home.

"This is not the men's store," Tess observed.

"No, ladies first," he reminded her. Sebastian walked into the middle of the dress department. He turned in a circle, looking at the various dresses displayed on the wall. An older saleswoman in a straight-cut black suit approached them.

"Welcome to Bergdorf Goodman. How may I help you?" she said to Sebastian.

Sebastian turned to Tess and asked, "What size do you wear?"

"Eight."

Sebastian then turned to the saleswoman. "She'd like to try on that one and that one," he responded, pointing to his selections. He had the uncanny ability to eye up a room and know exactly what he wanted to buy.

The saleswoman nodded and swiftly hustled through the door to the storeroom. She collected the dresses in Tess' size and showed her to the fitting room. Sebastian sat down in the brown suede chair in the outer room to wait patiently.

Finally, Tess emerged barefoot in Chanel. It was a simple black cocktail dress with a fitted bodice and a knee length skirt that flared out from the waist. The top was an overlay of sheer, black silk with cap sleeves and a round collar. Tess looked at him for approval. She was uptight, unsure how to react to wearing couture. It almost made him chuckle.

He nodded his approval. "That's nice. Try the other one on."

Several minutes later she stepped out in Calvin Klein. It was a stunning, strapless, gunmetal gray dress with thin tiers of organza on the skirt. He smiled appreciatively. Sebastian turned to the saleswoman. "We'll take them both."

Tess rushed over to him, whispering. "No, you can't."

"Why not?"

"These dresses cost over two thousand dollars. You just don't spend that kind of money on a whim."

"I do," he simply replied. "Now go get changed so we can go to the men's store and buy some jeans."

There was no arguing with him. She trudged back to the fitting room. Sebastian motioned for the saleswoman, who was now hovering intently. "Find out the rest of her sizes. Pick out lingerie—La Perla. She'll need black silk stockings with the seam up the back and black heels—something strappy." He handed her his American Express card. "I'll need them delivered to 1425 Park Avenue today." The saleswoman nodded and went about her task.

Tess observed the exchange between Sebastian and saleswoman when she exited the fitting room. She rolled her eyes in disbelief that he could act so nonchalantly about the shopping spree. "Gee, and you only have the gold card," she muttered under her breath. "I would have at least expected a platinum card."

Sebastian was not amused. "Mother has the platinum card."

"I'm just joking," she told him, gently touching his arm. "I don't have a credit card. Most people our age don't!"

"Well, I'm not most people our age. Will you please stop stressing out?" Sebastian pleaded.

"What will your mother say when she sees the bill?" Tess stopped for moment, placing her hand over her heart in a panic. "What will *my* mother think?"

He offered her his arm. She eagerly took it, as if Sebastian was a life preserver in a wild storm. He steadied Tess. "Platinum credit cards, the cost of a dress, the expense of the Jaguar…what does it matter? You can't fault me for living a privileged life. My mother and I are playing a game. She wants an obedient son. I go along just enough to have a comfortable life," he explained with malice.

"Most people would say your life is excessive."

"Maybe so, but it's the only way I know," he replied matter-of-factly. "Tess, you make me happy. Don't ruin this for me."

"Sebastian, you don't have to buy my friendship. You already have that."

They left the building and walked across Fifth Avenue to the men's store. Once they were inside, a salesman quickly approached the couple. "Welcome to Bergdorf Goodman. My name is Randolph. How may I be of assistance to you today?" he asked, addressing Sebastian and barely glancing in Tess' direction.

Sebastian noticed him eyeing his expensive suit and figured the salesman had found himself a hefty commission by offering his services. Sebastian smiled politely. "The lady would like to see me dressed in jeans and sneakers," he said, tilting his head toward Tess.

"Any particular designer?" he asked, finally acknowledging her presence.

"Tess?"

She shrugged, unsure how to reply.

"Bring what you like," Sebastian instructed him.

"I'd say a thirty-two waist and an eleven shoe," Randolph guessed aloud. "I shall return momentarily with a few selections. Can I have someone bring you a beverage?"

Sebastian acknowledged the correct sizing, and after an eyebrow lift to Tess, declined the beverages.

Tess took a seat and Sebastian sat next to her. He squeezed Tess' hand in an attempt to dispel her unease.

The salesman quickly returned with a small stack of denim jeans for Sebastian to try on. He returned a few minutes later wearing Calvin Klein jeans. The cut was loose and full. He stood on the small tailor's platform and looked into the three way mirror, turning his head this way and that to see his reflection from all angles. He frowned. "No." He stepped down and retreated to the fitting room to try on the next pair.

He returned in Armani slim-legged jeans. He repeated the mirror routine. This time he smiled. "These will do."

"And the shoes, sir?" the salesman asked, holding four shoe boxes in his arms.

"Let the lady decide," he replied, before returning to the fitting room.

After a light lunch, they walked back to the brownstone. Sebastian carried a shopping bag containing his first pair of jeans, a cashmere sweater, and sneakers. They didn't talk, and that was okay. Sebastian was so comfortable with Tess that he didn't feel the need to fill the silent space with idle chatter.

They heard the beautiful sound of piano music filling the foyer when they entered the house. The music abruptly stopped. "Sebastian, is that you?" Sigourney called from the front parlor.

"Yes, we're back," he responded, popping his head through the open doorway.

"Come have some tea before you get ready for dinner," she suggested.

Tess and Sebastian joined Sigourney, who stood from the piano to pour the tea. She handed them each a cup and motioned for them to sit on the sofa.

"I see you had quite a successful shopping trip by the number of boxes that Bergdorf's delivered. I had them put everything in your room, Tess. I hope you'll let me help you get ready. I can't wait to see what Sebastian bought you!" Sigourney sounded as excited as a six-year-old on Christmas.

"That would be great," Tess said.

"Oh, I almost forgot—Mummy called while you were out. She'll be here on Monday. She's sorry she won't get to see you this weekend. She did say she'll be in Pennsylvania the week before Christmas, and she decided to have the annual New Year's party there."

"Brilliant," he spat in disgust, quickly taking a cigarette out of his pocket and lighting up.

"Sebastian, don't be like that. She really loves you in her own way," Sigourney informed him. "And put that fag out."

"And I really despise her," he replied, ignoring her request to extinguish the cigarette.

"She wants you to be successful," Sigourney argued. "The fag, Sebastian, put it out."

"She wants me to be less like my father and more like her. I can't understand why, since neither one of them raised me," Sebastian seethed. He took another drag on his cigarette.

Sigourney leaned over and kissed his forehead. "I know you're in a quandary, but you're doing so well here in America. Nanny keeps me posted because you have no free time for me."

"Yes, well, Tess gets all the credit for that," he replied, motioning to her as she sat quietly, taking in the sibling interaction with great curiosity.

Sigourney looked to Tess for input.

"He's a changed man," Tess announced.

"See!"

Sigourney laughed. "You just took her on a shopping spree. Of course she'll be on your side."

Sebastian shot her a dirty look. Sigourney had gone too far with that comment. Tess took notice and quickly jumped in. "Sigourney, I'm well aware of Sebastian's life in England. He's made an amazing effort to focus on his grades and get into a good school. I'm really proud of him. Our friendship has nothing to do with money."

"I haven't gotten the chance to meet the new and improved Sebastian yet," Sigourney mocked.

"Well, he's right in front of you and he's a wonderful and kind person," Tess defended Sebastian.

"You must think I'm horrid for being so cynical. I'm sorry," Sigourney apologized.

"It's okay."

"Good," Sebastian interrupted, smudging out his Dunhill in the crystal ashtray. "Now that we have that sorted, will you two go and begin your primping? Our reservation is for seven o'clock."

Tess and Sigourney left the room and began their ascent to the second floor. Tess turned to face her as they climbed the stairs. "Are you coming to dinner, too?"

"Oh, no," Sigourney replied with a devilish smile.

"Then why did he just tell us to go primp?"

"I'm here to transform you into Cinderella."

At that moment, they reached the guest room to find a tower of white Bergdorf Goodman boxes neatly stacked in the middle of the room. Her face fell. "Oh, Sebastian, what did you do?" she muttered to herself.

"Open them up!" Sigourney urged cheerfully. "I'm dying to see what he bought you." Tess was frozen in place. "Tess, why do you look so terrified?"

"He just spent over two thousand dollars on dresses. What else could he possibly have purchased?"

"There's only one way to find out. Come on." Sigourney pulled Tess toward the boxes.

Tess opened the first box. Inside she found a pair of black leather Manolo Blahnik stilettos. She picked the shoe up by its strap and showed it to Sigourney. "How am I supposed to wear these and not break my neck?"

"Oh, look! French lingerie and silk stockings," Sigourney chirped, ignoring her while opening the next box. "I am going to have so much fun making you up!"

"I won't feel underdressed tonight," she mused, dropping the torturous heel back into the box.

Tess showered in preparation for what was to come. Sigourney primped and prodded her as if she were a Barbie doll. She was seated at the vanity as Sebastian's sister expertly applied makeup and styled her hair. "I don't know, maybe we should try an updo?" she pondered aloud.

"No, it's fine." Tess quickly dispelled, fidgeting in the chair.

"It just needs something." She thought for a moment and then reached into her jewelry box. Sigourney placed a diamond barrette in Tess' hair. "Perfect." She gleamed with satisfaction.

Tess stood up and gazed at her reflection in the full-length mirror. Sigourney stood behind her, smiling. "Sebastian does have exquisite taste," Sigourney proclaimed. "He's waiting for you. It's time to go."

Carefully, Tess descended the stairs, holding onto the railing for balance. She teetered in her new shoes. Sebastian stood below in the foyer, fixated. His breath hitched. He couldn't believe how beautiful and utterly sexy she looked in her Calvin Klein dress. The cut was perfect for her. The transformation from plain girl to society lady was astonishing.

As she hit the landing, Tess lost her footing on the slick marble floor. Sebastian quickly reached out for her arm to steady her.

"How do you expect me to walk in these damn things?" she questioned him in despair.

He merely smiled as he placed his hands on her waist to straighten her posture.

Sigourney walked down the stairs holding a fur coat. "Tess, wear this tonight. It's cold outside."

"Sigourney, I can't."

"Of course you can," she argued, sounding just like her brother.

Sebastian held out the soft mink and slipped it onto Tess. "Off we go. The taxi is waiting." With Sebastian's hand on her back, they stepped out into the chilly New York air.

The doorman welcomed them to Tavern on the Green. The hostess greeted Sebastian. "Mr. Irons, we will seat you at your mother's table."

He glanced at the hostess' name tag. "Thank you, Emily."

She nodded and sat them at a prime table. It was next to a large window overlooking Central Park. The fairy lights magically twinkled in the trees outside like thousands of tiny fireflies blinking on and off. Emily handed them both menus and discreetly excused herself.

"I'm not having a cheeseburger tonight, am I?" Tess asked before she even opened the green leather-bound menu.

"No, not tonight."

"Just order for me," she said, laying the menu on the table.

The sommelier opened a bottle of Cabernet Sauvignon and handed the cork to Sebastian before pouring an inch of wine into a crystal glass. Sebastian took a sip. He swirled the wine around his mouth. The rich, full flavors of black fruit, oak, and herbs rolled over his taste buds before swallowing it. He nodded to the waiter. "This is fine."

The sommelier poured two glasses of wine. It was perfect for what Sebastian had in mind for their meal. Tess politely took a sip.

Sebastian enjoyed the cabernet, while Tess switched over to water. The waiter arrived at their table. Sebastian placed their order without looking at the menu. "We'll, have a baby beet salad with arugula and mandarin vinaigrette. For the main course we'll have the filet mignon, wild mushrooms with white truffle oil, and grilled asparagus."

Once the waiter left them, Sebastian raised his glass to make a toast. "To you," he said softly, "for your friendship and encouragement."

Tess raised her glass. "You know you didn't have to do this."

"I know."

"I feel like a very uncomfortable Cinderella."

"Just try to enjoy the evening. I'll have you home before midnight. I just wanted to have the perfect day with you."

"So was it perfect?"

"I don't know. The day is not over yet," he replied with a sly smile.

"Fine, I'm just along for the ride. Protesting will do me no good."

"It's about time you sussed that out. This weekend you're all mine, and I'm going to show you this amazing city and all it has to offer."

The waiter placed the salad plates on the table in front of them. He took a chilled salad fork from the napkin-covered plate he held and laid one by Sebastian and one by Tess. Sebastian picked up his salad fork and Tess followed his lead.

"I'm sorry about Sigourney, earlier. She isn't very good at editing her thoughts before she speaks."

"I admire that she says what's on her mind. She's not like you in that regard. You are always thinking before you speak." She took a bite of her salad. "Sometimes it would be nice to hear what you're thinking in the moment."

"I could say the same of you, Tess."

"Fine," she responded, taking up the challenge. "You look very handsome in that suit. You look more comfortable and at ease in a suit and tie than in anything else I've ever seen you wear. It puzzles me." She sighed with satisfaction. "See—unedited thought. Now you."

He gazed at her for a long moment, taking in every inch of her: Tess' long, silky hair, luminous complexion, bare shoulders, and the perfectly fitted dress that hugged her in all the right places. "I think you have never looked more beautiful than you do right now. You put every other woman in this room to shame."

She swallowed hard. "I don't know how to respond to that, Sebastian," she said, her eyes glancing down on the table.

"A simple thank you will do."

Her self-consciousness prevented her from saying thank you. Instead she said, "Explain to me why you enjoy big fancy meals. You know I'm perfectly happy at McDonald's."

"That dress would be wasted on McDonald's. You Americans fail to realize the value of a good meal, good company, and lively conversation," he pompously announced.

"So you and your friends enjoyed fancy dining back in London?"

"Yes—food is to be savored, not eaten in fifteen minutes. Fast food is not a meal, Tess. There is a reason they call it 'fast.'"

"How long will this fine dining experience last?"

"A few hours. I promise I won't bore you."

"You never bore me, Sebastian." She waited until he broke eye contact, and they both returned to their salads.

Sebastian opened the front door of the brownstone and ushered Tess inside. The house was dark. He flipped on the light and spied a note from his sister propped up on the vestibule table. "Sigourney is out with friends. Guess we have the place to ourselves." Sebastian removed Tess' fur coat and placed it over the stair banister. "Sit down for a second," he instructed, pointing to the steps.

She gratefully took a seat, looking relieved to be off her feet. Sebastian knelt down on the floor in front of her. He lifted her right foot and began to caress her ankle. Slowly, he untied the leather strap until her foot was free. Gently, he massaged her tired and achy foot without breaking eye contact with Tess. "Does that feel better?"

She didn't speak. She simply nodded.

"You look absolutely stunning, Tess." His voice was soft and seductive.

She lowered her head, looking away to hide her flushed cheeks. Sebastian raised her chin with his right hand to re-establish eye contact. "Happy birthday." He leaned in and kissed her on the lips. It was sweet and chaste. Sebastian knew it was her first kiss and he didn't want to scare her away. He took off her left shoe and then reached for her hand and lifted her into a standing position.

Sebastian swept her up into his arms and carried her up the stairs. He placed her back onto her stocking feet just outside her bedroom door. He leaned in and kissed Tess again slowly, lingering for a bit longer this time, testing the waters to see if she would kiss him back.

Tess slowly placed her hands on his chest. "Thank you for a wonderful day. Goodnight, Sebastian."

He couldn't let her go that easily. He moved in closer to her body, pinning her against the bedroom door. "Your heart is racing," he whispered, feeling her body heat and thumping heart against his chest. He kissed her again, his tongue gently parting her lips. She was definitely kissing him back.

Tess turned the door knob with her left hand and snuck back into her bedroom, catching Sebastian off guard. He tried to follow her, but she quickly closed the door in his face. "I'll see you tomorrow morning," Tess told him through the closed door.

She left him standing there, his forehead against the doorframe, gutted. He swore he could hear her breathing on the other side. Would she change her mind and let him inside? Moments later he heard the soft creak of the floorboards as she walked away from the door.

Sebastian walked back to his bedroom alone. This was not how the evening had played out in his head. Right now their naked bodies should be tangled up in luxurious Italian sheets. He threw himself on his empty bed, glowering at the ceiling. Just how long could she resist him? He thought he had planned the perfect fairytale day for her. Sebastian couldn't hold out much longer. It had been months since he'd had sex and it was driving him mad. Sebastian could go to a club right now and easily find a willing sexual partner, but he only wanted Tess.

The simple fact that he was head over heels in love with her left him only two choices: a cold shower or a good wank. Honestly, he'd been doing too much of both lately.

He methodically undressed and carefully hung his custom-made suit in the closet. He turned the shower on and stripped off his boxers, then stepped into the tile stall and felt the warm water rush over his chilled body. It felt good. His mind still focused on Tess: the curve of her hips, the sexy silk stockings on her legs, the black strappy heels that drove him wild. It was sensory overload. He instinctively reached below his waist with his right hand, taking hold of his erection, and braced himself by extending his left arm against the tile wall.

Once he felt relief, he turned off the water and grabbed the towel to dry off. Rubbing his tired eyes, he let the bath towel drop onto the floor and crawled into bed naked. Sebastian drifted off to sleep quickly, yet erotic dreams of Tess did not escape his consciousness.

He had entered such a deep sleep that he didn't hear Tess knock on his door around 10:00 a.m. She slowly opened the door to find him snoring softly, sound asleep in the middle of the bed with a mound of pillows surrounding his head. She padded gently toward him and sat on the edge of the mattress without disturbing his sleep. Tess had never seen him without his shirt, and noticed the word *Libertine* tattooed on his bicep. She reached out to touch it with her fingertips. The movement startled Sebastian, who sat straight up. The duvet fell down around his waist, threatening to expose him. His normally perfect hair was standing out at various angles. Tess sucked in a breath.

"Tess?" he muttered in his hazy state of mind, somewhere in between dreaming and reality.

"I'm sorry, I didn't mean to wake you," she apologized.

"No, it's okay," he responded, reaching over to the bedside table to grab his wristwatch. He yawned deeply.

Tess caught a glimpse of his bare hip bone and quickly turned away. She realized he was naked under the sheet.

Sebastian looked at the time. "Damn, I overslept." He noticed her blushing and enjoyed it, making no attempt to cover himself up. He was getting under her skin, too, he realized.

"You promised me art today," she reminded him, focusing on his face and careful not to let her gaze move lower.

"Yes, I did." He stretched, and the duvet slipped another inch.

"Well, get dressed—and please wear your jeans so I don't feel so out of place."

"Yes, darling," he playfully replied. Grabbing the edge of the sheet with his fist, he began to lift the sheet. Tess was out of his room in a flash. Sebastian fell back onto the pillows laughing.

Thirty minutes later, he joined Tess downstairs in the living room. Even dressed casually, Sebastian was handsomely groomed. He wore a white shirt, navy tie, and a gray merino wool V-neck sweater, which he tucked into his belted jeans. "Ready?"

She looked at the tie and shook her head—at least he was wearing jeans. "Why aren't you wearing your sneakers?"

"They don't match my coat," he informed her as he opened the front door. They walked down the stone stairs onto Park Avenue and out into another beautiful New York City day.

Sebastian and Tess made their way toward Central Park and the Metropolitan Museum of Art, choosing to walk rather than hail a taxi.

"Tell me about the Libertine tattoo."

He looked over at her as they stopped on the street corner and waited for the light to turn green. "Do you know the definition?"

"Yes," she nodded. "It describes someone who is a free thinker in religious matters or a person who indulges in sensual pleasures or vices. Somehow I don't think the first meaning applies." She rattled the definition, sounding like a walking dictionary. "Why did you do it?"

"Alistair called our little trio the Libertines. One night we got really pissed and thought it would be a good idea for the three of us to get a tattoo to commemorate our bond. It seemed like a good idea at the time."

"So was it a good idea?" They stepped into the intersection and continued on their way.

Sebastian shrugged. "I don't know. When you're sober it's obvious that it was a stupid thing to do, but I don't regret it. It's a reminder of where I've been and how far I've come."

Sebastian enjoyed watching the people they passed as they made their way toward the museum. Mothers pushed baby strollers, people were jogging, some walked their dogs, and a sweet old couple walked hand-in-hand, slowly making their way through the park.

"Let's get a soft pretzel," she urged, stopping in front of the vendor's silver cart. "Two please." She reached in her pocket and grabbed a few dollar bills to pay.

Sebastian let her spend her own money. He knew it would please her to pay, and they hadn't eaten any breakfast. She handed him one of the pretzels.

"There not very soft," he mumbled as he choked on the hard, dry pretzel. They continued their walk and thankfully there was another vendor just a short distance away. He bought them each a bottle of water and pitched the half eaten pretzel in the rubbish bin.

"They are pretty awful, aren't they?" she said, also tossing hers in the bin.

"We'll have a proper lunch at the Met."

They continued on their way and soon came upon the entrance of the museum. They started to walk up the grand staircase when Sebastian stopped and said, "Wait." He gently took her hand and stopped her from walking any further ahead of him.

"What is it?" she asked, turning to look him the eye. She was a few steps above him, which actually made her petite frame the same height as Sebastian.

"I want to kiss you on the steps of the Met," he muttered, closing the gap between them and honing in on her lips.

"In front of all these people?"

He never spoke his reply. Instead he kissed her, taking Tess in his arms. The world around them faded away.

Chapter 12 - Mad World

It was the twenty-first of December and Sebastian wasn't feeling very joyous. He wished he could just speed up the calendar and the whole holiday would be over, and his mother would fly off to her next destination. She hadn't yet arrived in Pennsylvania and he was already consumed with dread.

"Hey, are you okay?" Tess asked, nudging him with the tip of her pencil.

"What?" he asked absentmindedly. He was having trouble concentrating on his homework and he squirmed uncomfortably in his chair.

"What's wrong? You've been unusually quiet and moody this week."

"You haven't seen anything yet," he muttered, closing the book in front of him.

"Do you want to talk about it?"

"No."

"Let's just call it a day."

"Tess, are you home?" her mom called from the living room.

Tess left the kitchen to join her mom and Sebastian followed, grateful for the distraction. Kate was standing in the middle of the room with a big smile on her face, holding a thick white envelope in her hands. "It's from NYU."

Tess quickly grabbed the envelope from her mom's outstretched hand and tore it open. Her eyes frantically scanned the letter. "I'm accepted," she whispered with relief. She hugged her mom and started crying.

Sebastian stood back, watching it all play out. He wanted to be happy for her, but he couldn't pull himself out of his own misery.

"Why are you crying?" her mom asked.

"I spent so many years working toward this one moment. I can't believe I did it. I mean, I was fairly confident, but you just never know."

"I always had faith in you, Tess," her mother said.

Tess handed her mom the acceptance letter. "Look at the cost of the dorm room! That doesn't even take into account the mandatory meal plan and books. How are we going to pay for all this?"

"I've been planning for your college education since you were born. Between the college fund and the scholarship, there's enough money."

"I should be going so you two can celebrate. Congratulations, Tess." Sebastian gave her a quick hug and showed himself out the door before she could protest. He got into the car and headed toward New Jersey. Sebastian needed a drink and remembered a liquor store on Route 73 just over the bridge. He needed to stock up for his mother's impending arrival. Alcohol would be the only way he'd make it through her stay.

He arrived at the Roger Wilco liquor store and picked a few of his favorite brands off the well-stocked shelves. With his brown bags of vodka and scotch safely tucked inside his tote bag in the trunk of the Jag, he crossed back over the Tacony Palmyra Bridge and headed for home.

Sebastian found Alice in the kitchen, looking through some cookbooks, trying to finalize meals for Lady Irons' stay. "Has she arrived yet?" he asked as he took off his coat.

"Her flight's been delayed. She won't be here until tomorrow morning," she answered, looking up from a Julia Childs cookbook.

"What time?"

"Seven in the morning."

"I'll be sure to leave for school early then." At least he had one more night of freedom.

"Are you hungry? I can make you something to eat," Alice offered.

"I'm fine, Alice. I just want to visit with Nanny." He took his tote bag with his books and the concealed liquor bottles and headed upstairs.

He knocked on Nanny's door. Inside he found her watching the telly. "Sebastian, I'm glad you popped in. Your mother's arrival is delayed."

Sebastian took a seat next to her and gave her a brief hug. "That was the best news I've had all day."

"You can't let her impending visit upset you. You've done so well here in America. This is your time to stand up for yourself—show your mother that you are in control of your life."

Sebastian gave her a melancholy smile. "You're brilliant to say so, Nanny, but you know six months away from her doesn't mean she's going to stop pushing me to do what she desires."

"You need to talk to her, Sebastian. You need to tell her what you want."

"And if she won't listen?"

"Sebastian, I've given you the money for your schooling." She paused before continuing. "You need to make a decision. Either you mend your relationship with your mother or you forego it all together."

"She could disown me."

"It's a strong possibility. Are you prepared for it?"

"How would we live, Nanny?"

"I have some money stashed away. If you continue to invest it wisely, you could live the remainder of your life off the interest alone."

Sebastian chuckled. "Have you got a million pounds stashed under your mattress?" It seemed ludicrous that his sweet, loving nanny could be so wealthy.

"Hiding money under a mattress is for old fools. I prefer the stock market and a good financial advisor."

Sebastian studied her face; there wasn't a hint of jest in her voice. Was it even possible? "You're completely serious, aren't you?"

"Of course I am, my dear boy. I never joke about money."

"So if we had to go it on our own, we'd be okay?'

"Yes."

"Nanny, there are so many things I don't know how to do. All my life, I've always had someone to do it for me." He shook his head in defeat.

"Well, then we'll just have to come up with a plan."

"So you'll still stay with me? Please tell me you won't go back to England and work for some other family."

Nanny patted him on the knee. "I'm getting old, Sebastian. I won't be around forever."

"Don't say that," he interrupted. "You're all I have."

"Nonsense! You have Sigourney, Henry, Alice, and don't forget Tess."

"I don't know where that relationship is going, Nanny. Just because I'm in love with her doesn't mean she loves me back."

"Well, of course she does, my dear boy. It's obvious."

"It's not obvious to me. We did have a wonderful time in New York, but ever since, it's been strictly school studies."

"You need to tell her you love her."

"I need to tell Tess I love her. I need to tell my mother I won't follow her wishes. I need to get accepted to NYU." He slumped forward and placed his head in the palms of his hands. "I can't do it. I don't have the energy or the strength to do it."

"You can," Nanny encouraged. "And you will."

Sebastian didn't sleep well that night. He had nightmare after nightmare. In one, he was destitute and homeless, living on the streets. His mother threw him a pound note as she was chauffeured through the streets of London in a bright and shiny Rolls-Royce Silver Shadow. Then the dream shifted. He was on his knees telling Tess how much he loved her. She responded with loud and echoing bellows of laughter, rebuffing his advances and walking off hand and hand with the quarterback. He awoke with a start, gasping for air, beads of perspiration covering his brow. It was still dark outside, but he shuffled to the shower, knowing he needed to start his day earlier than usual to avoid Lady Irons' arrival.

Sebastian left Edgewood and pulled up to the Hamilton home at 7:00 a.m. With his mind on his mother's arrival, he shook the thought away and knocked on the front door. Tess answered quickly and she looked at him skeptically.

"I brought you some hot chocolate," he said, offering her the steaming cup. "I'd like to drive you to school today."

Tess took the cup and stepped back, allowing him to enter the house. She was only half dressed, her white blouse still untucked and no shoes on her feet. "Give me ten minutes to finish getting ready," she said as she scurried away, leaving him to his own devices.

Sebastian settled onto the sofa and drank his coffee. His eye caught an invitation-sized envelope sitting on the coffee table. He could see that the postmark was from England and tensed up immediately, recognizing the script—it was from his mother. He opened it, although he knew it wasn't his place to do so. It was a personal invitation to dinner from his mother to Tess. She wanted to meet the tutor who had done such a magnificent job getting her son to buckle down and achieve good marks, it said. The date of the dinner was tomorrow.

He was still holding the card in his hand when Tess finally joined him. She was fully dressed and ready for the school day. "Oh, you found the invitation. Did you know about this?" Tess inquired, not bothered that he had opened it.

"I had no idea," he admitted. "You're not going, are you?"

"Of course I'm going," Tess told him, grabbing her coat from the closet.

"I'd prefer you didn't."

Tess gave him an odd look in return. "Sebastian, you need to tell me what's going on. You haven't been yourself lately."

"I don't want you to go because I don't want to be around you," he blurted out. Of course, that wasn't the way he meant to say it, but it was too late.

"Oh," was all she could manage to verbalize, confusion flooding her expression.

"Tess, I don't want to be around you because I don't like who I become when I'm with my mother. I go to a very dark place with her that I don't want you to see. I don't know how to stop it. I'd prefer you stay away from me while she's in town," he explained.

"She invited me to dinner. How can I refuse? How bad could it be?" She spoke in short bursts tinged with a hint of annoyance.

"I can't stop you, can I?" he sighed, defeated.

"No."

"You'd better wear the Chanel, then. Jeans are not permitted at the dinner table."

She leaned in and kissed him on the lips. It made his heart feel a little bit lighter. "Everything is going to be okay," she whispered.

He pulled her closer and kissed her again, wanting to believe her, but he knew better.

Sebastian arrived home after school. Alice cornered him when he opened the kitchen door and told him that his mother was in the library and wanted to see him immediately. He slowly walked down the hall with an uneasy feeling in the pit of his stomach. Sebastian reached for the library door and turned the knob, trying to collect himself before he entered.

"Sebastian, sit and have some tea with me," she instructed, her voice flat and serious.

"No, thank you," he replied, standing only a few feet into the room.

She looked up at him and began her discourse. "I must say, I'm very impressed with your marks ever since you began at St. Alexander's. I'm glad you took my warning to heart. I've invited your tutor to dinner tomorrow evening. I'd like to meet the person who influenced you so positively."

"Her name is Tess Hamilton and she has done a fine job of tutoring me, but do you really need to bring the hired help to the house for dinner, Mother?" he asked with a clipped British accent. He hoped that if he pretended to hate his tutor, maybe Lady Irons would cancel the dinner.

"I've taken from my discussions with the Cummings that you have befriended this girl."

"Of course, I've befriended her. If I have to be stuck with her for the entire school year, I might as well have her on my side."

"And what side might that be, Sebastian?"

He laughed. "I'm not fucking her, if that's what you're implying."

"Mind your language, Sebastian. Now go to your room. Dinner will be at seven o'clock." The discussion, as far as she was concerned, was over.

"I'm not hungry," he replied, turning on his heel and leaving the room, getting in the last word.

Sebastian slammed his bedroom door. He turned on the TV and lit a cigarette. Paul Young's *Come Back and Stay* video was playing on MTV. He wasn't sure what his next move should be. He had wanted his mother to think that he didn't like Tess, to prevent her from being invited to the house. Obviously, that hadn't worked.

Henry had started a fire in the fireplace and it helped to remove the chill in his bones left by the brief visit with his mother. The crackling sound and the aroma of burning wood were comforting. Alice had left him a sandwich on the coffee table and he smiled. These two people were more parental than the woman who had given birth to him. Sebastian had confided in them just how difficult this time with his mother would be for him, and here they were still taking care of him.

This house was his safe haven. It was the place where he found the family he'd always wanted. Now his mother was here to ruin it all. He sat on the floor in front of the fireplace with his back against the sofa. Sebastian reached under the furniture and pulled out a bottle of scotch. He poured himself a glass and let his mind slip away. There was a knock on the door. "Who is it?"

"Henry. May I come in?"

"Enter." He shifted the open bottle and glass behind him to conceal the liquor.

Henry found Sebastian sitting on the floor smoking a cigarette and staring at the TV. "I just wanted to see how you were doing."

"She invited Tess to dinner tomorrow," Sebastian said out of nowhere, still staring blindly at the image of U2 on the television. "I couldn't convince either one of them that it was a poor idea."

"I think Tess can take care of herself," Henry assured Sebastian. "It's you I'm worried about."

"I'll be okay when she leaves."

"If you need anything, just let me know." Henry stood up to leave. "Your mother has me running errands all day tomorrow in preparation for the holidays. You're welcome to join me if you want to get out of the house."

"Thanks, I'll think about it," he replied softly, lost in his thoughts.

He didn't have to think very hard. He left with Henry early the next morning, avoiding his mother. They finished the last of the errands around three o'clock and headed back home. Sebastian snuck up the servants' staircase and made a quiet dash to his bedroom. He closed the door without a sound and locked it behind him for privacy. He wished he had some pot so he could get stoned and numb himself to the impending dinner party. Instead he had to settle for a Dunhill. He lit up and walked into the closet to pull out his tuxedo. He laid the tux across the bed and frowned.

"Fuck it," he muttered in disgust. He lay down on the leather sofa, pulled the scotch out from under the furniture, and took a swig straight from the bottle. It immediately warmed him as it slid down his throat, but he knew that no amount of alcohol was going to sufficiently brace him for the hours to come.

Tess arrived three hours later. Alice greeted her at the front door. "Let me take your coat, and then I'll introduce you to Lady Irons."

"I'm a little nervous," Tess admitted. "Sebastian didn't want me to come to dinner tonight."

"I know. He's been out of sorts lately. I think he'll cheer up when he sees you."

Alice walked down the hallway and stopped at the library door. After a gentle knock, she opened the door. "Lady Irons, I'd like to introduce Tess Hamilton."

Tess stepped forward. "Hello, it's nice to meet you."

Lady Irons was sitting behind the desk, confident and imposing, like the President of the United States. "Miss Hamilton, welcome to my home. I'm very grateful for your hard work in tutoring my defiant son. I know he isn't an easy person to deal with. I applaud your patience. "

"Sebastian has worked very hard to turn his grades around. I'm very proud of him."

Just then, the phone on the desk rang. "Excuse me, I'm expecting this call. Alice, take Miss Hamilton to the sitting room. I'll be in as soon as I can."

Alice nodded and escorted Tess from the library. "Is she always that proper and stiff?" Tess leaned in and whispered.

"Yes."

"Where is Sebastian?"

"Upstairs in his room hiding. Why don't you go up and get him."

Tess dashed upstairs to Sebastian's room. She tried to open the door, but it was locked. "Sebastian, are you in there?"

He slowly stood up from the sofa. Buzzed from the alcohol, he weaved his way across the room and opened the door.

She entered the bedroom and said, "I saw your mother downstairs." Then she noticed the half-empty bottle in his hand, the intense aroma of alcohol on his breath, and the stench of cigarettes swirling around him. "What are you doing?"

"Drinking, obviously."

"Do you really think drinking is the answer?"

"It seems to help," he snapped. "Let he who has not sinned cast the first stone," he replied with a glib smirk on his face. He knew those incessant religion classes would come in handy at some point.

Tess didn't need to be reminded of her indiscretion at The Jug. "Do you think getting drunk is going to save you from your mother?" She reached out and took the bottle from his hand.

His anger raged. "Put it down!"

"No!" Tess stood up to him with both passion and concern. She moved toward the bathroom to pour the remainder of the bottle down the drain. "You don't need this, Sebastian."

"I don't need your help," he seethed. "This is my room and my home and my bottle of scotch and I will do whatever I bloody well please!" He grabbed her wrist and pulled her back to him. "Give me the bottle, Tess," he demanded.

Her face winced in pain from his grip, but instead of crying, she became more infuriated with him. "Far be it for me to stand in the way of the great Sebastian Irons," Tess mocked him as she shoved the bottle into his chest. He released her from his tight grip and clutched onto the scotch instead. "You're an ugly drunk. I'll be downstairs having dinner with your mother and sister."

And then she was gone, closing the door behind her.

Sebastian placed the bottle of scotch on his bedside table. He made a fist and slammed it into the wooden door. Reeling back in pain, he cursed. "Motherfucker." Looking down at his hand, he saw his knuckles begin to bleed. He stumbled into the bathroom and ran cold water over his throbbing hand. After wrapping it in a wet washcloth, he rang for Henry.

When Henry answered the page, Sebastian was sitting on the edge of the closed toilet seat, his head hung in shame. Henry knelt down next to Sebastian and slowly removed the bloodied wash cloth from his hand. "What the hell were you doing?"

"Had a fight with the door," he mumbled.

"And lost, from the looks of this." Henry examined the cuts and peeling skin. His hand was beginning to swell. "You might need an x-ray."

"No, just wrap it up for me."

"You smell like a distillery. Where did you get the booze?"

"Roger Wilco liquor store in New Jersey, where it's perfectly legal for me to buy it."

Henry shook his head in disapproval. "You were doing so well—why did you do it?"

"Because I fuck things up. That's what I do, Henry. Wasn't that what you were waiting for?"

"Grow up," Henry spat with disgust.

"Get out! I'm sorry I even called for you," Sebastian shouted.

Henry grabbed Sebastian by the arm and pulled him upright. "No, you don't get off that easy. You're coming downstairs and sobering up so you can apologize to Tess. How dare you leave her to fend for herself with your mother. She is completely out of her element down there, and has a look of sheer panic on her face all because you deserted her."

Henry escorted Sebastian downstairs to the kitchen and shoved him toward the table. "Sit down."

Sebastian did as he was told. He had never seen Henry so angry and wasn't enjoying being the object of his wrath. Loudly banging about the kitchen, Henry started a pot of coffee. Then he grabbed the first aid kit from the pantry.

Alice walked into the kitchen between serving courses to Lady Irons. She looked at Sebastian's hand and gasped. "What on earth!" She quickly rushed over to his side and examined his hand. "Tess said you weren't feeling well. She didn't say anything about the blood."

"Don't coddle him, Alice," Henry warned. "Dumbass decided to get plastered and use the door as a punching bag."

"Don't be so mean. He's hurt."

"If I weren't trying to sober him up, I'd do more than break his hand."

"Go on, then. Put me out of my misery," Sebastian whispered.

"That would be too easy. You're going to do the right thing." Henry opened the first aid kit and pulled out a bottle of iodine. Liberally dosing a cotton ball, he began dabbing the cuts on Sebastian's knuckles.

"Bloody hell!" Sebastian exclaimed as he jumped from the sting of the antiseptic.

"Sit still or you can take care of this on your own." Henry reached for a tube of ointment and squeezed it on the wound, then wrapped Sebastian's hand in white gauze and secured the bandage with tape.

Alice placed a mug of black coffee in front of Sebastian. He thanked her, and then took a sip. The sound of a ringing bell came from the dining room, beckoning Alice back to duty.

"I suggest you pull yourself together. Tess deserves an apology," Henry barked.

After the dessert plates were cleared, Lady Irons excused herself and bade farewell to Tess. She needed to call the UK to discuss business. Henry had entered the room with Tess' coat and purse. She took them silently and slipped out the front door.

Tess escaped into the cold December night. She fumbled for her car keys and dropped them on the ground, jolted from a voice whispering from behind.

"I'm so sorry." Sebastian was standing there against a tree, dressed in jeans and a flimsy sweater, his hands shoved in the pockets to ward off the cold and hide his injury. Tess turned around to face him, a burst of her white breath visible in the air. "I really am," he reiterated. "I had no right to be angry with you. I wish I could take it all back. Can you forgive me?"

Tess stared at him for a long moment. He was shivering in the cold without an overcoat, reaching out for help and wanting to be forgiven. In an instant, all the anger between them melted away. She quickly stepped forward and took him in her arms, burying her head in his quivering chest. "You have to stop drinking. It hurts me too much to see you like this." She lifted her head to look him in the eye. "I can forgive you if you promise to not act like this anymore," Tess pleaded.

He kissed her on the lips, the faint smells of scotch and mint toothpaste on his breath. "I love you."

It was the first time he'd said those words to her. In fact, it was the first time he had ever uttered those words to any girl. Three small words that could be exhilarating, dangerous, scary, and wonderful all at the same time. It may not have been the way he'd envisioned the moment in his head, but it was real and honest.

She stood there dumbstruck, unable to repeat it back, looking at him. He didn't know what she was thinking, couldn't read it in her face or her posture. Tess remained still, continued to stare straight at him—or perhaps through him. When she finally managed to speak, she said, "Okay. You're freezing. Let's get you inside."

Sebastian took his hand out of his pocket.

Tess noticed the bandage and let out a heavy sigh. "Honestly, can't you do anything right today?"

"Apparently not."

"What can I do to help?"

"An ice pack and aspirin would be good."

"Fine, but we're going through the kitchen so I can avoid bumping into your mother."

"You'll get no argument from me."

Henry and Alice looked up from washing the dishes when Tess and Sebastian came in through the back door. They were holding hands. Henry nodded at Sebastian with approval for working things out with Tess.

"Alice, do you have an ice bag I can borrow?" Tess asked.

Alice scurried from the room and returned in short order. Filling the bag with ice cubes from the freezer, she handed the bag to Tess. "Thanks. I'm going to see he gets to bed. I'll be back down in a few minutes."

Tess poured him a glass of water and took some aspirin from the bathroom cabinet while Sebastian warmed himself in front of the fire. The tables had turned: now she was taking care of him, just as he had done for her that night at The Jug.

"How's your hand?"

"The ice is helping." He put the aspirin in his mouth and took a sip of water.

"I really am sorry," he apologized again. "The one thing I never wanted was to have you get involved with mother. Instead I pushed you right into her lair."

"Dinner was brutal. She just stared at me the whole time, badgering me with questions, making me feel inadequate and not worthy to be in her presence. Maybe now I have some small understanding of what she must put you through," Tess admitted. "It still doesn't excuse your behavior."

"I know. Henry already gave me my comeuppance."

"Good." She nervously looked at the clock. "I need to get home. If you'd like to come over for Christmas Eve dinner, I'd like to see you. You can bring Nanny Jones, too."

"I'd like that very much," he admitted, quickly accepting the invitation.

"I'll see you tomorrow." She stepped next to him, leaned in, and kissed him on the cheek. A moment later, she was gone.

She seemed so eager to leave him that he didn't have a chance to find out what she was thinking. He'd told her he loved her and she couldn't even say it back. She did invite him to dinner. That was something—a tick on the plus side. He was grateful for the chance to redeem himself yet again. Why was he so flawed? It gnawed at him. Why was he always apologizing? He figured he should change his name to Sebastian "I'm sorry" Irons. Maybe one day she'd get so fed up that apologizing would no longer work.

Tess closed his bedroom door softly. Sigourney came up behind Tess unexpectedly and startled her. "Tess, what's going on with Sebastian? I've been knocking on his door all afternoon and he just repeatedly told me to go away."

"He's been drinking."

"That's not good. It's one thing to go out with your mates and get pissed; but drinking alone…"

"He'll be all right. He's got to be all right," Tess said. "Goodnight, Sigourney." She turned on her heel and walked away.

Sigourney watched Tess head down the hall toward the servants' staircase until she was out of sight. She turned and opened Sebastian's door, not caring to knock or announce herself. He was sitting on the sofa with the ice pack on his hand. "Dear brother, what is wrong with you?" she questioned, joining him on the sofa.

"Please, Sigourney, just go away," he pleaded, not turning to look at her.

"No. I want you to talk to me."

"What do you want me to say? I'm a complete fuckup."

"Well, I know that already," she agreed.

"Cheers."

"Will you let me finish!" she interjected. "I think you were a complete fuckup, but you really are turning things around for yourself." Sigourney grabbed the pack of Dunhills off the coffee table and lit one, letting the smoke billow up from her red lips.

"I wish she'd go home," he told her, referring to their mother. "I don't want Tess involved in this mess."

"Tess can fend for herself. Don't worry about her. You, on the other hand, could certainly have handled yourself better this evening. It's shameful of you to leave the poor girl all alone with Mummy during dinner," Sigourney admonished him, blowing another column of smoke into the air.

"You were there," he countered.

"Yes, well, I may have let the cat out of the bag."

Sebastian leaned his head back on the sofa and groaned. "What did you say?"

"Mummy was admiring Tess' dress and I let it slip that you bought it for her at Bergdorf Goodman."

"For Christ's sake, Sigourney. My relationship with Tess is none of her business."

"I don't even know what your relationship with Tess is. Do you?"

"Oh, bugger off." He wanted nothing more than to end this conversation and be alone.

"I have a great idea. Come on." He looked at her as she stood. Sigourney roughly pulled him off the sofa, snatching the cashmere blanket and wrapping it around her shoulders. She took his good hand and ushered him out the door, down the stairs, and outside into the cold night air.

"You're completely mental," he muttered as she led him across the frozen ground, past the wilted gardens, far away from the house. All they could hear was the crunch of their feet on the packed earth. The glowing moonlight was a beacon to a clear field surrounded by nothing but trees. Sigourney let go of his hand, inhaled deeply, and let out a shrill scream. Sebastian stumbled backwards. She laughed. He stood still, shaking his head in disbelief. "What the hell are you doing?"

"Go on then, have a go," she challenged him. "We're on a private estate. There isn't another house or person around for miles. Scream, Sebastian. Just let yourself go."

He paused, and then inhaled deeply. Cold air rushed down his windpipe and filled his chest. He screamed at the top of his lungs. It was exhilarating. He was in awe that something so tribal and feral could be so freeing. He repeated it and Sigourney joined in, their voices bouncing off the trees and getting lost with the wind. They let go a flurry of screams and yells until they were finally out of breath. They dropped to the ground, panting and laughing. Lying on their backs next to each other on the cold earth, they looked up at the stars.

Sigourney turned her head to face her brother. "Don't give up, Sebastian. Everything will work out in the end." She leaned in and kissed him on the forehead.

Chapter 13 - Please, Please, Please, Let Me Get What I Want

Christmas Eve morning, Sebastian made his way into the kitchen. It was 8:00 a.m. and Alice and Henry were preparing breakfast for Sebastian's family.

"Good morning," Alice greeted.

"Good morning." Sebastian poured himself a cup of coffee and selected a danish from the silver tray Alice was preparing.

"You're up early," Henry observed.

"I have some last minute shopping to do."

"Have you smoothed things over with Tess?"

"I think so. She invited me to dinner tonight."

"Your mother will be none too pleased about that."

Sebastian grinned. "Yes, I know."

Henry shook his head. "I don't know what sort of game you two are playing, but if you're not careful, things could get very messy."

Sebastian didn't respond. He sat down at the table and ate his breakfast. Henry was still angry with him, but at least he was talking to Sebastian. Henry was right—things could never end happily ever after for Sebastian and Lady Irons. With any luck, maybe he still had a chance with Tess.

Alice leaned in and looked at Sebastian's hand. The swelling was gone and there were a few traces of yellow bruising around the knuckles, but it was healing nicely. "Your hand looks much better."

"Yes," Sebastian agreed.

"You best get going. The mall will be packed with last minute shoppers." Henry chimed in as he picked up the tray of danish to take it into the dining room.

Sebastian braved the mall along with all the procrastinating male shoppers to pick up some holiday gifts. Nanny had agreed to attend dinner at the Hamiltons' later in the day, so he couldn't show up empty handed. It was also a perfect excuse to get out of the claustrophobic house. Sebastian knew it was wrong to let his mother have this kind of control over him. He needed to get his emotions in check where she was concerned, but had no idea how to accomplish it. Maybe Nanny was right—maybe he needed to talk to his mother. But what would be the point in that? For whatever reason, he was the 'chosen one.' She had deemed him the heir to Irons Electronics, and the more Sebastian rebelled, the tighter Lady Irons' grasp became.

After picking out the appropriate gifts, Sebastian returned home. He entered through the kitchen and came to a quick stop. His mother was standing next to Alice, going over a menu.

Lady Irons looked up. "Where have you been?"

Sebastian looked down at the shopping bags he held and then back at this mother as if she were daft. "Shopping—it is Christmas Eve, and I can't go to the Hamiltons' empty handed."

"The Hamiltons'?"

"Nanny and I have been invited to dinner. It's the least I can do to make amends for not escorting Tess to your dinner party." Sebastian smiled victoriously. Surely, his mother couldn't deny his logic. She valued etiquette above all other things.

"Yes, you must go," she coolly replied. "Your behavior last evening was unconscionable."

"Yes, it was," Sebastian agreed.

Lady Irons blinked. Sebastian *never* agreed with his mother, and it effectively silenced her.

She bounced back a moment later. "You'll be here tomorrow for Christmas dinner." She said it more as a statement of fact than a question.

Several different retorts filled his brain: *No, Mother, I'll be joining the circus* or *I'm having dinner with the Queen.* Instead he decided to keep his mouth shut.

It was a wonderful Christmas Eve dinner. The Hamiltons' house was decorated with fresh garland and a small but perfect tree shining with multicolored twinkling lights. They dined on roast turkey with all the trimmings.

"Mrs. Hamilton, the dinner is delicious," Sebastian complimented.

"Thank you. I'm so glad you both could join us tonight. It's wonderful having company during the holidays. My family live in Florida and Tess and I don't see them very often."

"Do you have a large family?" Nanny Jones inquired.

"No, just my younger sister and her husband."

"I tend to find that blood relatives are often quite taxing, and the close friends you choose tend to make a better family."

Sebastian smiled as he reached to clasp her hand. "Well said, Nanny."

The meal was easy and relaxed. Everyone laughed and talked at great length. When the last morsel of chocolate cake was consumed, Mrs. Hamilton stood. "Let's go into the living room."

Everyone sat near the Christmas tree. Gifts were passed around. Sebastian opened his present from Tess. It was a photo she had taken of them at Edgewood back in October when he'd taught her how to ride a horse. She had placed the photo in a five by seven wooden frame.

"I love it," he whispered in Tess' ear, while hugging her. It was a personal gift, something she had made, and it meant far more to him than anything she could have purchased.

"You next." Sebastian handed her a square package with an ornate bow. Tess opened the LP collection and was very happy with his selection.

As the evening wound down, Tess picked up some empty glasses and looked at Sebastian. "Come to the kitchen with me?"

He followed, picking up a few empty plates as he went. Once they were in the kitchen and the dishes were placed into the dishwasher, Tess leaned against the counter. "Tonight was perfect. Thanks for coming and for bringing Nanny Jones."

"I love my photo."

"I love my records. I'm so glad you didn't do something extravagant." She leaned in and kissed him. Something hard pressed against her chest. She slowly pulled back and carefully patted the breast of his suit coat, feeling something small and square. "What's that?" she asked.

Sebastian smiled. "Something extravagant," he slowly responded. "May I show you?"

She shook her head in disbelief. "I should make you return it right now."

"But the stores are closed," he fretted. "Tell me you're not dying of curiosity." His hand closed around hers, which was still on the box.

She rolled her eyes in exasperation and gave in. "Go on."

He pulled the small, blue Tiffany box out of his breast pocket and offered it to her as it rested on his open palm.

She pulled on the white satin ribbon and it unraveled in her shaking hand. Slowly, she pulled off the box top. Inside was a black velvet box. Tess lifted the hinged top to reveal a pair of exquisite solitaire diamond earrings. She held her breath. Again, he had left her speechless.

Sebastian watched as her expression changed from trepidation to relief. "You can breathe now," he playfully reminded her.

She sucked in a big gulp of air and then closed the lid on the box.

"Oh, God, you hate them," he lamented.

"No! I just thought…" She could not finish her sentence.

"Thought what?"

"Nothing."

"Do you like them?"

"They're beautiful. How could I not like them?"

"You'll keep them?"

She didn't answer him verbally. She merely leaned in and kissed him again.

Sebastian was happy and he wished he could stay like this forever, in this cozy little house, with the girl he loved. When they pulled apart, Sebastian said, "My mother is throwing this big New Year's Eve bash. Say you'll come. I need your company or I fear I might not survive the evening." He knew his mother already suspected Tess was more than just his tutor, but he didn't care. All he knew was that he needed her by his side. Tess didn't respond. "Don't tell me you have a date with some other guy— someone better looking and richer than me."

Tess chuckled. "I don't think that's possible. Yes, I'll come to the party."

Tess and Sebastian stood in the corner of the room as the guests mingled at Lady Irons' annual New Year's Eve gala. "It's amazing how many people your mother knows. Does she actually get a chance to talk to all of them?" Tess wondered aloud.

"Yes, it's amazing the number of people she has in her exclusive circle," Sebastian said, scanning the room.

Lady Irons made her way across the room to their private corner. She gave Tess the once over, examining her from top to bottom, as if ready to judge her in a beauty pageant. "Tess, you look lovely this evening." She was wearing the Calvin Klein dress Sebastian bought her. Her hair was slicked back in a ponytail with a black satin headband to show off her sparkling diamond earrings.

"Thank you."

"Sebastian, come with me. I want to introduce you to a few people." Lady Irons took him by the elbow. He shot Tess a helpless look as he was pulled away from her.

Tess watched as Lady Irons escorted Sebastian through the crowd like a prized show dog on a leash. She stopped at a small congregated group of partygoers to make introductions and then moved on to the next group, pulling Sebastian along. He looked miserable. Sigourney walked up beside her and sighed. "I see the horse and pony show is under way," she said as she tilted her head toward them in emphasis.

"Does she always do this?"

"Every chance she gets. She's grooming him to take over Irons Electronics," Sigourney explained, taking a sip from her crystal champagne flute.

"But what if he doesn't want to take over the company, Sigourney?"

"It's his duty," she simply replied.

"But what about your older sister and brother? Don't they work for the Irons Electronics? Why not one of them?" Tess inquired, a bit confused.

"Mummy has her sights set on Sebastian. There will be no changing her mind. There is no escaping his fate, I'm afraid," she mused with an air of sadness.

"Can't you do anything to stop her? He doesn't even like her. Why is she so persistent?" Tess shook her head and continued to watch the farce. "I don't understand your family."

"Of course you don't, you poor thing."

Suddenly breaking free, Sebastian came toward the girls at a brisk pace. He took Tess by the hand and led her out of the room and up the staircase without a word.

They stopped at the top on the landing. Sebastian grabbed two champagne flutes from a passing waiter and handed one to Tess. He downed his in one gulp, putting his empty glass on the waiter's tray. His hands tightly gripped the railing. Tess certainly couldn't deny him a glass of champagne after the scene she had just witnessed. In fact, she took a drink herself.

"That was intense," she muttered, referring to his mother. He lit a cigarette and inhaled deeply, blowing a long stream of smoke out above his head and watching it disperse in the air. Tess put her arm around his waist and leaned her head against his shoulder. "Smoking is bad for your health, you know."

"Yes, but I've given up drugs and I've cut back on the alcohol, so please leave this one vice," he pleaded.

"I just care what happens to you," Tess reasoned. "And I don't like kissing you after you've had a cigarette. You reek of smoke."

"I know."

"I'm sorry she's making you unhappy. Isn't there anything you can do?"

"If I knew what to do, I wouldn't be in this predicament. If only that NYU acceptance letter would come in the mail."

"When it does come, will that change her mind?"

"No, but at least I'd have a plan," he explained. He waved a server over and helped himself to another glass of champagne. Finishing again in one gulp, he extinguished his cigarette in the last few drops of alcohol with a sizzle. Sebastian set the glass on the carpeted floor.

The crowd began to count down to midnight and usher in 1986. At the stroke of midnight, the crowd erupted in cheers. People hugged and kissed, others made champagne toasts. "Happy New Year, Tess," he whispered, slowly pulling her into him and kissing her. Neither realized that Lady Irons was watching them from the foyer below. "Let's get out of here," he suggested, still locked in their embrace.

Tess nodded her head in agreement. He took her hand and steered her away from the party, down the long hallway, toward his bedroom. "I can't run in these shoes," she laughed as she stumbled, grabbing onto his arm for support. The champagne had made her a little giddy.

"No problem," he responded, lifting her up and placing her over his shoulder. Her hair fell forward and her black satin headband landed on the floor. Sebastian opened his door with his free hand and kicked it closed with his foot. He set her softly on the leather sofa and lay on top of her. He hadn't bothered to turn on any lights.

He was slightly out of breath, and their proximity made the mood suddenly serious. He leaned in and kissed her glossy lips. She tasted of strawberry lip gloss and champagne. Sebastian was heady with excitement as their kissing became more urgent. They heard footsteps coming down the hall. Whomever it was stopped in front of each door to open and then close it. Sebastian placed his finger over Tess' lips to silence her. His bedroom door suddenly opened and the light from the hallway flooded the room. They were completely silent, still lying on the sofa, hidden away in the deep shadows since the back of the sofa faced the door. Whoever was on the other side of the door didn't find what they were looking for. A few moments later, the door closed. Sebastian assumed it was his mother, looking to pull him back to the party and away from Tess. They remained quiet until they could no longer hear the footfalls.

They looked at each other and began to chuckle. Sebastian sat up and removed his tuxedo jacket. Tess slowly pulled on his bow tie until it unraveled and fell around his neck. She took hold of the loose tie and pulled him toward her. They continued kissing, their soft lips touching and parting to allow the tips of their tongues to touch. Sebastian was so aroused he couldn't think straight. He was operating on raw instinct as he reached for the zipper on the side of her dress and started to pull it down.

Tess quickly pushed him away. "No! Don't do that," she exclaimed, struggling to sit up, his tie still in her hand.

He scrambled to get off her and scurried to the far corner of the sofa. "I'm not going to hurt you," he faltered. "I love you, Tess."

"I *know*," she said quickly, deep with emotion. She moved to the opposite end of the sofa, as far from him as she could manage. "I'm just not ready to have sex with you."

"You're killing me—you realize this, don't you?" he groaned in frustration.

"It's not my intention," she assured him. "Look, I know you are very experienced in this situation, but I'm not."

"You took off my tie. We were lying on the sofa. What was I supposed to think? I tell you I love you and you won't say it back." Closing his eyes, Sebastian pushed his hand through his hair. "I'm so tired of always apologizing to you."

After a long awkward pause, Tess spoke. "You're right. I led you on. It was wrong of me to even let myself get into a situation like this."

"Stop," he whispered, unwilling to hear the disappointment in her voice.

"No, we have to talk this out."

"That's all we do—talk!"

"Sebastian, you turned my world upside down. My stomach does somersaults when I know I'm going to see you. When you kiss me, my brain goes fuzzy. This wasn't a part of my plan," Tess tried to explain.

"Love isn't always convenient."

"I feel something for you, that's for sure. I just don't know if it's love yet."

"You need more time, then?"

"Yes."

"How much longer?" At least she'd admitted having romantic feelings for him, but her lack of commitment was discouraging.

She shot him a dirty look. "Don't push your luck."

"I'm not giving up, Tess," he simply informed her. "I will have you."

Tess gave him an intense look. "God, you can be an arrogant ass sometimes, you know that?"

Sebastian stood from the couch and offered his hand. "Come on, I'll drive you home." He didn't want to argue with her anymore and thought it best to remove the source of his temptation from the bedroom before he did something he would regret.

The house was quiet when Sebastian arrived back home after dropping Tess off. The plethora of party guests had either left for the evening or were sound asleep in their guest rooms. Unfortunately, Lady Irons was still awake and Sebastian had the misfortune to bump into her.

"Sebastian, I'd like to speak with you."

"I'm tired. I'm going to bed," he said as he began to walk up the staircase.

"Did you and Tess have a nice evening?"

Sebastian stopped midway up the stairs and turned to face his mother. "Delightful."

"You said there is nothing going on between you two, yet I saw you kiss her and then you ran off together. I was looking for you. Where did you go?"

"I drove Tess home."

"I wonder if you're getting too close to Miss Hamilton. I think I should contact the school and let them know we no longer require her services."

"Fine," he coolly replied. "I don't need good marks since I have no intention of going to Oxford. Send her packing if you wish. I only kissed her because I knew you were watching and I wanted to make you angry." He turned around and continued up the stairs. "Have a lovely flight home. I won't be up to see you off."

Christmas vacation was over and the students of St. Alexander's returned to school facing midterm exams. Jordan, Courtney, Tess, and Sebastian sat at the lunch table discussing their holiday.

"I got some totally killer deals at the after Christmas sales," Courtney gushed, showing off her new shoes.

"What did you get for Christmas, Tess?" Jordan asked.

"My mom bought me an electric typewriter."

"Is that *all*, Tess?" A sly smile crossed Sebastian's lips.

Tess didn't respond. Jordan rolled her eyes, saying, "Will you two get a room already?"

Tess grabbed her tote bag and stomped out of the cafeteria without even looking back. Sebastian sighed. "Nice, Jordan."

"I'm only joking. She shouldn't be mad if it's not true," Jordan replied, defending her comment.

Sebastian shook his head in disgust and went after Tess. He spied her walking into the girls' lavatory. The hall was clear, so he ducked in behind her, not thinking who else might be in there. He found Tess clutching onto the edge of the sink, eyes closed, taking deep breaths. She sensed someone nearby and quickly turned. He was standing next to her when she opened her eyes.

"What are you doing?"

"Oh come on, this isn't the first time I've been in the ladies' toilet with you," Sebastian reminded her. He pointed to the empty stalls, her eyes following his finger, and said, "We're alone." She looked back at him and he continued. "Jordan was only joking. If you had stayed, she would have apologized. Honestly, why can't you just tell them we're together? Am I that awful that you don't want to be associated with me?" he asked in exasperation.

"No, of course not."

"Then say it. Tell me you love me," he pleaded.

"I'm not there yet, Sebastian."

"Then admit you consider me your boyfriend," he challenged her.

She hesitated for a long moment then finally agreed. "I consider you my boyfriend," she said, looking him straight in the eye. "I'm just not ready to tell anyone yet—especially Jordan and Courtney, okay? I'm not even used to the idea myself. I wasn't looking for this. You were supposed to be my student, nothing more."

"I'm way more than that, Tess." He looked deep into her eyes, imploring her. "I want to tell them. I don't even understand how you became friends with those two. Jordan is boy-crazy and Courtney's just daft. "

The sound of a bell ringing jarred them. Tess looked relived to end this conversation before it became any more difficult. Classes were changing and Sebastian needed to duck out of the girls' bathroom without a teacher catching him. Wordlessly, they headed to the door. Tess stepped into the hallway and blocked Sebastian from view as he crept out.

After the final bell, they met in the library. There was a low buzz in the quiet confines of the room as students found places to sit, pulled books off shelves, and whispered to fellow students. Tess had worked out a study schedule for their midterm exams, which would begin in just a week. She handed him the paper with its well-organized time grids and reference notes. "Ready to get started?" she asked Sebastian.

He put the sheet down without looking at it. "No," he replied. "I want to finish our conversation from earlier today."

Tess laid her head on the table and muttered, "What else is there to say? I admitted to you what you wanted to hear."

"Then why can't we tell everybody? Are you ashamed of me?"

Her head popped up from the table. "No! Why would you say that?" A few students turned in their direction as Tess raised her voice a bit too loudly. She closed her book and stood from the table. "Please, let's get out of here," she begged, self-conscious of the scene she was making. She didn't wait for his reply, but gathered her books and quickstepped to the exit.

He stood and followed her into the empty hall. "I love you. I'd shout it out to anyone who would listen," he hissed in a low tone. Sebastian walked briskly to keep up with her, the sound of their footfalls echoing off the metal lockers.

She flung open the glass exit door and walked outside into the parking lot. "Sebastian, when we're here, this is business. I was asked to be your tutor and I take that responsibility very seriously."

"As do I."

She stopped walking and faced him. "Good, then I hope you'll understand why I need to keep 'Sebastian the student' separate from 'Sebastian the boyfriend,'" she said under her breath, afraid of drawing any more attention to herself.

"Why do you have to compartmentalize everything? Why can't I be both at the same time?" He was eager to know. This always confused him about her.

Tess resumed walking, not answering his question. She stopped again when she reached her car, putting her key in the door keyhole to unlock it. "If you want this relationship, this is how it has to be." She sat in the car and put the key in the ignition in an attempt to end the conversation for good.

"Fine," he surrendered. "I'll see you tomorrow."

Sebastian turned on his heel and walked to his car. He couldn't understand her reasoning and was angry that he had no choice in the matter if he wanted to keep her in his life. How long would he be asked to keep their relationship a secret? Maybe if he kept this relationship *all business* he could wear her down. If he played hard to get, she might just change her mind about going public. Anything was worth a try. Sebastian's mind was reeling. He drove home without even remembering the journey.

For the next two weeks, he studied diligently with Tess in the library and did not accept invitations to her house to study, nor did they go to Edgewood. Sebastian was all business: he didn't hold her hand, attempt to kiss her, or see her socially on the weekend. It must have been working because Tess was becoming noticeably antsy as their exams wound down.

Sebastian spent Saturday morning eating breakfast in the kitchen with Henry, Alice, and Nanny. Alice had whipped up a feast of buttermilk pancakes served with maple syrup, scrambled eggs, and crispy bacon. He enjoyed these casual meals in the kitchen. It was nice to have everyone together. It made him feel like he was a part of a normal family.

"How were your exams?" Nanny asked, taking a sip of her tea.

"I believe I did well."

"I haven't seen Tess in a while. Is everything all right with you two?"

"She's been stressing over exams. I reckon if I just let her be, she'll come around when she's ready."

Henry smiled. "In other words, you're playing hard to get?"

"Exactly." Sebastian took a bite of his pancake. "Can either of you ladies explain why she insists on keeping our school relationship separate from our romantic relationship?"

"Did you ask Tess?" Nanny inquired.

"Yes." He reached for the basket of homemade biscuits. "She didn't have an acceptable answer."

Henry chuckled. "Women are mysterious creatures, Sebastian. Sometimes you just have to hold on and go along for the ride." He looked at Alice out of the corner of his eye then took a deep swallow of coffee, trying to hide his grin.

Alice nudged Henry in the ribs. "Henry, don't depress the poor boy!" She turned to Sebastian and said, "She'll come around when she's ready, and when she does you won't have a moment's peace."

"I can't wait," Sebastian admitted.

A week later, report cards were issued. "Did you see the board?" he asked as Tess neared.

"You got honors again, congrats!"

"Thanks," he replied, keeping his distance from her.

"What are you doing tonight?"

"I don't know yet," he said, acting cool and aloof. They hadn't seen each other outside of school since New Year's. Sebastian was playing by her rules now and he guessed she was about to break.

"Do you want to go out tonight?" Tess leaned in closer, and in a soft, barely audible voice said, "I miss you."

He felt a pang of triumph swell in his chest. Staying away from her might just have made her heart grow fonder. He knew he certainly longed to have her in his arms again and kiss those soft lovely lips. "It's supposed to snow tonight. Maybe we should wait," he suggested. Her face showed her disappointment. Damn, she was irresistible. "What did you have in mind?"

"You could come over to my house. We can get a pizza and rent a movie."

"I'll be there at seven," he said, not caring what they did—only that they were together.

Sebastian pulled up in front of the Hamiltons' house promptly at seven o'clock. The snow had already begun to fall in soft swirls. It was creating an effervescent white coating on the bushes and trees but it wasn't yet sticking to the streets or sidewalks. He rushed to the front door holding the steaming pizza box and a few VHS tapes—*The Breakfast Club* and *St. Elmo's Fire*, which he'd picked up at the video store. Tess opened the front door. Sebastian handed the pizza to her and shook his head, allowing the wet snowflakes to fly off his hair.

He followed her into the kitchen and took off his jacket, hanging it on the back of a chair. Tess took plates from the cabinet and placed them next to the pizza box on the kitchen table. Sebastian got two Diet Cokes from the refrigerator and snatched the glasses she had filled with ice. She balanced the plates on the pizza box and they went into the living room. Tess put a video in the VCR and they sat back on the sofa.

An hour into the *The Breakfast Club*, the phone rang. Tess stood to answer the call. Sebastian pushed the pause button, leaving the image of Molly Ringwald frozen on the screen. A few minutes later, Tess was back on the sofa, sitting next to Sebastian. "That was my mom. Since the weather is supposed to get pretty bad, the hospital asked her to pull a double shift. She's not coming home tonight. She also said you should stay. She doesn't want you driving in the snow."

"Are you okay with that?" he asked, a little shocked.

"You're sleeping on the sofa," she smirked, resuming the movie.

They finished watching in silence, sitting close to one another but not touching. The video automatically rewound when it reached the end. The TV defaulted to the cable channel and MTV appeared on the screen. "Ready for the next movie?"

"No, not just yet," Tess replied as she moved closer to Sebastian. "Tell me, why haven't you tried to kiss me tonight?"

"I thought you invited me over to watch a movie."

"You haven't kissed me in weeks. Is there someone else?" she asked, peeking up at him through her thick eyelashes.

"You have me on such a tight study schedule, there isn't time for anyone else," Sebastian gently reminded her. He figured she was about to break and desperately wanted Tess to make the first move.

She slowly leaned into him until her lips finally touched his. Tess was kissing Sebastian and he was so overjoyed he took her in his arms and pulled her closer. Eventually, Sebastian found the strength to pull away, although it was the last thing he wanted to do.

"Don't give me that look," she pleaded.

"What look?"

"The desperate 'let me sleep with you' look."

He ran his hand through his hair. Sebastian didn't want to have this conversation again. "I should go home now."

"You can't. Look at it out there!" she said, pointing toward the winter weather blowing outside the window. "The snow is already sticking to the roads and visibility is practically zero."

"Fine." He sat there for a long moment thinking, his foot nervously tapping on the floor. "Tell me something. Did you really mean it when you said you missed me?"

"Of course. What kind of question is that?"

"I just don't understand. If you miss me, then why can't I kiss you?"

"Because you want more. You're not satisfied with just kissing," she tried to explain.

"I'm a guy. I haven't had sex in months. There's only so much masturbation one can do," he blurted out.

"Oh, God." Tess put her hands over her ears, not wanting to hear any more details.

Sebastian let out a groan of frustration. "Tess, I'm just being honest. I love you. I'm incredibly attracted to you." He stood and paced the floor with nervous energy. "I've played by your rules and I haven't pressured you to have sex. I'm keeping 'student Sebastian' separate from 'boyfriend Sebastian'—and you just made me refer to myself in the third person!"

He was in such a state, it made her laugh. At first it was just a small chuckle and then it turned into full-blown laughter.

"You think this is amusing?"

"Yes," she said almost in tears. Tess was laughing so hard that she could barely breathe. "You're so cute when you're all riled up and speaking in an English accent."

"I'm happy you're finding humor in my misery," he muttered, sitting back on the sofa with a thud.

"I'm sorry," she apologized, finally ceasing her laughter.

"I think I'll go to sleep now."

"Yeah, okay," she agreed.

Sebastian watched as she made her way up the stairs to her bedroom. A few minutes later, the light from her bedroom was extinguished and he heard her bed creak as she climbed into it. He wasn't sleepy. He just wanted to be alone. She'd laughed at him. Maybe he was a little hysterical with his outburst, but did she really have to laugh? Having a bruised ego was a new experience for him.

Sebastian made a quick call to Henry to let him know that he would be staying at the Hamiltons' overnight. Then he turned his attention back to the glow of the television. Turning the volume of MTV a little softer so it wouldn't bother Tess, he stretched out on the sofa. Kevin Rowland from Dexy's Midnight Runners was walking down the street, dressed in denim overalls, one strap hanging loose over his left shoulder. He was wearing a red bandana around his neck and his black hair was big and curly. He was singing a desperate plea for his girlfriend to take off her dress and have sex with him. Sebastian wondered if she ever said yes. Did she ever give in? The video seemed to parallel his own life, only he wore designer suits instead of denim. The video ended and VJ Mark Goodman appeared on the screen. Sebastian hit the mute button. The snow seemed to blanket the earth with silence. He gazed out the window at the falling snow which glowed in the light of the street lamps. It was beautiful but he was not in the state of mind to enjoy it.

Tess crept down the darkened stairs keeping time with Neil Finn as he walked down the steps in the Split Enz video for *One Step Ahead*. The flickering light of the TV was the only thing that illuminated the room. Tess joined Sebastian on the couch. She was wearing pink plaid flannel pajamas and had fuzzy slippers on her feet. He had stripped down to his boxers and T-shirt under the warm cotton comforter he'd placed over his lap.

"I thought you said you were going to sleep." Tess said, unfolding the comforter to cover them both.

"I changed my mind," he replied. "Why aren't you sleeping?"

"I'm not tired either."

They sat watching an endless barrage of music videos until Tess finally fell asleep on his shoulder. Sebastian didn't have the heart to wake her, so he ceded the couch to her. He gently placed the crocheted blanket that hung over the back of the couch on top of her to keep her warm as she slept. He watched as it rose and fell with her soft breaths. Sebastian took the comforter and stretched out on the lounge chair directly across from Tess.

Mrs. Hamilton walked in the front door at around eight o'clock in the morning to find the pair sleeping in her living room on their respective pieces of furniture. Sebastian was startled by the creaking of the front door opening and sat up, rubbing the sleep out of his eyes.

"Good morning," she whispered.

Sebastian stretched as he let out a large yawn. "Good morning. How are the roads?"

"Not very good. The plows haven't been out everywhere and it's been snowing all night. One of my coworkers has a four-wheel drive and drove me home."

Sebastian rose and wrapped the comforter around himself, padded to the big picture window and looked out. He spied his car covered in snow. "That's not going to be fun digging out," he muttered in dismay.

"No, you've got that right," she agreed. "Come into the kitchen. I'll make us some breakfast. Tess can sleep through anything."

He knew that all too well, but refrained from commenting. He couldn't tell her mother that Tess had spent the night at Edgewood after a drunken escapade at The Jug. "I'll join you in a moment."

Sebastian picked up his clothes and made his way to the toilet to freshen up and dress. Taking Tess' hair brush, he tried his best to smooth out the tousled, brown mess. He found some mouthwash to rinse away his morning breath. After splashing some warm water on his face and looking in the mirror, he was satisfied with his appearance. He smoothed out his sweater and headed for the kitchen.

Tess was stirring on the sofa when he made his way through the living room.

"Good morning," he said, taking up a seat on the edge of the couch next to her.

"I smell French toast," she said, still groggy from sleep.

"Your mom is home. Come have breakfast with us."

"Mmm," was all that she could manage but she slipped her feet into her fuzzy slippers and allowed him to help her up. She stumbled into the kitchen and Sebastian smiled.

Chapter 14 - Tempted

After school, Sebastian rushed home and dashed into the house, holding his overcoat closed for protection against the wind. He entered through the kitchen door, where he found Alice preparing dinner. "It's bloody freezing out there," he said, pulling off his leather gloves and shrugging out of his coat.

"I'm making your favorite tonight—beef Wellington."

"So what did I do to deserve Wellington?" he asked putting the kettle on for a cup of hot tea.

Alice pointed to the thick white nine by twelve inch envelope placed in the center of the kitchen table. Sebastian slowly walked over to the table and sat down on the wooden bench. It was from NYU. He ripped it open and scanned the letter. A smile crossed his lips.

Henry walked in as the scene unfolded. "Good news, I take it?"

"I've been accepted," Sebastian announced. "I've been accepted," he repeated, as if not believing it the first time. He put the envelope on the table and clutched the letter, grinning like a fool.

Henry patted him on the back. "Congratulations!"

"Dinner's at six," Alice added with a wink.

"I have to tell Nanny." He bolted from the table and bounded up the servants' staircase to take the shortcut to her room.

Sebastian knocked on Nanny's door and barged in before she could respond. "How is the most amazing woman in the world?" he greeted, plopping down on the sofa next to her. He handed Nanny the NYU letter.

She read it in silence and squeezed his hand with pride. "I knew you could do it, my dear boy."

Sebastian sat there savoring his own victory. He had accomplished what he had set out to do eight months ago and was accepted to the university of his choice. "Do you suppose it's too boastful to say I'm very pleased with myself?" he wondered aloud.

"Not at all!"

Finally, he could start making plans for the fall. He would break the news to his mother later—much later. Maybe he would wait until September, once he had already started his first semester. He perused the letter further and starting tallying the assorted charges for room and board. When you multiplied the number by two and then factored in inflation, he could understand why Tess was worried.

"What concerns you, dear?"

"I'm adding up all the costs above and beyond tuition. I don't feel right letting you pay for my education."

"As long as we continue to make sound investments, the dividends will pay those expenses." Nanny thought for a while, then suggested, "We could take the money that you'd be spending on a dormitory room over those four years and use it to buy a flat. You could live there while you're at university and sell it for a profit if you decide to leave New York after you graduate. Real estate is a sound investment, Sebastian."

She was brilliant! Why didn't he think of that? Then he realized it never occurred to him because it wasn't his money to spend—it was Nanny's savings, and she was already being too generous by paying for his college education. "If you buy the flat, will you come and live with me?"

"No, you need to be with Tess. There'll be no room for an old lady like me."

His face fell. "I can't let you do that. You've already done too much."

She leaned in and whispered, "You are the son I never had. This is an investment in you and your future. I know you won't let me down. Let me grow old knowing you've brought me great happiness by living up to your potential."

"But where will you live?"

"I want to go home to England. I want to live out my days in the fresh country air surrounded by the rose gardens."

"But I won't see you."

"We'll talk on the phone and you can always come home to visit."

Sebastian forced a smile. Somehow he didn't think he'd be traveling back to England once his mother was privy to his plan to attend NYU and the fact that Nanny was bankrolling it.

Sebastian made an appointment with a prominent Manhattan real estate agent, named Margo Milton, to show him potential properties near NYU to purchase. He had already narrowed down a large list of available units to a manageable group he wanted to see. Margo had made appointments and he was eager to have a look. He wanted to bring Nanny with him to get her opinion, but she wasn't feeling well. Henry joined him instead and they headed into Manhattan.

Margo had five properties to show them in two boroughs. They started with a townhouse in Brooklyn. Sebastian wasn't happy with the house or the neighborhood. The house would need a great deal work and there would be little time for domestic projects while they were going to class and studying. They visited several condos and studio lofts in SoHo and Greenwich Village. They were all very small and dated, considering the astronomical asking prices. Sebastian shook his head as they left the final property on his list, a fourth-floor walk-up with a stunning view of a brick wall.

By early afternoon, Sebastian was exhausted and irritated. In a last ditch effort, Margo suggested they take a look across the Hudson in Lincoln Harbor and Weehawken, New Jersey. Sebastian wasn't thrilled about the suggestion, but Margo persisted, telling him it was an up and coming area. Many young urban professionals were moving into the newly built condos. The location was perfect because it offered easy ferry access to the city, modern amenities, and sweeping views of the Manhattan skyline. Against his better judgment and with a bit of prodding from Henry, he relented. He looked at the printout of property information that Margo showed him.

Okay, he thought, they were larger and newer than anything he had looked at today. Many were new construction and he even had the option of picking appliances, wall color, and flooring.

When they reached the condo complex, Margo pressed the button for the doorman. She recited her credentials and the electronic gate opened, allowing them to enter.

Sebastian held the door open for Henry as they trooped into the building. Inside, it smelled like new carpet. The walls were clean and free of marks and the elevator was just steps away.

They rode to the second floor. Margo found the combination lockbox and turned the dials to the proper letter code, opening a door and revealing a set of keys. Margo opened the door to number 4B and Sebastian and Henry walked inside. The afternoon sun shone through the large floor-to-ceiling windows, the skyline of the city bright and magnificent across the rippling water of the river. They wandered from room to room. Henry opened the circuit breaker box and looked under counters to examine the plumbing. For the first time that day, Sebastian felt comfortable. He knew he had found his new home. Margo was right—it really was the nicest property she had shown him. The condo had two bedrooms, two baths, and a large living space which would easily accommodate his furniture. The kitchen was well equipped with good quality appliances and even a stacking washer and dryer so they wouldn't have to go to the laundromat. Henry agreed it was the best option as they drove back to Edgewood to share their findings with Nanny.

Once home, Sebastian found Nanny with her knitting, sitting in a sunny corner of the day room, watching the squirrels playing in the garden while her hands expertly worked the needles. He told her of their day, talking her through each property they'd looked at. When he got to the condo in New Jersey, he went into great detail, showing her the builder's brochure and floor plan. She pored over them with great interest, but she seemed tired. She waved off his concerns and made him continue with the description. At the end of his presentation, she agreed: the condo in Lincoln Harbor was, by far, the best choice.

Sebastian phoned Margo Milton and made an offer. She would overnight him the required paperwork to start the sale. Sebastian was happy and confident in his decision. Now all he had to do was persuade Tess to live with him. He pondered various ways to broach the subject and the conclusion he kept coming to was the same: she would never agree unless her mother was on board, so a conversation with Mrs. Hamilton was in order.

Friday afternoon, Sebastian drove Tess home from St. Alexander's. As she went upstairs to her bedroom to change out of her school uniform, Sebastian headed for the kitchen and greeted Mrs. Hamilton. She, in turn, gave him a hug. "I'm glad you're here. Can I talk to you for a few minutes?" He didn't want Tess around for the conversation.

"Sure, what's on your mind?"

He sat down at the kitchen table while Mrs. Hamilton put on the tea kettle. "Tess has been so stressed out about NYU and how much it's going to cost to go there."

Mrs. Hamilton nodded, her hands busy with pulling out tea mugs, milk, sugar, and tea bags. "I know. I've told her not to worry. It's been a real struggle, but we have the college fund and her scholarship. Tess might need to get a part-time job, but we'll manage."

"May I make a proposition?"

"Of course."

"Mrs. Hamilton, I'm crazy about your daughter." It was done: he'd said it aloud—now to get to the difficult part.

"That is obvious, Sebastian. I'm very pleased Tess had the good sense to choose you as her first boyfriend."

"Thank you for saying so." He fidgeted in his seat, a little nervous to continue, but plucked up the courage. "I've been calculating the cost of the dormitory, food, books, and other living expenses for two people. I realized that money could be better spent if I were to buy a two-bedroom flat in New Jersey. I'd like Tess to take one of the bedrooms." He stopped for a moment to try to judge Mrs. Hamilton's reaction. She kept a straight face, but was intently listening. "There will still be some bills to be paid, of course, but in four years I'll have an investment that will produce a profit when it is sold. If you would agree, I'll take care of all the house bills. Tess won't need to get a part-time job. She can study in a quiet environment. I know I'm only eighteen, but I've had, um, experiences that most people my age have never had. Those experiences have made me more mature." He took a deep breath after his awkward, rambling speech and waited for her to respond.

"Buying a home is a big responsibility. Are you prepared for that?" she asked with great curiosity, as well as concern.

"I have a lawyer to help with the paperwork. I have the money to pay for it. Nanny always said two of the best investments you can make are art and real estate. What do you think of my idea?"

"I think it is a wonderful idea, Sebastian. I would be very grateful to know that you would be with Tess and she wouldn't be alone in that big city. She's my only child. I want her to be happy and safe. Have you asked Tess yet?" The tea kettle was whistling a shrill note. She turned off the burner, leaving the kettle on the stove untouched, her attention still fully focused on Sebastian.

"No, I wanted your blessing. For some reason, I think convincing Tess will be far more difficult than this conversation."

Kate brought the tea kettle over to the kitchen table and poured the hot water over the tea bag in each mug. Then she poured some milk in his mug and placed it in front of him. "I think you're in love with my daughter."

"I am!"

"I raised an ambitious, strong willed, intelligent, and independent girl. Sometimes she's so focused on one thing that she forgets to live in the moment. I think Tess has yet to admit that she's in love with you."

"Right again," he confessed, sipping his tea.

"I met Tess' father when I was in high school. Our parents didn't encourage our relationship. They thought we were too young to be in love. To this very day I am so grateful that I followed my heart. I had a wonderful husband for fifteen years and he gave me my daughter.

Now, sadly, he's gone, but I'm left with wonderful memories." She walked behind Sebastian, gently placed her hand on his shoulder. "Life's too short. You need to take every opportunity you can get. None of us can foresee the future. So for now, love her, be her best friend, and take care of her for me."

He turned to face the mother of the woman he loved. "I will. I promise." He was blown away by her compassion, wisdom, and implicit trust. He felt he didn't deserve her amazing confidence in him, but it strengthened his resolve to be the person Mrs. Hamilton believed he was.

"You will what?" Tess asked, walking into the kitchen.

Her mother smiled. "Who said, 'Better to have loved and lost…'"

"Then never to have loved at all," Sebastian finished the quote for her. "It was Tennyson."

Tess gave them both a weary glance. "Mom, poetry, really?"

"I'll leave you two alone now," her mom said, making a hasty retreat to allow them to talk in private.

Tess sat back in her chair, crossed her arms, and glared at him. "Spill it, now."

Sebastian sat across from her and took a sip of his tea to give him a few moments to formulate just how he wanted to explain. "I promised your mother that I would look out for you when we go to NYU in the fall," he partially confessed.

"You got in?"

Sebastian reached under his sweater and took the acceptance letter from his shirt pocket. He handed it to Tess without a word.

She unfolded the paper and read it. "Oh my God. You did it! You got into NYU." Overcome with emotion, she instinctively hugged him before kissing him on the lips. He held her in his arms, not wanting to let her go. "I think you don't need me anymore," she said, her brow furrowed.

"I'll always need you," he reassured her. "You're a big part of the reason I got into NYU in the first place." Sebastian leaned in and kissed her again.

She still wasn't satisfied. "And what about the Tennyson quote?"

"Your mom was telling me how much she loved your dad and how lucky they were to have found each other when they were so young."

Her expression softened. "They really did love each other." She was lost in a faded memory for a few seconds.

"Well, I should be going."

"So soon?" she asked him with disappointment in her voice. "There's something you're still not telling me about the conversation with my mom."

"You have that Future Business Leaders of America thing tomorrow. I'm sure you need to do some work to prepare for it. Did you write your speech yet?"

"No, but this doesn't mean you're off the hook. Can I stop over tomorrow after the meeting?"

"I'd like that."

"I'll be expecting an explanation."

"Yes, darling."

Tess walked him to the front door. Sebastian bade farewell to Mrs. Hamilton, then stepped onto the front porch with Tess. After a goodbye kiss, she watched him walk to his car, get in, and drive away, before she returned inside.

Tess' mother looked at her daughter intently and said, "He's a very special person."

"Hmm."

"Do you love him?"

"I think I do."

"Maybe we should make an appointment with the gynecologist and get you some birth control."

"We're not having sex, Mom."

"I know," her mom responded. "And if you were, I know I've taught you well and you'd be responsible. I remember what it's like to fall in love, Tess. It's new and exciting. The feelings are intense and overwhelming."

"Does it stay that way?"

"Time changes love. It twists and turns and shifts it into something different," her mom tried to explain.

"Is it better?"

"I think so. You get a deeper understanding of the person you're in love with—the things that make that person tick. The sex is amazing when you have that kind of deep connection with someone." She smiled to herself.

"Okay, I'm not really comfortable discussing your sex life. I've got a speech to write," she told her mom and eagerly ran up the stairs.

The FBLA meeting wrapped up around four o'clock. Tess found a pay phone outside the gym and dialed Sebastian. "Hey," she greeted him.

"Hey, are you finished?"

"Yep, I'll be there in half an hour."

"Stay for dinner?"

"Yes, I'd like that," she replied and hung up the receiver.

The grandfather clock standing guard in the marbled foyer chimed on the hour, and at the same time there was a knock at the front door. Alice bustled in from the kitchen to open it. "Hello, is Sebastian in?" the tall, slender beauty asked in a clipped British accent.

"Yes, please come in," Alice replied, inviting her inside. She took the young woman's designer coat to hang in the closet. "I can get him for you if you would like to wait."

"No, please just tell me where I might find him," she commanded with a sense of urgency, her eyes straining to see up the long staircase to the second floor.

"His room is up the stairs, third door on the right."

"Thank you," she breathed as she scurried up the staircase.

Her knock on Sebastian's door was brief before she opened it. Sebastian was seated in front of the fireplace, his head buried in a book. His back was to the door. "That was quick," he quipped, assuming it was Tess who entered.

"How did you know I was coming?" Penelope asked in confusion.

Sebastian dropped his book and sprang out of the chair. He quickly turned to face her, stunned to see her in his room. "Penny, what are you doing here?" She was standing in the doorway wearing a white wool dress and black pumps. Even though she had just stepped off a seven-hour flight, she looked impeccable. He noticed the distress on her face.

She rushed across the room and into his arms, holding onto him so tightly that he found he could barely breathe. "Oh, God, how I've missed you," she muttered to him, burying her face into his neck.

The smell of lavender filled his nostrils as she clung to him. It was nice to have her in his arms again.

She pulled back slightly, looking into his eyes for a long moment before kissing him. He'd forgotten what a good kisser she was and momentarily lost his mind, kissing her back until he shook himself free, coming to his senses. "Penny, wait," he blurted breathlessly.

"I've thought about this moment for so many months," she purred, tugging at his sweater in an attempt to remove it.

"Pen, stop. I need to tell you something," he reiterated, gently pushing her away.

It was at that very moment, with Penelope's hands still tugging at his sweater and his hands on her shoulders, his hair slightly tussled, that Tess walked into the doorway. She went unnoticed by the former lovers and quickly backed out into the hall and out of view.

"Pen, I'm very happy to see you again and I would like nothing more than to take you to bed right now, but I can't. I love Tess."

"Who is Tess?" Penny asked, trying to hide her rejection.

"Tess Hamilton is my girlfriend," he informed her, stepping away from Penny.

Penny's body suddenly swayed and the she fell onto the sofa with a complete lack of grace. "Girlfriend? You, in love? In a monogamous relationship?" she spurted out in one breath.

Sebastian burst into laughter as he joined her on the sofa, propping his feet on the coffee table. "God, Pen, I wasn't that bad!"

"Yes, you were," she retorted, disagreeing with him. "I was there. Who were those twins you spent that one weekend shagging?"

"Well, I'm a changed man. Tess makes me want to be a better person—a different person. She's amazing," he announced, grinning from ear to ear.

There was a quiet moment between them. Penny sat distraught, shaking her head. "What happened to us, Sebastian? We were the Libertines."

"We grew up, Penny," he responded, putting his arm around her shoulder to comfort her. "Why are you here? Where's Alistair?"

"We broke up." As soon as she said it aloud, she burst into tears. "He cheated on me."

"Can you forgive him? After all, we did have an affair behind his back," Sebastian reminded her.

"Yes, but he never found out. I had to suffer the humiliation of finding out about his tryst in *The Sun*. Everyone knew before I did. I was gutted, Sebastian. In my anger, I confronted him, told him to bugger off, and caught the first flight out of London."

"You're too good for Alistair and you really don't want to lead a life of duty to the public anyway. Penny, you are a stunning beauty. You could have your pick of any man you want," he finished, trying to build up her confidence.

"I can't have you," Penny lamented. "And you were so much better in bed."

Sebastian smiled. "I'm glad you came to visit. I'm always here for you," he reassured, taking her slender, delicate hand in his.

A sudden thud came from the hallway. Sebastian jumped up to see what had happened. He found a vase had fallen off the credenza, with Tess crouching over it, trying to clean up the shards of broken porcelain. After the initial shock of seeing her there, he had a sudden realization that she had been listening to his conversation with Penny.

"Tess, leave it. Alice can clean it up." He bent down next to Tess and took her hand. "Come with me. I want you to meet someone."

"No, I should go. You have a guest." She stood up, straightening the simple blouse and skirt she wore.

"How much did you overhear?" His attention was distracted by the sight of Penny appearing in the doorway. He took a deep breath. He couldn't handle two mental girls at the same time. He didn't have the strength.

"You must be Tess," Penny announced, forcing a smile.

"And you're Penny," Tess coolly replied, eyeing the other girl.

"Where are my manners?" Penny said to herself as she wiped her tears away and extended her hand to Tess. "I'm Penelope Stanton."

"The Libertine," Tess said, shaking her hand.

"And you're the girl who's won his heart."

"I'm standing right here, you two." Sebastian ushered them both inside his bedroom and closed the door behind him. He glanced at his mattress and let his mind wander for a brief moment, imagining what it would be like to take them both to bed right now. He quickly shook the thought away. The girls sat on the sofa, as far away from each other as possible. Sebastian poured them each a small measure of scotch. He handed the girls a tumbler of golden liquid and said, "You really should drink this." He directed his words specifically to Tess.

She swallowed it in one quick gulp and shook as the warm alcohol slid down her throat. "Well, this is awkward," Tess chimed in, breaking the silence.

"Having past and present lovers in the same room usually is," Penny added.

"I'm not his lover," Tess tersely replied, as if repulsed by the idea.

"Sorry, I just assumed."

"Can we please not discuss sex?" Sebastian pleaded. "It's not good decorum."

"Fine by me," Tess agreed. "I could really use a Diet Coke," she said, looking at Sebastian and handing him her empty glass.

He looked at the girls with a great deal of suspicion. Against his better judgment, he left them to fulfill Tess' request.

Once alone, Penny turned to Tess and said, "I don't know how you did it, but you made that man fall completely in love with you. It's quite a feat." Tess didn't respond, so Penny continued. "He's a good friend. It's nice to see him happy. Take care of him." She stood and picked up her handbag and began to head for the door.

"Wait, Penny, can I ask you something?"

Penny stopped and turned around to face Tess. "Yes."

"I know about his past. All those girls and he was never in love before?"

She had a sad look in her eyes. "Never, not even with me. But I'd like to think that if I had chosen Sebastian over Alistair, we would have fallen in love," she replied with a wistful smile.

"What's it like—having sex with him?" Tess asked before she could stop herself.

"You Americans are certainly straightforward."

"I'm sorry. It was rude of me to ask."

"It's been on your mind, though."

"Yes."

Penny remembered fondly, momentarily lost in thought. "It was lovely. He was passionate and giving." She stopped when she heard steps in the hall. Sebastian was carrying a tray with crystal goblets filled with ice and two bottles of Diet Coke. He had also added a bowl of strawberries and another of chocolate. Nothing soothes an irritated woman better than chocolate, he figured.

Sebastian stepped into the room, only to find Penny about to leave. "What are you doing?"

"I'm going to the airport. I shouldn't have come unannounced."

"You can't," Tess interrupted, standing up from the sofa. "You came a long way. You must be exhausted. You should stay."

"Please stay, Pen," Sebastian agreed.

"Thank you, both of you," she said grateful for their kindness.

Tess walked over to Sebastian and took the Diet Coke from the tray. "I'm heading home. Take care of Penny. She needs you right now."

He couldn't believe how amazing Tess was acting. There seemed to be no jealously, only understanding.

Sebastian leaned in and kissed her on the lips. "I love you."

"Okay," she smiled. "I'll call you in the morning." And then she was gone.

Penny watched the whole incident play out and was gobsmacked. "You tell her you love her and her response is 'Okay?'"

Sebastian chuckled. "Yes, it's her thing. I know she loves me. She just hasn't mustered the courage to say it yet."

"She's one of a kind."

"That she is," he agreed. "How about we get you a nice, hot bath?"

"Yes, but only if you'll pull up a chair and talk with me."

Sebastian raised his brow with suspicion. "Just talk?"

"Yes, but bring the scotch and cigarettes and the chocolate, too."

He gently kissed her on the forehead. "Deal."

Penny sunk into the deep tub brimming with iridescent bubbles. She let out a heavy breath and closed her eyes. There was a knock on the door. "Are you settled? May I come in?" Sebastian asked.

"Yes."

He entered carrying a tray with food and drink. Sebastian set it down the on the floor, then handed Penny a glass of scotch.

She took a small sip then placed the glass on the ledge of the tub. "Light me a cigarette, will you?"

He did as requested, then sat down on the closed lid of the toilet. "Feeling better?"

"Yes, thank you for letting me stay." She took a deep drag on the Dunhill and slowly let the smoke escape her parted lips. "I like your Tess Hamilton. Though I have to admit, she's nothing like the girls you dated back home. What made you fall in love with her?"

Sebastian contemplated the question. There were so many things he loved about Tess; he wasn't sure how to verbalize them. Finally he said, "She's everything I'm not and everything I want to be."

"You've got it bad and she hasn't even had sex with you yet."

"It's a bone of contention between us."

Penny began to giggle uncontrollably, water splashing around her breasts. "Bone of contention."

Sebastian eyed her wearily, and then began to laugh, too. "Penis jokes, Penny? Honestly?"

"Sorry," she apologized as the giggles faded away. "I really did miss you, Sebastian. My offer still stands, if you want to relieve some tension. We were good together, remember?"

"Please, don't tempt me."

"Can't blame a girl who's just flown seven thousand miles for trying."

"You're a wicked vixen. You know that, don't you?" he teased right back, picking up her hand and kissing it.

"I don't understand how Tess can resist your charms. How far have you gotten with her?"

"Penny! I'm not going to answer that."

"When you left the room, she asked me what it was like to have sex with you."

"She did?" Sebastian asked in disbelief.

Penny nodded her head as she took another sip of scotch. "She's been thinking about it a lot. I reckon it won't be long before she says yes."

Penny and Sebastian talked as old friends do, catching up on the latest gossip, reminiscing about old times and filling each other in on their lives apart. Several hours had passed before her eyes became heavy with sleep and Sebastian put her to bed in a guest room down the hall.

When he was back in his own room, he picked up the phone and rang Tess. It was already ten thirty in the evening. Thankfully, she answered. "You're still up," he muttered, exhausted from the day, but happy to hear her voice.

"How's Penny?"

"She's sleeping. Thank you for being so supportive today. She's pretty upset about the breakup."

"Is she going to be okay, Sebastian?"

"She'll be fine. I was going to let her stay here for a while. Are you all right with that?" For some reason, he wanted her approval.

"It's your house. You don't have to ask my permission."

"I love you. If you're uncomfortable in any way, just say it. She can stay with Sigourney. I know Penny's always keen on shopping, especially when the exchange rate is in her favor." He tried to make light of the situation.

"I'm fine with her staying. I trust you."

"Come over tomorrow for brunch. I'd like for you two to get to know each other better."

"I'd like that," Tess agreed. "I'll see you tomorrow."

Sebastian hung up the phone when he heard the click on her end. He closed his eyes, laid back, and took a deep breath. More than ever, he was glad to have Tess in his life.

Chapter 15 - Need You Tonight

Spring break had finally arrived and Sebastian was relieved. The countdown had begun: less than three months left of high school. Less than three months until his new life began with Tess. He was very excited about his condo purchase, even if he hadn't had the nerve to tell Tess yet. When the time was right, he would know, and then they would have a conversation about moving in together.

It was Saturday morning. Sebastian made his way to Nanny's room to escort her to breakfast with Henry and Alice. He knocked on her bedroom door and waited for a response, but there wasn't any. He knocked again, louder this time. When there was no answer, he entered the room. Nanny was still asleep in bed.

Sebastian smiled. "Wake up, sleepyhead. Breakfast is ready." She didn't stir. He suddenly got a sinking feeling that something was terribly wrong. Sebastian sat on the edge of the bed and took her hand. It was ice cold and her fingers had begun to turn blue. "No, no, no," he muttered, closing his eyes tightly, hoping this was nothing more than a bad dream.

Slowly opening his eyes, the scene remained the same. This wasn't a dream. Panic set in and he ran into the hallway and shouted at the top of his lungs. "Henry, call 911!"

Henry and Alice raced up the back stairs when they heard his cry for help. Sebastian leaned against the wall for support. When his knees gave out, he slowly slid to a sitting position on the floor in the hallway. Henry began to administer CPR. Alice dialed 911 and then called Nanny Jones' physician. Sebastian repeatedly banged the back of his head against the wall to try to drown out the noise inside Nanny's room.

Alice made her way downstairs to wait for the ambulance. Henry continued to administer CPR until the paramedics rushed into the room, with a police officer following close behind. Relinquishing his post, Henry walked into the hall and knelt down in front of Sebastian. "I'm so sorry…" His voice trailed off.

"Don't say it," Sebastian pleaded.

Alice escorted Dr. Wexler into Nanny's room. He was carrying a black leather medical bag and soon joined the other personnel. Sebastian walked back into the room and watched as the doctor examined the lifeless body. Looking at her ashen face, all he could think was, *not again*. It wasn't supposed to end this way.

Henry, who had stepped up beside him, put a hand on his shoulder and eased him aside. "Do you want me to call your mother?"

"I don't have a mother anymore," Sebastian replied in a daze.

Henry rephrased his question. "Would you like me to call Lady Irons?"

"No! She has no say in this." His eyes glazed over in disbelief. "Nanny wanted to be cremated and her ashes scattered in the rose garden at the castle. It was here favorite place."

"Does she have any family?"

"I was her only family." How could he possibly call a funeral home and ask them to take her away? "Henry, will you help me take care of the arrangements?"

"Anything you need."

Doctor Wexler called the time of death at 9:42 a.m. Solemnly, he approached Sebastian and Henry. "I'm very sorry for your loss. We can transport the body to the coroner if you would you like an autopsy, or you can have the body sent directly to the funeral home."

"Get out!" Sebastian yelled, deeming him an insensitive oaf.

Henry quickly ushered the offending man out into the hall so they could talk in private. The paramedics packed their equipment and left the room.

"I have some questions we need to go through," the police officer announced, stepping in front of Sebastian.

The two of them went back and forth as information was assimilated. Sebastian hardly remembered any of the questions, he just answered as they were asked. When the officer was satisfied with the questioning and deemed no foul play was evident, he left Edgewood to file his report.

Alice gently took Sebastian's hand to comfort him. "Are you sure you don't want an autopsy?"

"What's an autopsy going accomplish? It won't bring her back. She died in her sleep. Does it really matter how?"

"No, it won't bring her back, but some people like the closure from knowing the cause."

Henry walked in shortly thereafter with a business card in hand. "Doctor Wexler gave me some information. He said if you didn't want a service you can do a direct cremation. That means we can take the body to the crematorium and get the cremation permit. The doctor will provide a copy of the death certificate. If you'll sign an authorization form, we can probably get this taken care of quickly."

"Good, I want it done today," Sebastian instructed in a slow monotone voice. "Lily can't know. If you tell her, she'll take over. There will be hideous flower arrangements and a fancy coffin. She won't honor Nanny's last wishes."

"Okay. Let me make the call."

Alice nudged Sebastian. "Come with me."

Sebastian had no energy to fight back, so he just let her guide him along.

The cold breakfast sat uneaten on the kitchen table. Sebastian took a seat as Alice moved away the place settings so Sebastian could have some room. She handed him a cup of tea, which he took with a word of thanks but did not drink. He laid his head on the table and closed his eyes.

"In the top drawer of her bedside table you'll find a manila folder. Can you get it for me? I need to ring her solicitor and make an appointment. I'm the executor of her will."

Henry got on the phone and arranged for the cremation. There would be no funeral service per Nanny's request. Once he finished the call, Henry sat next to Sebastian. "You're in shock right now. Let me call the lawyer for you."

"I need to make this call on my own, Henry." He was focusing on what he had to do rather than thinking about his loss. It was going to be the only way to get through it.

"You don't have to go through this alone."

"I know." Sebastian got up from the table and made his way back to his bedroom.

Sebastian slid to the floor and sat on the plush carpet with his back leaning against the side of the bed. He grabbed the phone cord and yanked the phone to where he sat. Opening the manila file, he found the solicitor's information and punched in a long number. Sebastian waited while the phone rang with short, brief English tones.

"Rupert Hume, here," the voice on the end of the line responded.

With all the restraint he could manage, he cleared his throat and began to speak. "Mr. Hume, this is Sebastian Irons. I'm calling to inform you that Martha Jones has just passed away and as executor of her will I was hoping you could meet with me as soon as possible to sort out the necessary paperwork. I'm living in The United States at the moment, so I will need to make some travel plans." He took shallow breaths. His stomach was clenched in knots and he had a raging headache pounding through his temples.

"I'm sorry for your loss, Mr. Irons. Will you please hold while I look at my calendar?"

"Of course."

"I have an opening at ten o'clock on Monday morning of this coming week. Will that give you enough time to make your travel arrangements?"

"Yes, I appreciate your sense of urgency. I'll see you Monday morning." Sebastian hung up the phone as tears uncontrollably streamed down his face. He buried his head in his hands and sobbed. Why was this happening to him now? Who was going to be his rock? Who was going to give him sound advice? Thoughts were running through his mind at such a rapid pace as he was overwhelmed with fear and grief. Sebastian frantically wiped the tears away with the palms of his hands and took a few deep breaths. He picked up the receiver again and called Tess. Thankfully, she answered on the second ring. "Hello?"

"Tess," he began in a shaky voice. "Can you come over straight away?"

"What's wrong?" she asked in a panicked tone.

"Please just get here as soon as you can," he muttered quickly before being overcome by tears again and hanging up the phone before waiting for her response.

* * *

It was only half an hour, but the drive to Edgewood seemed like an eternity. Tess burst into Sebastian's room unsure of what she would find. His hand was still gripping the phone as he sat cross-legged on the floor. He wasn't crying, but his eyes were bloodshot and puffy and the tip of his nose was red. Tess fell to her knees in front of him. "What's happened?" she asked frantically.

"She's gone," Sebastian whispered.

"Who?"

"Nanny. She passed away in her sleep last night. I found her this morning." He choked out the words.

Tess placed a hand over her mouth to hide her gasp of shock. There wasn't anything she could say to comfort him—she knew this from her own personal experience. He wanted her here and right now that was the most she could do for him. Tess took Sebastian in her arms and held him tightly as he began to cry again, wet tears seeping through her cardigan sweater. She tried to quell his shaking body with soft caresses.

"How do you go on?" he needed to know.

"You just do," Tess replied softly. "Every day it gets a little easier, but it's been three years since my dad died and I'm not over it yet. You'll think of her every day, but it really does get easier. I'm sorry I can't say something more comforting," she admitted as a few tears ran down her cheeks.

"All this money and I couldn't do a damn thing to save her."

"It was her time, just like it was my dad's time. It's never fair," Tess reasoned, pulling away. She handed him a tissue then sat on the floor next to him, holding his hand. Silence passed between them.

"Do you have a passport?" he randomly asked. There was a sudden clarity in his eyes, as if he were compartmentalizing things, just as she did.

"Yes," she replied with confusion. "I got one so I could take a semester abroad when I go to NYU."

"I need to take her ashes back to England. It was her final wish. And I need to see her attorney and settle her estate. Please come with me?" he asked in desperation. "I can't do this alone."

"What about Sigourney?"

"I need *you*. You're the only one who really understood what Nanny meant to me and what I'm going through now."

"Okay," she acquiesced. She could not refuse him when he was overcome with grief and she did understand exactly what he was going through.

During the course of the day Alice, Henry, and Tess cared for Sebastian: Alice made sure he ate; Henry set about arranging their air travel and London hotel; Tess held his hand and gave morale support. The sun began to set and Sebastian let out a yawn. The day had exhausted him.

"Come on, you should try to get some sleep before we fly out tomorrow," Tess encouraged.

"Fine."

She walked him up to his bedroom, trying to support him as they climbed the stairs together. "I'm going to head home. I need to talk to my mom about this trip. I need to make sure she's okay with it."

"Don't go. Just lay with me like Nanny used to when I was young so I can fall asleep."

"Sebastian, I really don't think it's a good idea," she gently told him, even though he was utterly defenseless and could cause her no harm.

"I need you tonight. Please, Tess. I promise I won't try anything," he pleaded his case earnestly. "Call your mother. Try to explain."

She gave a heavy sigh and nodded her head. She wanted to be out of earshot so she went back into the hall to make the call. She dialed home. "Hi, Mom," she greeted in an exhausted voice.

"Tess, what's wrong?"

Her own stomach was in a knot as she laid out the details for her mother. "It's Sebastian. Nanny Jones died last night. He's so upset, Mom. It's like going through Dad's death all over. He's been crying all day. Alice, Henry, and I have all been here, but there just doesn't seem to be anything we can say to help."

"In times like these, all you can really do is be there for him. Remember how your Aunt Karen came and stayed with us when your dad died?"

"He wants me to go back to England with him to scatter her ashes. He's so devastated. I couldn't say no. Would you be okay with that?" Tess asked, unsure of her response. "Sebastian will pay my airfare."

"Tess, you're eighteen years old. I trust you. I think you might be one of the few people who have actually experienced what he's feeling right now. He needs a good friend like you. You have the week off from school. Do what you need to do," she encouraged. "I can pack a bag for you, if you like. How long will you be gone?"

"We'll probably be gone four or five days. I guess it depends on how quickly he can get everything in order." Then Tess smiled. "You know you're a totally awesome mom, don't you?"

"And you're a totally awesome daughter. You should stay at Edgewood tonight. I don't want you driving home when you're so exhausted, and Sebastian will feel better knowing he has a friend close by. Give him my sympathy."

"I love you, Mom. I'll be over tomorrow to get my bag on the way to the airport."

"I love you, too."

Tess hung up the phone and noticed Alice approaching. She was carrying a small silver tray with a glass of water and a small blue pill. "Has he fallen asleep yet?" Alice asked.

"No, not yet. I'm going to spend the night here. I'm worried about him."

"Do you want to take this to him? It's a sleeping pill. And make sure he drinks the whole bottle of water. He needs to stay hydrated. Oh, and make sure he's not mixing this with alcohol." Alice was so sweet and knew all his tricks and still cared for him anyway. Just like Tess did.

"Alice, you and Henry were amazing today. I know Sebastian appreciates it more than he can verbalize."

"We're quite fond him, Tess. You need anything, just call us. Goodnight."

Tess bade her goodnight and walked back into Sebastian's bedroom, closing the door behind her. He was under the covers wearing his T-shirt and she assumed he had stripped down to his boxers as his trousers were in a ball on the floor. She handed him the tray. "Alice said you need to take the pill and drink all the water. You haven't had any alcohol have you?"

He shook his head no and did as instructed while Tess kicked off her sneakers and removed her cardigan to reveal a short sleeved gray T-shirt. With some hesitation, she took off her jeans and quickly got under the covers, sitting up against the headboard. Sebastian handed her the tray, which she placed on the bedside table.

Sebastian took a pillow and laid it on her lap then placed his head upon it, extending his left arm over her knees. "Is everything all settled with your mother?"

"Yes."

His face was long and drawn. His eyes were puffy. There was sadness emanating from them, which forced her to look away in pain. "Sebastian, you're breaking my heart."

"Mine's already broken," he murmured as he closed his eyes and drifted off to sleep.

She sat there for the longest time watching him sleep. The pill had done its job. He lay still and was sleeping soundly. She worried that he might be prone to nightmares like she had been after her dad died, but they did not invade his sleep this evening. Eventually, Tess dozed off, too.

During the night, they changed positions, ending up sleeping on their sides. Tess curled up around his back, enveloping him like a cocoon, keeping him safe and warm.

The light streaming through the window woke her. She was unsure of the time. She tried to strain her neck to see the clock.

Sebastian instinctively held onto her arm. "Don't go," he said in a hushed voice, still groggy from the sleeping pill.

"Did you get any sleep last night?"

"Yes, what about you?"

"Not really, I'm worried about you."

"As long as you're here with me, I'll be okay."

Tess kissed his cheek and then placed her chin on his shoulder. "I'm hungry. Do you want me to bring you something?"

"I'll come down with you," Sebastian replied. "I need to see how Henry made out with the travel plans." He rolled onto his back and looked up at Tess. He gently touched her cheek with his hand. "Thank you for staying last night."

"You're welcome," she replied, placing a small kiss in the palm of his hand. "I have to use the bathroom before we go downstairs," she told him, hopping out of bed. She grabbed her jeans and cardigan off the floor and dashed across the room, closing the bathroom door behind her.

Tess washed her hands and splashed some warm water on her face. She noticed his toothbrush holder contained two brushes: one was Sebastian's, the other was hers. He had given it to Tess the night he took care of her after the drinking fiasco at The Jug. Sebastian had left it there all those months. It made her smile as she gratefully grabbed it to brush her teeth. Finally sneaking a peak at herself in the mirror, she wasn't too horrified. She smoothed down her hair using his hairbrush before stepping back into the bedroom.

* * *

Sebastian didn't bother to dress—he simply threw on a maroon robe and patiently waited for her on the bed. When she returned, they walked to the kitchen together. Alice smiled when she noticed them and handed Sebastian a cup of coffee. They sat at the table and two plates of scrambled eggs and bacon promptly appeared in front of them. Tess poured herself a glass of orange juice from a carafe and turned down the offer of a hot drink. Sebastian eyed the plate with suspicion. His appetite hadn't returned and he wasn't sure he could keep bacon and eggs down. Alice saw his face and offered him a plate of toast with a fine coating of butter and cinnamon sugar instead and he took it with relief and appreciation.

Henry stood next to Sebastian and placed his hand on his shoulder. "How are you holding up?"

"I've been better," he replied with a halfhearted smile. "Were you able to make the arrangements?"

Henry studied the notes he'd made on a yellow legal pad. "I booked you on a British Airways flight leaving Philadelphia today at one o'clock. I was only able to get business class," he said apologetically. "You have a reservation at The Savoy for this evening. I rented a car for you to pick up on Monday after you meet with the lawyer so you can drive home. You're scheduled to return on Friday. If you need more time, you can always call the airlines and change the ticket."

"Thank you so much, Henry. I couldn't have done this without your help."

"I arranged to collect Mrs. Jones' ashes this morning. When I return, I can take you and Tess to the airport."

"We'll need to stop by Tess' home to get her suitcase," Sebastian reminded him.

"Can you be ready by ten thirty?"

Both Tess and Sebastian nodded in unison. "We don't have much time. Tess, do you want to shower?"

"I don't have any clean clothes."

"Oh, I'll take care of that," Alice offered. "Come on, you can hop in the shower and give me your clothes to wash."

"That would be great," Tess agreed appreciatively.

Sebastian pulled out an overnight bag and began to pack while Tess took her shower. He packed his Paul Smith suit, an assortment of shirts, a jumper, and the pair of jeans Tess had made him buy.

He heard the water turn off. Tess cracked the bathroom door open and popped her wet head out as clouds of steam surrounded her. "Can you hand me something to put on until Alice comes back with my clothes?"

He went back to his closet and grabbed the first thing he saw and handed it to her. A few minutes later, Tess walked into the room wearing his navy pinstriped shirt. It was oversized on her. The cuffs hung down, covering her hands—they were longer than usual because they were made for cuff links. Her damp curls cascaded over her shoulders. She looked spectacular and Sebastian was lost for words. Tess sat on the edge of the bed where he was packing and rubbed her arms up and down, feeling the extra soft fabric.

"This feels amazing. Where did you get it?"

"My Savile Row tailor. It's custom made with a blend of cotton and cashmere."

"It's very comfortable." Then she observed, "You're packing light."

"The last time I took an impromptu trip, I didn't even take a bag," he said, absentmindedly zipping the top compartment.

"Where did you go that you didn't need a bag?"

"Spain. I sort of left England in a hurry."

"What were you running away from?"

"Everything: my mother, my future, death."

"That's oppressive."

Sebastian silently nodded. There was a knock on the door and Alice entered the room carrying Tess's clothes. "Here you go, Tess."

Tess took the warm clothes from Alice's arms and ran off to the bathroom to get changed, the sleeves billowing as she moved.

Henry returned home from his errands at 10:30 a.m. to find Sebastian and Tess waiting for him in the foyer. Sebastian was wearing his black suit in mourning. Henry took Sebastian's bag and the three of them walked out to the car together.

Sebastian opened the back door for Tess. He walked to the other side of the car and got inside. A small box made of satin rosewood with a golden hinge sat on the backseat. Sebastian picked it up and placed it on his lap with loving care. He felt tears beginning to well in his eyes, but quickly blinked them away. He looked at the box for the longest time, then ran his fingers across its top. *So this is how it ends. Seventy years of life on Earth and you end up in a small wooden box. We're taking you home, Nanny*, he thought to himself.

Henry pulled up to Tess' home about thirty minutes later. She and Sebastian exited the car and went into house while Henry waited outside with the car running.

Tess' mom was sitting on the sofa relaxing with her Sunday newspaper, *The Philadelphia Inquirer*, when they walked through the front door. She rose quickly and hugged Sebastian tightly. "I'm so sorry." She pulled back and looked at him. "I really enjoyed getting to know Mrs. Jones. You were very lucky to have her in your life."

He nodded in agreement, then said, "Thank you for letting Tess accompany me home. I really can't do this alone right now."

Tess spied her bag on the floor and picked it up. "We should go. Henry is waiting." She tugged on Sebastian's elbow. He was riveted to the spot, lost in thought.

Mrs. Hamilton handed Tess a bank envelope. "Here's some spending money, just in case." Then she hugged her daughter. "Have a safe flight. Call me when you land."

"I will, Mom. Thanks again."

They arrived at the airport an hour later. Tess stood on the curb outside the departures terminal while Henry and Sebastian got the bags out of the trunk. "Sebastian, the mortician thought you might want this." Henry reached into his pocket and pulled out an item. He placed it in the palm of Sebastian's hand.

Sebastian stared at the thin 14-karat gold wedding band. He hadn't even thought to take it off her finger when he said goodbye. It was nothing fancy. She was married during the Second World War and her husband was killed in action in Normandy. They never had any children, so shortly after his death she became a governess. He closed his hand and clutched it tightly. "Thank you. I'm very happy to have this memento." He carefully placed the ring in his jacket breast pocket and gave Henry a hug. He turned on his heel, picked up the bags, and escorted Tess into the terminal.

"Do you think I have enough time to run to the ladies' room and change? I feel very uncomfortable wearing jeans when I know we're going to be sitting in business class."

"Fine, but please make it quick. We still need to get our boarding passes."

"Great." She squeezed his hand, took her bag, and rushed to the toilets. Ten minutes later, she emerged wearing a simple black skirt and crème colored blouse matched with black ballet flats.

"Feel better?"

"Much, thanks." They queued up and waited for the next available agent.

Once they received the boarding passes, they made their way to the gate just as the boarding process began. Tess and Sebastian took their adjoining seats after stowing their carry-on bags in the overhead locker. They sat back in the soft leather seats. They were larger and more comfortable than coach class, but not first class, to which Sebastian was accustomed. It didn't matter; in seven hours they would touch down in London. He never thought it would be under these circumstances. He looked at Tess, who let out a small yawn. She had been such a trooper over the past twenty-four hours. She really had come through for him.

"Tess, lay your head on my shoulder and try to get some rest. It's a long flight."

"No, I'm okay. I want to stay awake. I don't want you to be alone."

He leaned in and kissed her temple. "I'm not alone. Try to sleep for a while."

The plane taxied down the runway for takeoff. Tess leaned into Sebastian's arm and nodded off to sleep before the wheels left the ground.

Chapter 16 - Don't Dream It's Over

The British Airways plane landed in London seven hours later with a smooth bump, and taxied to the gate. "Stay close, Tess. It's a very crowded airport." Tess took his hand and together they walked to customs. "We'll need to split up here so you can go through the visitors' queue. I'll meet you on the other side."

Tess watched Sebastian follow the lines through customs like a zombie, tightly clutching his small wooden box. She couldn't imagine how hard this was for him. How could he mourn if he was so focused on travel plans and settling an estate? Tess smiled at the customs agent as he methodically stamped her passport. She found Sebastian standing on the other side the partitioned wall. They walked outside to the taxi stand and took a black cab into London.

"I'm still tired," Tess admitted. "How are you holding up?"

"I'm okay, just nervous about meeting with the lawyer tomorrow."

"It will be over soon." Tess looked out the window as they neared the city, with its many lights and ancient architecture. If she weren't so tired, she'd be giddy with excitement. Tess had never dreamed her first excursion overseas would be to scatter Nanny Jones' ashes. The taxi pulled up in front of The Savoy, an upscale hotel located on The Strand in London's West End.

Inside, Tess marveled at the black and white checkered tile floor, art deco furnishing, and marble columns. They checked in at the front desk then made their way to their room. The guest room was furnished with Edwardian furniture, rich and warm fabrics, and two beds. She sank into the closest bed and sighed. "I can't believe how beautiful this place is." The nicest place she had ever stayed was the Holiday Inn.

"Are you hungry? I can order room service."

"No, I'm okay. Let me call my mom, and then we can go to sleep."

"Okay," he agreed, kissing her on the lips. "I'm going to get a shower. We'll have breakfast at The Savoy Grill in the morning before we head out to meet Mr. Hume."

Fifteen minutes later, Tess had finished her phone call and put on her pajamas. She was sitting up in bed, under the soft down duvet, waiting for Sebastian to return from the bathroom. He appeared, in chambray cotton pajama bottoms and a white T-shirt, his wet hair slicked back.

"Do you want to call Henry?"

"I called him from the bathroom," he replied.

"There's a phone in the bathroom? That's just crazy."

"Yes, but handy."

Tess pulled back the covers on the empty side of her bed. "Stay with me tonight?"

Sebastian switched off the lights and lay down. He took Tess in his arms and she dozed off to sleep within minutes, feeling safe in the warmth of his arms.

* * *

The next morning, they woke and ate breakfast in the hotel restaurant, and then took a cab to Kensington to meet with Mr. Hume. Sebastian dressed in his Paul Smith suit. Tess chose her black skirt and crème blouse. The receptionist escorted them into Mr. Hume's office promptly at ten o'clock for their scheduled meeting.

"Mr. Irons, I'm sorry for your loss," he stated, standing from behind his desk. He extended his right hand first to Sebastian and then to Tess for a handshake.

"Thank you," Sebastian replied, taking a seat on the opposite side of the lawyer's desk. "This is my partner, Tess Hamilton." Tess sat next to Sebastian, her hand on his forearm for support.

The desk was clear except for one file, which Hume opened without any drama. He began: "I will now read the last will and testament of Martha Jones."

"I, Martha Anne Jones née Simpson, do declare to be of sound mind and body and thus bequest upon my death all my personal belongs to Sebastian Andrew Irons. Said belongings include a joint Barclays bank account and various mutual funds and stocks issued through the same Barclays account. Funds will remain in trust for Mr. Irons until his eighteenth birthday. At

273

said birthday they are to be distributed as follows: Only monies in the bank account will be available for Mr. Irons' personal use but with restriction. Mutual funds and stocks will be administered by Killik Stockbrokers, 2A Downshire Hill, London. Quarterly dividends will be placed in the bank account if available. Special access must be granted by Hume and Leavenworth, trustee for the estate of Martha Anne Jones nie Simpson, for major purchases in excess of £20,000 and can only be considered for education, home or medical emergencies. All funds, stocks and monies will be released in their entirety to Sebastian Andrew Irons when he reaches the age of twenty-five."

Hume cleared his throat and continued. "There is more legalese, but this is what you need to know. I have a copy of the will for you. Do you have the death certificate?"

"Yes." Sebastian opened the manila envelope he'd brought with him and handed Mr. Hume the document.

The lawyer glanced at it and then tucked it in the file. He removed three envelopes from the file and placed them on the desk, sliding them across to Sebastian. "You should know that the funds and stocks Mrs. Jones has left you are in excess of one million pounds."

"Excuse me?" Sebastian sputtered.

Mr. Hume shuffled through some papers, pinpointed the page he was looking for, and repeated, "The funds and stocks' current value is one point three million."

"How much is that in US dollars?" Tess whispered, leaning into Sebastian.

"Approximately one million dollars," Sebastian responded in disbelief.

"These envelopes are for you. First, this your Barclays card, which gives you access to your bank account. It can be used worldwide at any cash point," he explained, pointing to the first of the three envelopes. "As Mrs. Jones saw fit to have all accounts in both your names, you have avoided a hefty inheritance tax and filing with the court for probate of the will. Second, I have two letters from Mrs. Jones that were sent to my office just a few weeks ago. One is for you and one is for Miss Hamilton. You will see your names on the front of the respective envelopes."

Tess looked at Sebastian in shock. "Did you know about this?"

He shook his head. "No. Why would she send letters here when she was with us every day?" Sebastian wondered aloud, looking at Mr. Hume for an answer.

"I do not know what is in those envelopes, but she wanted you to have them." As he had no further information on the contents of the envelopes, he changed the subject. "I will need your current contact information, Mr. Irons."

He recited an address in New Jersey, which Tess did not recognize, and then added, "I'll be attending New

York University in the fall and spending the next four years there."

"You're on a student visa, then?"

"Yes."

"You'll need to extend the visa. I can make those arrangements for you. If you decide to stay in America after the student visa runs out, be sure you contact me. Of course," he said, almost as an aside while taking a final glance in the folder, "if you do marry an American citizen, you'll have no need for a work visa."

For an interminably long thirty minutes, the lawyer continued with more information and legal drudgery. There were forms to sign and documents to read. Although the lawyer was quick, succinct, and no-nonsense, Sebastian's head was swimming by the time they wrapped up their business. They bade their farewells and rushed out of the office for some much-needed fresh air.

* * *

Tess and Sebastian stood on the crowded London street and looked at each other, not knowing what to say about the whole experience, the city rushing by them as they stood overwhelmed with legal overload. Finally Tess managed to mutter, "I need a Diet Coke."

"I could use something a little stronger," he countered.

"But you're going to be driving," Tess reminded him.

"Yes," he sighed. "Come along, I'll buy you a Diet Coke."

They walked across the street, dodging the double-decker buses and black cabs, and ducked into a Tesco. Sebastian grabbed a packet of crisps, a Cadbury bar for

Tess, and two sodas. He paid the cashier and exited the shop.

They collected the rental car and made their way up the M1 toward Sutton on Ashfield. They were going back to the castle—back to scatter Nanny's remains. They didn't talk. The only sound came from the radio. *Stripped* by Depeche Mode played through the speakers.

Tess drank her Coke in silence and pondered the whole unbelievable scene they had just encountered with the lawyer. Suddenly she said, "You're a millionaire."

"Apparently so."

"You don't seem surprised."

"I did know about the account. I just didn't realize she had amassed that kind of fortune. She worked for Lily for thirty years and invested every dime Lily ever gave her. She was going to pay my way through NYU. I never thought of it as my money," he quickly confided.

"Well, that doesn't happen every day." She turned sideways in the car and stared at him. "Okay, I can't wrap my mind around this. Why are you so calm?"

"All I keep thinking is this can't be real. None of this seems real," he repeated. "Now you're going to see where I grew up and you're going to be even more overwhelmed than you are right now," he worried. "Please just remember: whatever you see, whatever happens, I'm still the same person you've come to know. I'm still the same person who loves you. That will never change." He said it as if he knew there was some impending doom looming ahead.

Her answer was quick and heartfelt. "I promised to be here for you, and that hasn't changed."

Tess leaned back in the leather seat and looked out the window. The cars they passed were so much smaller than the cars in America. She looked at the little towns as they drove and the snippets of rural land as they made their way along the motorway. The sun was setting as they turned onto the private road.

* * *

They drove along, finally cresting over a hill until the castle came into sight. It looked different to Sebastian; it appeared sad and lonely. It was a fixture of past greatness that was becoming old and worn. Even though he had been there less than a year ago and nothing significant had change architecturally, his outlook on life had changed and he saw it with new eyes. He had a premonition that this would be the last time he ever set foot on the castle's grounds.

Sebastian pulled up to the entrance and turned off the ignition. "Are you ready for this?" he asked, looking at Tess. He knew he wasn't.

She nodded and opened the car door. He took her hand and they walked into the house unannounced. A uniformed servant nearly dropped the glass vase of fresh cut flowers she was carrying when she noticed Sebastian walk through the front door.

"Sir, we didn't know you were coming home!" she squeaked, standing still and waiting for him to say something.

"Is Lady Irons here?"

"No, she's in Paris."

"Good, please have the bags in the boot of the car taken to my room." He left the servant and guided Tess up the staircase to Nanny's room.

* * *

He opened the door and walked into Nanny's room. Sebastian flipped the light switch, then he removed the white sheet that was protecting the love seat, neatly folding it and placing it on the coffee table. The room was quaint and cozy, perfectly matching Nanny Jones' personality. Several knickknacks had been left behind, as the move to America was only meant to be temporary and they hadn't bothered to pack everything.

"I love it," Tess announced as she turned around, taking in all the little details of the room. "It feels like she's still here."

He smiled for the first time in forty-eight hours. "You feel it, too? It seems as if she could walk into the room any minute and start talking about *EastEnders*." Sebastian took a seat on the sofa. "I want to scatter her ashes in the rose garden early tomorrow morning. She always made a point to have her daily walk just at sunrise."

Tess walked over to the fireplace mantel and studied the photographs. She picked up the one of Sebastian as a young boy, holding his teddy bear, sitting on Nanny's lap. "You were such a cute kid," she said, showing him the photo.

"I was happy then," he simply replied. "If you want the photo, you can have it."

"I'd like that very much. Thank you." Tess sat next to him. "She was an amazing woman. We had some interesting conversations about you."

"Like what?" he asked, turning toward her. His curiosity was piqued.

"She told me you were most happy when you were a child. I think her exact words were 'Sebastian was in love with his childhood.'"

"I had no problems," he reminisced. "Lily was rarely around. I never knew my father. I didn't realize that my life wasn't normal, so I was relatively happy. I did love my childhood, but I'm *in love* with you." He'd told her many times that he loved her, but his time was different and it surprised Tess.

"But what does that mean—*being in love?*"

A beautiful smile graced Sebastian's face. "The first day I met you there was something in your eyes. They were kind and didn't judge me. It was the first time in my entire life that someone looked at me and didn't have some preconceived notion of who I was. You believed in me and you didn't give up on me." He gently took her hand. "For us, being in love is friendship, loyalty, forgiveness, understanding—so many different things I can't even verbalize."

Tess was moved by his words but didn't know what to say, so she remained silent and kissed him.

He took her hand and stood. "Not here, not in this room."

They walked down the hall hand in hand. His bedroom door was already open and he stepped back and allowed Tess to enter first. Several household servants were busily preparing the room for his return. "Go now," he tersely instructed them. The last thing he cared about at this moment was dust on the furniture or having his bag unpacked. At his command, they promptly left. He closed the heavy door and turned the lock, leaving them alone.

The servants had arranged a light supper. The tray consisted of a sampling of cheese, crackers, and fresh fruit. There were finger sandwiches, a pot of tea, and a bottle of wine. Tess eyed the tray with a pang of hunger, but needed to finish the conversation with Sebastian.

"You told Penny I make you want to be a better person."

"It's true. I've told you everything, Tess. I feel naked, with my heart on my sleeve, yet I still have no idea how you feel about me. You never tell me." He gave her an intense gaze, pleading with his deep blue eyes for an answer. "We've been through so much together. Don't you at least owe me that?"

Tess hesitated. Her mouth opened and closed silently as she tried to search for the words. Sebastian was right—he had always been forthright with his feelings and desire for her. She, on the other hand, kept her feelings of desire clamped down deep inside. Those feelings were bubbling close the surface now. Suddenly, the words tumbled out of her mouth so quickly it seemed she had no time to form a coherent response. The torrent of emotion escaped and flowed freely. "I'm afraid of how much I like being with you. I'm afraid of how much I want you. I'm afraid of losing myself to you."

"You could never lose yourself," he reassured her softly.

"How can you be so sure?"

"Because you are the strongest, most self assured person I have ever met."

Moved by his simple yet honest words, Tess leaned in closer to him. "This is so complicated," she muttered, her lips just inches away from his. A moment later, she kissed him on the mouth, her stomach doing little flips-flops while her heart wildly palpitated.

"I suspect life never gets easier, but I know that I'm in love with you. I don't want you to be afraid to love me back," he whispered between their quick urgent kisses. "Please let me make love with you?"

She had no energy left to resist him; Tess wanted this just as much as he did. Swallowing hard, she surrendered with an affirmative nod of the head.

Sebastian smiled and sighed simultaneously. He swiftly pulled Tess into an embrace and looked into her eyes to be sure she had not changed her mind.

Tess assured him in hushed tone with a single word: "Yes."

* * *

She said yes. He had to stop for a moment to make sure it wasn't wishful thinking. After so many months of failed attempts, he found it hard to believe his wish was about to come true. For some unknown reason, Tess always let down her guard when she was away from home, and this time was no different. It was as if they were immersed in their own little world where no one else existed. This was the place that he was happiest. Somehow he sensed it was the same for her.

Tess placed her hands behind his neck and ran her fingers through his perfectly coifed hair. Oh, she definitely said yes. He was going to make love to her right now. He would finally be able to show her how he felt in his heart and every fiber of his being. He turned her around so he was facing her back and gently placed his hands on her shoulders, kneading his thumbs into her shoulder blades, massaging away any stress she might harbor. He leaned down and kissed the erogenous spot on her neck below her left earlobe.

"You know you drive me crazy when you do that?" she helplessly murmured.

He playfully bit her earlobe and then let his tongue trace a trail down her neck to the base of her shoulder. Sebastian could feel her pulse race under his touch. He spun her back to face him and unbuttoned her blouse until it opened up to reveal a simple, beige cotton bra. He unzipped her skirt and she slowly shimmed out of it, letting it drop to the floor.

It was a strange ballet, a movement of arms and legs intertwined. They fell onto the bed with Sebastian on top. He pulled away to look at her. She was only wearing her bra and panties; her long hair was fanned across the bed.

"I love you so much. We can go slowly. Just talk to me. Tell me what you like and don't like. This is about the two of us," Sebastian explained.

Tess tugged at his tie and pulled off his suit coat. Sebastian knelt on the bed frantically unbuttoning his own shirt and threw it on the floor. Then he removed his trousers and boxers, leaving himself naked. He covered her bare skin with little kisses, lingering at the curve of her breast. With a quick, expert motion, he unhooked her bra, sliding the straps over her shoulders until it fell away. He then removed her panties and she was finally naked. His eyes danced in the wonder of her beauty. Sebastian had always imagined what Tess might look like without her clothes; the reality was so much better than what he pictured in his mind. He wanted to burn the memory into his brain so he could treasure it for all time. Not taking this moment for granted, Sebastian was determined to show her how amazing sex could be. He wanted to give himself to her completely, without conditions or demands. This desire had never occurred with any other woman, and it was both terrifying and exhilarating.

He ran his hand along the inside of her thigh. Her skin was soft and silky under his fingertips. When he rubbed her clit, she let out a soft moan.

He hesitated before she gasped, "Don't stop."

Sebastian kissed her again on the lips while his hand continued to explore below her waist. Their tongues danced as her temperature rose. Her skin was warm to the touch. First he inserted was one finger inside her, then another. He felt Tess completely aroused by him and he wanted to make her come, make her feel ecstasy.

Sebastian trailed kisses down her body, starting with her neck and moving down to her breasts, tummy, and thighs. Soon the combination of fingers and his tongue between her legs made her quiver and pushed her over the edge. She called out his name. It made him smile, looking at her glowing in pleasure, her gorgeous full breast heaving with a shortness of breath. "Are you happy?" he whispered, crawling up toward her face.

"Yes," she replied. "I love you, Sebastian."

He had waited so long to hear those three little words come from of her beautiful mouth. Sebastian laughed with joy. "Say it again."

"I love you," she whispered breathlessly, three times. "I want to feel you inside me."

He fumbled with his bedside table drawer and grabbed a Durex condom. Ripping the foil packet, Sebastian rolled the condom over his erection. Ever so slowly and gently, he entered her. The sensation was overwhelming. He had been with other girls, but this, this was the most amazing feeling he had ever experienced. Warm, tight, home—this was how it felt to be inside her. It was a perfect rhythm of two people coming together as one. It seemed as if they were meant to be together, Tess instinctively arching her back to meet his slow thrust.

"Does this feel okay?" he asked, concerned about her comfort.

"Oh, yes," she managed to say between ragged breaths.

Sebastian picked up the pace as a small tingle of excitement began in the pit of his stomach. Suddenly he felt Tess' muscles contract, squeezing him until he could hold back no longer and climaxed. He stayed there on top of her, waiting for his pulse to regulate and his breathing to return to normal.

"I didn't hurt you, did I?" he questioned with concern, brushing the hair out of her eyes.

"No," she replied, holding onto him, clasping her hands on his lower back. It seemed as if she didn't want him to leave her.

He slowly pulled out and rolled over onto his back, exhausted. Sebastian wrapped his arms around Tess, placing her head on his shoulder.

"Is it always like that? Is it always that wonderful?" Tess asked.

"I have never felt this type of intense passion with anyone, Tess. I love you," he whispered as his eyelids became heavy with sleep.

"I love you, too."

"Thank you for being here with me. Thank you for trusting me and letting me love you like this."

In the morning, they dressed in their best clothes and walked down to the rose garden. It was sprawling—so much bigger than the garden at Edgewood. "I understand why she loved it here," Tess observed as they walked up and down the pebbled paths, which were arranged in neat vertical rows. In the center of the garden sat a small water fountain. Stone fish flanked the North, South, East, and West sides, their mouths spouting a steady stream of water into the large basin. Several small birds, which were enjoying a dip in the cool water, took flight when Tess and Sebastian approached.

Sebastian knew just where he wanted to go. He stopped in front of the Heritage Roses, which were just beginning to show beautiful buds. He was clutching Nanny's remains in the rosewood box. He had so many thoughts coursing through his head that he wasn't sure where to start or what to say. He stared into space, unmoving.

Tess held onto his arm. "Can I say something?" He nodded and she began, speaking from the heart. "Nanny Jones, I have a lot to thank you for. You may not have been the catalyst that brought Sebastian into my life, but your guidance and support made Sebastian give me a chance. To this day, I still don't understand why he puts up with me. I can be pretty tough on him sometimes."

Sebastian chuckled, his shoulders easing forward slightly, the tension abating.

"But you raised a beautiful boy who became an amazing man—someone who I fell in love with. Thank you for always being there for Sebastian." She couldn't contain her tears, so she let them flow, wiping them away with a tissue she held in her hand.

Sebastian leaned down and kissed the top of Tess' head. He drew strength from her words and began his own farewell. "Nanny, there are no words to express the deep and utter devastation I feel with your loss. You were my mother. You taught me so many things that I can't wait to pass onto my own children someday. I hope you are at peace. I know you'll be happy here for all eternity. I love you."

He opened the box and slowly scattered the ashes. Sebastian didn't want to let Nanny go and took his time, watching the gray ashes fall upon the rose petals. When the box was empty, he handed it to Tess. Sebastian took a pair of shears out of his coat pocket and snipped a few roses. He placed them inside the rosewood box and closed the lid. They walked to the fountain and sat on the stone bench, silently remembering Nanny. They stayed until storm clouds began to gather overhead. Sebastian put his arm around Tess and together they walked back to the house.

When they entered the house, a valet approached them. "Sir, would you like to have breakfast in the dining room?"

"No, could you just bring a tray up to my room?"

"Of course, sir." The servant nodded and went on his way.

Tess and Sebastian went back to his bedroom. "That was tough," he admitted, placing the box on the bedside table. He reached inside his coat pocket and took out Nanny's wedding band. He placed it in the box along with the roses and then closed the box with a soft click.

"What you said out there was really beautiful," Tess said.

There were tears in his eyes as he accepted the complement from her with a smile. "That was the hardest thing I've ever had to do, Tess."

"I know, but you did do it. You did exactly what she wanted. You need to be happy with that."

He was about to take a step toward her when a knock echoed from the bedroom door. "Enter," Sebastian said as the door opened, revealing a kitchen servant with a large round silver tray replete with two plates sporting shiny silver domes. He placed the tray on the sideboard table and quietly left the room, closing the door behind him.

"Come on, we should try to eat something." Sebastian pulled out a chair at the small table.

He poured them both a cup a tea, adding sugar and milk to hers just as she liked, and set it in front of her. He removed the domes and placed them on the floor. Steam wafted from the fine china plates. The cook had prepared fried eggs, crisp bacon, beans, fried potatoes, and a baked tomato. A toast rack sat in the center of the tray, holding its perfectly cut wedges of crispy white bread. "Traditional English breakfast. You don't have to eat it if you don't want to," Sebastian said, explaining the odd combination of food sitting before them.

"It's fine, thank you."

They halfheartedly ate their breakfast. Tess pushed the beans around on the plate while Sebastian managed a few bites of each item but nothing more. The somber mood of the day left them little appetite. "I'm not sure I can stay here any longer," Sebastian admitted. "Do you mind if we shower and leave this morning?"

"Sure," Tess agreed, pushing her chair away from the table.

Sebastian took the remains of breakfast, put all the dishes back on the silver tray, and placed it in the hallway on the floor. He didn't need someone interrupting them as they showered and packed to leave.

* * *

He turned his attention to Tess. Without words they undressed, this time being sure that they placed their fine clothing on hangers so it wouldn't wrinkle, and stepped into the shower together. Tess sat on the teakwood shower stool while Sebastian washed her hair, gently massaging her scalp.

"That feels so good," she told him, tilting her head back. He rinsed the shampoo out of her hair then pulled her up from the stool. He took the French milled soap and lathered it up in his hands before he began to clean Tess' back.

Tess couldn't believe this was happening to her. Three days ago she had agreed to spend the night with Sebastian out of concern for his well being. Last night, they finally made love, and it was spectacular. She had heard other girls talk at school about how the first time was quick and uncomfortable. This was definitely not Tess' experience. Sebastian made her feel desirable, special, and loved. How was she ever going to go back home and pretend this didn't happen—that her life hadn't been changed forever?

The sadness they felt turned into concern and care for one another. The events of the past few days threw them into a hurricane of emotion. In the eye of that hurricane, there was an eerie calm. It was a place of quiet oneness. They no longer felt like separate individuals; they moved and thought as one person. It was an overwhelming feeling that was new to both of them.

Sebastian turned off the water. They stood there in the shower kissing each other, the steam rising from their wet bodies. "We should get going," Tess whispered as she kissed his bare chest, which was beaded with drops of warm water.

"We can wait a little longer," he said, pressing up against her, aroused again.

"Okay," she agreed breathlessly, feeling the same pangs of excitement.

They made their way back to the bed. Sebastian lay on his back and Tess straddled him, her hands splayed over his smooth chest. She didn't think she could ever get tired of looking at his naked body, with his sculpted abs and strong arms. He felt so good inside her—warm, hard, home. They were so in tune with each other, lost in the moment, feeling the power and passion of their lovemaking. They didn't hear the key turning in the lock.

Lady Irons walked into Sebastian's room, catching them completely off guard. Tess quickly lay down on Sebastian's chest to avoid Lady Irons' stern glare—as well as the embarrassment of the situation.

"Sebastian," Lily said in calm, even voice, "I want to see you in the library immediately." She turned on her heel and left, leaving an aura of darkness in the room.

Tess apologized for something she had no control over, but it was the only thing she could think to say. "I'm so sorry, Sebastian."

"She had no right barging in here. You didn't do anything wrong. That door was locked and I'm not a child."

"Your mother walked in on us making love. I'm so embarrassed!" Her cheeks were red from the combination of exertion and awkwardness. She unconsciously covered her breasts with her arm, should the woman return.

Sebastian began to laugh and Tess playfully punched him in the arm. The lingering tension suddenly subsided. "I thought it was quite amusing. You should have seen the look the on her face." He sighed, leaning his head back into the pillow. "I guess I'll have to go see what she wants."

He put on his white shirt, but didn't button it. He grabbed his jeans and slipped them on. Sebastian ran his fingers through is wet hair instead of using a comb and properly styling it. "Here I go. Wish me luck."

"Should I get dressed?"

"Don't you dare! Stay right there, darling." He kissed her forehead. "I'll be back soon."

"Good luck."

He grinned. "The game is not over yet."

Sebastian left the room, closing the door behind him. Tess fell back onto the mound of pillows covering the bed. Sebastian always compared his relationship with Lily to a game. Tess was sure this move was checkmate, but she didn't know who was about to lose the game.

Chapter 17 - It's My Life

Lady Irons paced the hand-knotted Persian rug in the library, taking broad steps back and forth, her head held high and demanding. Sebastian entered the room, his hair disheveled and white shirt untucked and unbuttoned. "Don't grin at me young man. I don't find this situation very amusing. Thank goodness the house manager had the sense to call me when you decided to drop in for a visit."

Sebastian smiled. "Why did you summon me?"

"I don't take kindly to the scene I just witnessed. Sebastian, I will not have you being seduced by some middle-class social climber. You said you weren't sleeping with her."

"I believe my exact words were 'I'm not fucking her,'" he reminded Lily. "Now I am. Maybe you should have knocked before you barged into my room. The door was locked. Good manners of the elite upper class dictate a knock on the door and permission to enter."

With one swift move, she closed the distance between them and slapped him across the left cheek with a loud *crack*. "You never cease to disappoint me. You're no better than your father."

Sebastian was stunned by her outburst. The slap was hard and he bit his lower lip to stop from crying out in pain. He would not give her the satisfaction of emotion. A red imprint of her hand was beginning to rise on his skin. "Bitch," he muttered under his breath. "You never gave me the opportunity to know my father." Something clicked in his brain as he spoke the words. Finally it all made sense: Sebastian had just repeated the same sin as his father. All these years she was domineering because she feared he would be a carbon copy of his father. She had no right to project her fears and anger onto him.

"Sebastian, this is highly uncalled for. Have you lost your senses?"

"Why do you even care? You didn't raise me," he spat. Sebastian walked over to the sideboard and poured himself a scotch. He downed it in one gulp and slammed the glass on the table. "And for the record, Tess did not seduce me. If I'm going to sleep with someone, then it will be with whomever I damn well please. All my life you've done nothing but make me feel worthless and miserable. When I finally find someone who makes me happy, you want to ruin that, too. I'm not going to let you. Not this time." Sebastian balled his fists in determination.

"That's not true," she fought back. "I have done nothing of the sort."

"I don't want to hear it!" he yelled. "I've always acquiesced to you. This time I'm going to fight because I *hate* you and I *hate* Irons Electronics."

"You never complained while you were spending *my* money."

"You can keep your sodding money. I don't want it," he shot back.

She ignored all that he said and grilled him again. "What are you doing here? Why aren't you in school?"

He shook his head in disgust. Of course she had no idea of Nanny's passing—not that she would care if she knew. Nanny was just a hired governess, after all. He didn't want to tell her. Losing Nanny was too private; it was too painful. Tess was the only one who understood what he was going through.

"I'm waiting for an answer," she chimed in, snapping him back to reality.

"She's dead, and I came to scatter her ashes. Are you happy now?"

"Who died?"

"Nanny."

"But how can that be? Henry Cummings didn't inform me."

"I asked him not to inform you. I knew what Nanny wanted. You never did."

"You have no right to speak to me like that, Sebastian."

"I have nothing else to say to you," he replied, turning to leave the room.

"Sebastian, if you walk out that door you will never be welcomed back into this family," she said, giving him the final ultimatum.

He knew it was coming and he welcomed it. "I don't need your family," he spat back. "You don't even like me. I'm just an unwanted reminder of your failed marriage and philandering husband. All I've ever been to you is someone to carry on the family name and tradition. I'm in love with Tess. She's all I need."

"What could you possibly know about love?" she asked with a shrill and cruel laugh. Lady Lily Irons was standing before him, judging him, demeaning him. "You're only eighteen years old."

His eyes met hers. "Nanny taught me all about love. I don't think you even know the meaning of the word." He turned on his heel and walked out of the room with his head held high.

"That whore upstairs will be your undoing!" she exclaimed. "You'll come crawling back, begging for my forgiveness." He was already halfway up the stairs, heading to his salvation. Lily's words simply rolled off his back.

Sebastian walked back into his room with a smile on his face. He was finally free. Any trepidation about the future was washed away by the fact that he no longer felt confined by his mother and her rules. Sebastian would find his own way in the world, just as Nanny had wished for him. He could ask Henry and Alice to help him, teach him how to run a household and balance a budget. For as long as he could remember, it felt as if a heavy steel anvil sat upon his chest. Now that the pressure was gone and he could finally breathe.

He found Tess fidgeting on the edge of his bed, fully dressed and expecting the worst. She stood up and he wrapped his arms around her.

"It's over."

She pulled back and looked at him with concern in her eyes. "Who won?"

"Are you packed? We need to go now," he told Tess. "I'll explain everything in the car."

"What happened to your face?" Tess exclaimed, noticing the red mark on his cheek.

"It's nothing." He brushed off the question. "Let's go."

Tess collected the few things strewn about the room and threw them in her bag. Sebastian buttoned his shirt and tucked it into his jeans, put on a black leather belt, and grabbed his suit coat. He placed his remaining toiletries in his bag and looked at his room one last time.

"Are you sure you have everything you need?" Tess inquired, standing beside him.

"Everything I need is right here," he replied, squeezing her hand.

In the course of four days he had lost his beloved Nanny, traveled between two continents, inherited a million pounds, made love to his beautiful girlfriend, laid Nanny to rest, and been disowned by his birth mother. It would have been the perfect plot for one of Nanny's romance novels, but Sebastian couldn't have made up this story if he tried.

He guided the rental car out of the driveway and pointed it away from the bad memories as they set course toward London. "What happened to your face?" Tess asked as the color began to fade from his cheek.

"Lily slapped me when I antagonized her. She disowned me. I'm glad it's over. I'm very happy never to have to see her again," Sebastian admitted.

"Disowned! Are you okay?"

"Tess, it's out of my hands. We'll deal with the fallout when we get back," he said, trying to reassure her. "I may be disowned, but at least I have Nanny's money to fall back on. I'm not destitute."

"Technically, you can live off the interest. You don't actually get access to all the money until you're twenty-five."

"Yes, darling." He turned to her briefly and winked.

"Don't patronize me. This is serious. Can you please be serious for once?"

"What are you upset about? I'm the one who just got kicked out of my family?"

"Exactly! What will we do now?"

"Considering we just left the castle fifteen minutes ago, I haven't had time to formulate a plan. We can fly back to America early, I suppose," Sebastian offered. He hadn't given any thought to where they would go other than putting as many miles as possible between them and the castle.

Tess took a deep breath. She wasn't helping the situation by hounding him for answers. She tried a new tactic: "I've got an idea. Let's go back to the hotel. We have a few days before we have to leave. Show me what you love about London."

Sebastian pulled off to the side of the road and bounced along the gravel and ruts until the car came to a complete stop. He turned off the ignition, quickly unbuckled his seatbelt, and turned to her. In one graceful movement he leaned over the gear shift and kissed her with great intensity.

"Wow, what was that for?" Tess sighed, after finally coming up for air.

"You are absolutely amazing. You always know exactly what to say to make me feel better," he beamed.

"Well, it seems a perfect waste to go back early. Furthermore, your mother did interrupt us and I was hoping we could pick that up again," she admitted, only slightly embarrassed by her newfound desire for Sebastian.

He kissed her again. "My God, I will throw you in the backseat of this car and make love to you right now if you keep talking like that," he whispered.

"That would be very interesting—not to mention illegal and cliché. I think we better get back on the road or I might take you up on it."

They pulled into The Savoy an hour later. The neon green art deco sign was a welcome sight. Sebastian left the car running for the valet to park it. He took Tess' hand and led her up the steps. The concierge greeted them. "Welcome back, Mr. Irons."

Sebastian nodded his head in acknowledgment and continued to the front desk. "Three nights, please," he said, pulling the billfold out of his breast pocket and offering his American Express card.

"Superior or suite?" the clerk inquired.

"Superior will be fine." He was doing his best to be thriftier. 'Thrifty' to Sebastian was to pay three hundred pounds a night for a room instead of seven hundred and fifty.

The clerk ran the card through to preauthorize it. He frowned and discreetly leaned over the counter. "I'm sorry, sir, the card has been declined," he announced in a low voice.

Of course it had been declined: Lily was serious when she said she would cut him off completely. He wondered if he would even have a home to return to in Pennsylvania. "Here, use this one." Sebastian handed over the Barclays credit card that was linked to his own bank account. The card was processed without issue and soon Sebastian held the shiny brass key for room 501 in his hand. The bellman joined them with their bags. The three of them rode the lift to the fifth floor in silence.

After entering their room, Sebastian handed him five pounds as a tip. The bellman bowed and closed the door behind him.

"I have to call Henry and Alice. If she canceled the credit card, it won't be long before she changes the locks on the house and I find myself homeless," he told Tess as he sat down at the desk and pulled the phone toward him.

"She wouldn't do that, would she?"

"Yes, she would." He picked up the receiver and dialed home.

"Hello?"

"Henry, it's Sebastian."

"I'm glad you called. What's happening there? We just had a call from a real estate agent asking to take a tour of the house tomorrow?"

"Have you heard from Lily yet?"

"No."

"You will be soon. I've been disowned. I won't be surprised if she fires you and changes the locks by the time I return," he explained. "I didn't mean to put your jobs in jeopardy, Henry. I'm very sorry if I caused you any pain."

"You don't have to apologize," Henry insisted. "Lady Irons hasn't even called me. You don't know what will happen."

"Can you ring a mover and see if they can come out today and pack up my room and Nanny's? Have them put it in storage until I get possession of the condo. I can settle the bill when I get home."

"I'll take care of it right away," Henry reassured him.

"If it all goes wrong, call me back at The Savoy—we're in room 501—or leave a message with Mrs. Hamilton. We'll be back in Philly Friday evening, just like you booked the original tickets."

"I'll be waiting at the airport for you."

"Goodbye, Henry, and thank you for everything." He put the receiver back into the cradle and stretched his back and neck.

Tess sat perched on the edge of the bed. "We need to talk about this. We need a plan." There was an edge to her voice. "What will you do if we get home and you really don't have a place to live anymore?"

"We only have three more months of school. I can rent an apartment or get a hotel room."

"You can stay at my house," she offered.

Sebastian sat down next to her. "I love you for offering, but I don't think it's a very good idea. Your mother may like me, but I doubt she'll allow me to sleep in your bed every night. And honestly, it will just be too hard to be so close to you and not be able to be with you like that." He changed the subject. "Now, you wanted to see what I love about London, right?"

"Yes."

"First, I love The Savoy—they have the most amazingly comfortable beds," he explained, shifting his weight to lie on his back, pulling her with him.

Tess stared at him with disbelief. "You just lost your family and you're thinking about sex?"

"It's more like I just gained my freedom and I'm thinking about sex," he corrected. "Weren't you the one who told me you wanted to resume where we left off?"

She slowly smiled and leaned in to kiss him.

The sun was beginning to set when they roused to shower and dress for an evening out. Sebastian was taking her to his favorite pub, The Coal Hole, for a pie and pint. After that they would be off to the Gielgud Theatre to take in a West End play. It was a lovely night, so they decided to walk to the pub as it was only a few blocks away.

Sebastian opened the heavy wooden door to The Coal Hole and Tess stepped inside. The ceiling was high with heavy black beams. Medieval banners hung from the walls; below the beams was a beautiful marble frieze of wistful maidens picking vines. Beside the long bar, in a corner, was a magnificent fireplace decorated with a rustic wooden mantel. They grabbed a small table in the corner of the room near the fireplace.

A buxom server walked over straightaway to greet them. "Sebastian, I haven't seen you in months! How are you?" she asked, genuinely happy to see him.

"Siobhan, it's good to see you, too. I want to introduce you to my girl, Tess Hamilton. I've been studying abroad this year. This is my first time back in ten months."

"What can I get for you?"

"Tess will have a meat pie and Diet Coke. I'll have fish 'n' chips and a pint."

"Coming right up," Siobhan said and then headed for the bar.

The drinks were brought to the table. Sebastian took a long swallow of his draft.

Tess' eyes were roaming the room as she took it all in. "This is what I always imagined a London pub to be," she observed. "What a great place."

"I'm glad you like it. Wait until you taste the food."

Siobhan placed their plates on the table and Sebastian waited for Tess to take a bite of her meat pie. "Well, what do you think?" he was eager to know her thoughts on the British favorite.

She broke into the flakey crust with her fork, spearing a bit of potato and meat. The thick gravy dripped back onto her plate as she put it in her mouth. The bold flavors swirled around as she chewed it. She nodded with a smile. "It's good."

He reached for the malt vinegar bottle and splashed it over his fish and chips. Sebastian took a bite and smiled as if he were in heaven. "Oh, how I missed this. This is amazing. You have to try it." He put a chip on his fork and fed it to Tess. "Don't worry, I won't make you try the fish." Sebastian knew she refused to eat it.

She grimaced as she chewed the fried potato. "You put a lot vinegar on it!"

"I know, it's brilliant, isn't it?"

After the play, they walked along The Strand, back to their hotel. "I had a great time tonight. I forgot how much fun this could be," Sebastian admitted, putting his arm around her and leaning down to kiss the top of her head.

"I enjoyed my quintessential London night out. I'm glad you shared the places you love with me."

"I can't wait for you see what I have planned for tomorrow."

* * *

They lay in bed between the soft sheets, the duvet rumpled on the floor. Tess was gently running her hand up and down Sebastian's chest. "You're fantastic, you know that?" she said.

"No, I'm not. I'm terribly flawed, but you love me anyway." The light from the street lamps filtered in through the sheer curtains and lit his grinning face.

"What happened back at the castle between you and Lily? You never really went into detail."

"I did the exact same thing my father had done before me. She found me in bed with you, just like she found him in bed with another woman all those years ago. I think she put so much attention on me taking over Irons Electronics so I would turn out to be more like her and less like him. That didn't happen, of course. She said if I walked out on her, I was never welcomed back into the family. So I walked out."

"You're okay with that?"

"Yes. The moment I made that decision, I felt such relief. It's like I hadn't been able to breathe for years, and then there was this clarity and the weight was lifted. I don't know how else to describe it."

"Won't you miss your brother and sisters?"

"I was never really close to anyone but Sigourney. I can still see her in New York."

"I could never be as calm as you are right now, if I were in your position," Tess admitted.

"What can I do?" He shrugged. "It's a big relief to be out from under her thumb. God bless Nanny. Without her, I'd be penniless—and I assure you I wouldn't be so calm."

"What was that address you gave the lawyer the other day? Then you said something to Henry about a condo. I meant to ask you about it earlier, but you distracted me."

The time was finally right to tell her about the condo. "Remember how you were worried about the living expenses at NYU?"

"Yes," she said nervously.

"Well, I started looking at the numbers for two people to attend NYU for four years. When I saw the total and shared it with Nanny, she suggested I take that money we would have spent on temporary housing and buy something instead." He waited a long moment, trying to judge her reaction.

She mulled over what he said and finally said, "You bought a house?"

"Actually, a condo—with two bedrooms," he quickly added. "Move in with me. You'd have to have a roommate in the dorms anyway. Why not have a roommate who you already know and love?"

She was shocked. He had put so much thought and action into this while she had just been stressing over it. "Can I talk to my mom before I give you my answer?"

"She's on board," Sebastian informed Tess.

"What? You talked to her about this!"

"Yes. I wanted her to know how much I care about you and that I would always be there for you. She was happy to know you wouldn't be alone in New York City. She thought it was a good idea."

"That's what you two were talking about in the kitchen when you were quoting whatever dead poet it was." The clues were there and she only just realized it.

"Yes, and the dead guy was Tennyson," he corrected her with a smirk. "You don't have to give me an answer right now about living together, but I hope you will seriously consider it."

"I can't believe you waited this long to tell me! That happened weeks ago."

"I was going to tell you that next day, but Penny showed up unexpectedly." He tried to defend his actions.

"And the ensuing weeks after that?"

"The time never seemed right. I guess I was too afraid you would say no, and I wasn't prepared for that let-down."

"I wish you wouldn't keep things from me, Sebastian—especially not now."

"You're right. But it is rather ironic coming from you when I had to beg you to tell me how you felt about me." With that he let the conversation drop, and she was more than grateful. She needed some time to digest this.

* * *

The next morning Sebastian escorted Tess through the mazes of underground subway tunnels known as the Tube. They ended up at Pimlico Station and walked a few blocks to the Tate Gallery, one of Sebastian's favorite museums in London.

Tess looked up at the imposing stone building, with its white columns and numerous steps. Seems all they had done that day was walk up and down stairs—no wonder no one in the city seemed to be overweight. "It reminds me of the Met," Tess said as she began to climb the steps.

Sebastian took her arm and pulled her back. "Well, then I guess I have to kiss you," he said with a devilish grin before his lips touched hers.

"If you're going to kiss me on every set of stairs we take today, you'd better get out your Chapstick."

They walked into the marble atrium. "Welcome to the Tate. Here you'll find the world's most extensive collection of Pre-Raphaelite paintings in the world." He ushered Tess to the right and continued. "Today you will see works by William Holman Hunt, Edward Burne-Jones, Ford Madox Brown, and Dante Gabriel Rossetti."

"Why do English painters always have three names?" Tess wondered aloud.

"I have no idea. I never really thought about it."

The art lesson continued as Sebastian enthralled Tess with stories of the artists and their muses. He was happy to share his passion with her and she seemed eager to learn.

"You're really good at this. Did you ever think of working in a museum?" she finally chimed in during a break in his lecture.

"No, this is just something I love. I never thought about it as a job."

"That's exactly why you should do it for a living—you love it and it doesn't feel like a job. I bet any museum in New York would love to have you on staff."

He gently caressed her cheek, beaming. "I love you."

"Come on, I want to look in the gift shop."

They split up; Sebastian headed for the art books and Tess walked over to the posters. She flipped through the large metal rack until she stumbled onto one of Sebastian's favorites. Tess grabbed the rolled poster tube from the corresponding slot below and paid the cashier. When she was finished, she found Sebastian.

"What do you have there?"

"A present for you," she replied, handing him the tube. "It's a poster of Edward Burne-Jones' *The Golden Stairs*. And before you complain, it only cost five pounds—and the real painting is not for sale, so the copy will have to do. You need something to hang in that condo of yours."

He was touched by her simple gift and gave her a hug. "Our condo," he whispered before releasing her from his embrace. "Thank you, Tess."

For the next few days, Sebastian acted as Tess' personal tour guide. They visited The National Gallery at Trafalgar Square and took a cruise along the Thames. They even had a fun outing at the London Zoo—it had been a favorite of Sebastian's since he was a child. They walked through Hyde Park and lingered in front of Buckingham Palace with the tourists who were hoping to catch a glimpse of the Queen or the changing of the guard. Sebastian never really appreciated his hometown until he saw it through Tess' eyes. She was filled with excitement, wonder, and awe. This was the least he could do for her, since she had become his constant companion since Nanny's passing.

They sat together on a bench along the Thames overlooking Parliament and Big Ben. The sun was bright and the clouds were few. It was a perfect day—a rare occurrence in London.

"I can't believe how beautiful this is," Tess commented. "I wish we could stay here forever."

Sebastian had passed this spot many times, but until Tess drew it to his attention, he had never really noticed. He had a fresh perspective, and he realized there were many wonderful things about his country that he took for granted. Too bad he wouldn't be back for a very long time, he reflected. His future was in America. He took her hand and turned her to face him. "Tess, I have no idea what I did to deserve you. Marry me and I swear I will adore you every day for the rest of our lives."

"Yes," she simply replied, without hesitation.

Sebastian looked at her quizzically. It was the first time since he'd met her that she had no doubts or trepidation. He couldn't believe what he'd heard. "What?" he asked, needing to hear the simple word again.

Tess sat on Sebastian's lap and placed her hands on his face. "I said, yes."

"Yes!" Pulling her closer, he kissed her. Then panic set in. "I don't have a ring!" he gasped.

"I don't need a ring, Sebastian. I said yes because you didn't plan some grand event or fairytale moment to propose to me. It was spur-of-the-moment, sincere, and from the heart." She let out a melancholy sigh. "We've lost so much already. I don't want to wait any longer. Life's too short. I'll marry you. I'll move into the condo with you."

Chapter 18 - Time For A Change

The plane touched down in Philadelphia Friday evening. Henry and Alice were waiting for Sebastian and Tess at the baggage claim carousels as planned. Henry snatched their bags and they all walked out to the parking garage.

"How bad is it?" Sebastian inquired.

"It's not good," Henry responded, confirming Sebastian's fears.

"Well, go on," he encouraged.

"Edgewood is for sale. Lady Irons has allowed Alice and me to stay there for the next four weeks until we can find new employment or a new place to live."

"That was generous of her," Sebastian muttered.

"She's had all the locks changed and has forbidden you access. She's hired a live- in groundskeeper to keep tabs on us and make sure we don't let you on the premises. Your car has been returned to the dealer and she terminated the lease."

"She's an evil woman," Alice chimed in with contempt.

"Alice and I found an efficiency apartment a few blocks from St. Alexander's for two hundred and fifty

310

dollars a month. This way you won't need a car. You'll be moving into the condo after you graduate, so hopefully you can deal with the apartment for a few months. It's nothing fancy, but it will be a roof over your head," Henry conceded.

Sebastian was astounded by their care and concern. They had no idea Nanny had left him a substantial amount of money, even if most of it was tied up in investments. The fact that they used their own money to make sure he would be okay showed a loyalty that he would never forget.

"I'm so sorry," Sebastian apologized. "I selfishly put myself before you. I never stopped to consider you would be residual fallout."

"It's done," Henry said.

They set off from the airport in silence.

Henry pulled up to apartment complex half an hour later thanks to relatively light traffic. He reached into his front pocket and pulled out a key. "Here you go," he said, and handed Sebastian the key.

They walked up the cobbled pathway, and Sebastian opened the door with caution and slowly entered his new home. He flipped on the nearest light switch. Alice, Henry, and Tess followed a few paces behind him. The walls were a dingy white. The single room had a slightly worn tan carpet and one small window looking out onto the street. Alice and Henry had moved his bed, night stand, TV, and stereo into the room. There was barely enough room to walk with his belongings furnishing the space.

Sebastian took in his surroundings. There was a small galley kitchen to the right of the entrance. The floor was yellow vinyl, dull and grimy from age. The walls were painted an off-putting shade of avocado green. The cabinets were made of white metal and it was all topped off with a Formica green speckled countertop, circa 1970.

On the other side of the kitchen wall was a narrow hallway that contained a tiny clothes closet and the bathroom. The bathroom walls were adorned in pink tile. The floor was covered in small black and white hexagonal tiles. There was a standard white toilet and tub. Suspended from the ceiling was a silver metal bar, which held a clean plastic shower curtain.

Although the unit was definitely dated, it was immaculate and clean; Alice and Henry had done a great job turning it from a bland space into a home. Sebastian turned and hugged them both simultaneously. "Thank you so much. I love you both." He knew that these two people had ceased being employees to him and had become family a long time ago, and he was grateful more than words could describe.

Alice kissed him on the cheek. "That woman has been a real witch. If you look in the kitchen cabinets you'll find the china, crystal, and silver from Edgewood. I've tried to make your stay here as comfortable as possible. Oh, and there are two cases of champagne under the sink, that were left over from the New Year's party."

"Alice, you're magnificent."

"There's still a lot to sort out, Sebastian. We'll come over tomorrow morning to make plans," Henry said.

"I'll make breakfast," Alice piped in. "Nine o'clock?"

"Perfect," Sebastian agreed.

"Tess, are you ready to go?"

Tess glanced at Sebastian.

"Please stay one more night. It's late. I don't want you driving home alone." Her car was still at Edgewood, so it would be a long night of driving back and forth. She nodded in agreement.

"We'll bring your car over tomorrow morning, Tess," Henry reassured her.

"Thank you, Henry."

Sebastian locked the door after Henry and Alice departed. Tess was already on the phone calling her mom. The answering machine picked up, so she left a quick message and hung up the receiver. Sebastian sat next to her on the bed—there was nowhere else to sit. "So here we are."

"I can't believe Henry and Alice did all this over the span of three days," Tess commented in utter amazement. "You're so lucky to have them."

"I know. I can't lose them, too. Do you think I can persuade them to move to New Jersey?"

"Maybe." Tess yawned. "I'm tired and hungry and I'm dying for a hot shower."

"You go have a shower and I'll see what Alice left in the refrigerator."

"You could come with me," Tess invited, taking his hand.

"If I come with you, we won't get to eat or sleep," Sebastian reasoned as he tried to back away.

"I know." She gave him a sly smile and pulled him down the hallway toward the bathroom. He didn't need much convincing.

They lay in bed naked under the ivory sheets, Sebastian holding Tess in his arms. "I don't want to let you go. I don't want to be alone," he whispered in her ear, taking in the scent of shampoo from her damp hair.

"I'm going to miss waking up with you in the morning," Tess admitted. "When do you make settlement on the condo?"

"June. Are you willing to move with me then? Won't your mom be expecting you to spend the summer at home?"

"I don't know. We have a lot to talk about. Come to dinner tomorrow night. We'll talk to her together. We can tell her about the engagement."

"Really?"

She nodded.

"Can we set a wedding date? You can have whatever you want—money is no object. I'll rent St. Patrick's Cathedral. We'll get you a couture wedding dress." He was so excited, he squeezed her in his arms.

"I want to wait until we graduate NYU," she slowly responded, hoping not to upset him.

"That's four years away!"

"Yeah, but we're going to have to get used to living together. Adjusting to college is something else we have to worry about. You can't go spending all the money Nanny left you. We can't have an extravagant wedding," Tess explained, trying to illustrate her point.

"So you never dreamed of your wedding day: the dress, the church, and the flowers? Every girl dreams about that, don't they?"

"I'm not every girl, Sebastian." She leaned in and kissed him on the lips. "I love you and I will marry you, but first I need to focus on college. I want to graduate and begin my career."

"Then tell me your plans for world domination," he prodded, deciding to drop the subject of the wedding for now.

"I want a journalist position that will let me travel. I want to see the world and write about it." She looked up at his face. "What are your plans? Have you given any more thought to working for a museum?"

"I'll raise the children and be a house husband, like John Lennon."

She raised her eyebrows with great curiosity. "Oh, really? And how many children will I be having?"

"Two: a boy and a girl. We'll name the girl Martha, after Nanny. We can call her Mattie for short—that way she won't be ostracized by the children at school."

"And the boy?"

"What was your father's name?"

"William—his name was William."

"Then William it is," he agreed with pride. "Let's forget the wedding. Let's go to the justice of the peace. We can keep it simple and very inexpensive," he suggested.

"Stop! I want the wedding! But I want to plan. I want to do it right. I only expect to do this once in my lifetime."

"What about next summer? I want to marry you now and you want to wait four years, so maybe we can meet somewhere in the middle," he suggested. "We'll have three months off. We can plan a small wedding and then we can spend two months traipsing through Europe for our honeymoon. We can even get a Euro rail pass and stay in budget hotels if you're worried about expense."

She smiled at the thought of his grand plan. It was certainly appealing. "Maybe. Let's see how things go over the next year," was all she could manage.

It appeared they had reached some sort of compromise as they drifted off to sleep.

The alarm sounded at 8:00 a.m. Sebastian reached over and hit the top of the clock with the palm of his hand. Tess nuzzled into his chest. "Good morning," he muttered. "We should get up. Henry and Alice will be here in an hour."

"All right."

"I need caffeine. Do you think Alice nicked the coffee pot, too?"

"You go start the shower. I'll start the coffee."

He sighed with relief. "Good—I don't know how to make coffee. I have a lot to learn, don't I?" He slowly got out of bed. Tess chuckled as she watched his naked ass saunter down the hall.

They showered and washed away the morning haze under a trickling stream of hot water. Padding back to the bedroom wrapped in soft Egyptian cotton towels kindly proffered by Alice, they dried off and dressed for the day. Tess slipped into her jeans and cardigan; Sebastian wore his jeans and a navy plaid shirt, which was uncharacteristically untucked.

He walked into the kitchen, barefoot, and poured himself a cup of hot coffee. He inhaled its rich aroma and took a sip. "This is delicious." He placed an arm around Tess waist and gave her a squeeze. "You're the official coffee preparer. I bow to your perfection and complete competence."

"It's not rocket science. It's just coffee. If you read the directions on the package, you can make it too," she reminded him, holding the metal coffee can up to his eyes with one hand.

Alice and Henry knocked on the door, jarring them from their chatter. Sebastian unlocked the dead bolt and let them enter. Alice was carrying an overflowing bag of groceries and Henry was holding the metal bistro table from the greenhouse. Sebastian slipped on his shoes and helped Henry bring the table inside.

Alice joined Tess in the kitchen. "I put some coffee on," Tess told her. "Want a cup?"

"Thank you, Tess." Alice unpacked the bag and placed the items on the small counter. One by one she pulled out a dozen eggs, a pound of butter, a variety of cheeses, a loaf of bread, a bottle of orange juice, and finally one very expensive French copper omelet pan. "Lady Irons won't be needing this either," she remarked with a smile.

In the other room, Henry and Sebastian unfolded the table and set up the four chairs. It took up the only remaining floor space in the small room.

"How did you sleep last night?" Henry inquired with a knowing smile.

"Well, thank you." Sebastian hesitated, then said, "I don't know what I'm going to do tonight when Tess has to go home and I'm left alone. I've never been alone before, Henry."

"Sebastian, I wanted to tell your mother off so badly, but Alice stopped me. She said we could help you more if we stayed on Lady Irons' good side instead of alienating her," Henry tried to explain.

"You did the right thing. You need time to figure out where you'll go next. Do you have any idea?" He sat down at the table and placed his coffee cup on top of it.

"You know, Manhattan is a big place with a lot of rich people. We thought we might try our luck in the Big Apple. I hear they have these great condos in Lincoln Harbor."

Sebastian couldn't believe they would do that for him. "I would love that. You and Alice are my family now. I am going to need you both to teach me how to have a normal life. How to cook, clean, balance a budget, be a good husband." He rattled off the list of things and waited for what he said to sink into Henry's brain.

Henry sat there and processed it item by item. It took perhaps a minute or two, but slowly a smile broke out on Henry's lips. "You asked Tess to marry you?"

Sebastian nodded. "She said yes, Henry."

"Congratulations!" Henry slapped him on the back. He stood and squeezed into the narrow busy kitchen. Henry took a bottle of champagne out of the refrigerator and plucked four crystal flutes from the cabinet above the stove. "Ladies, I need you in the other room now, please."

They put down their breakfast preparations and Tess and Alice followed in Henry's wake. He stripped the foil and popped the cork and poured a glass for each of them. "To Sebastian and Tess—may you have a beautiful life together." They raised their glasses to toast the pending nuptials.

Tess left the apartment a few hours later to go home and fill her mother in on everything that had transpired since

Nanny Jones' death. Henry and Alice remained behind with Sebastian to discuss the future.

Taking control of his life for the first time felt good. Sebastian began by arranging to repay Henry and Alice the money they'd put out for the apartment, the movers, and the storage space. They set up a budget for him to follow and then went over a list of things at Edgewood that he might need. Lily might have kicked him out of the house, but Henry and Alice would make sure he had all the things necessary to live on his own and in as much comfort as possible.

Tess and Mrs. Hamilton arrived at the apartment around five o'clock. He answered the door with a broad smile. He was dressed in a gray suit accented with a light blue striped silk tie. "Welcome to my new temporary home," Sebastian said as he opened the door for his soon-to-be mother-in-law. "I know it doesn't look like much, but it is home." He was embarrassed to be seen in this light—embarrassed they had to pick him up because he no longer owned a car. It was hard for him to think of himself as young male adult when he relied so heavily on others.

Kate smiled, placing her arms around him to give him a hug.

"I'd give you the tour, but you can stand right here and see everything," he told her shrugging his shoulders. "Shall we go to dinner?" He felt awkward and wanted to leave quickly.

They sat in the corner of the local Italian restaurant at a round table. They started with Caesar salad, and selected baked ziti with sausage for their main course. It was served family style. They finished their salads and were waiting on the entrée to be served. Mrs. Hamilton chose this pause in dinner to say what was on her mind. "Sebastian, you've had a grueling week. It appears you've handled everything well. I just wanted to let you know that if you need anything, please don't hesitate to ask."

Funny that you should mention that, he thought to himself before he cleared his throat and began. "I couldn't have gotten through this past week without Tess. Thanks for letting her come with me to London."

Mrs. Hamilton gave a melancholy smile. "Losing someone you love so dearly is never easy. I do understand what you're going through."

"I know you do." He took a deep breath. "I love Tess, and I asked her to marry me. I hope you can support that decision, too."

"I was staring at the same decision you are right now when I was eighteen. You know the path I chose, and I don't regret it for a minute. I trust you both." She looked back and forth between them. "I know you realize that this commitment is not an easy decision. I think you're strong enough to deal with the good and the bad."

Sebastian let out a sigh of relief. Tess took his hand under the table. "Thank you so much. I think you're the only mother in America who would be so understanding."

"I couldn't be a hypocrite, you know. I believe you two are meant to be together. I'm very happy for you. Just promise not to make me a grandmother too soon." It came out as a little more of an order than a light-hearted joke. She raised an eyebrow to soften the comment a bit.

"Mom! You're going to have to wait a long time for that," Tess exclaimed. "We have to graduate college and start to make a living first."

"I assure you there will be no children in the near future. Tess will need to win the Pulitzer Prize first," Sebastian chimed in. "I think she has the timeframe for our life already written down, so I'm powerless to argue." He gave Tess a crooked grin.

Tess looked at him and smiled. "Yeah, the Pulitzer."

The entrée was brought to the table in the nick of time. It provided a welcome relief from talk of babies. Tess quickly spooned a large portion of the cheesy concoction onto her plate and took a bite. It was their cue to dig in and so they did, nary speaking a word as they enjoyed their dinner. They left room for dessert, of course. The house specialty was homemade tiramisu, and they enjoyed each and every bite of the rich chocolaty decadence. When they finally had their fill of good food and pleasant conversation, Kate drove Sebastian back to the apartment. He thanked her again, kissed Tess on the cheek, and wished them a good evening.

Tess watched as he walked, alone, back to his front door. Her mother sensed her sadness. "He's never been alone before, has he?" Tess shook her head. "Go spend the night with him. I'd still like to you stay at home during the school week, but you can spend the weekends with Sebastian."

Tess reached over and hugged her mother. "Thank you! You're amazing."

"I'm not going to be like my mother, who forbade me from seeing your dad. I always want to be a part of your life with Sebastian. I'll pick you up tomorrow night."

Tess jumped out of the car and raced to Sebastian's door. She knocked frantically until he opened it.

"What are you doing?" he asked with great surprise.

"I don't want you to be alone. Mom said I could stay."

He picked her up and swung her around her around in a circle. Mrs. Hamilton smiled and slowly pulled away.

Monday found them back in school, sitting at the lunch table with Courtney and Jordan. So much had transpired since the last time they eaten lunch together. Sebastian didn't want to go through three more months of high school before he could move on to his new life with Tess, but he had no other choice.

"Where did you disappear to? I called your house and your mom said you went away for the week," Courtney inquired.

Tess looked at Sebastian, unsure how to answer. He gave a nod as if to say it was okay to tell them. "I was…" she stopped mid-sentence and grappled to find the right words to explain. There was a strange vibe at the table and Jordan and Courtney waited impatiently for her to finish.

Finally Sebastian stepped in and saved her by saying, "She was with me in England burying my mother, who passed away last week." It hurt him to say it aloud. The words were a glaring reminder that she was really gone. Tess placed her hand on top of his as a sign of support.

"Oh God, I didn't know. I'm sorry," Courtney apologized. She and Jordan surmised every conceivable notion as to why they disappeared—from being arrested to going on a bender in Atlantic City to eloping in Vegas. The reality had never entered their minds.

"If one more person says they're sorry to me, I think I'm going to bloody scream," he whispered, standing up. "Excuse me. I need to get some air." He walked toward the double doors and then stepped outside, inhaling the fresh spring air.

Tess shot Courtney an annoyed glance.

"I'm sorry!" Courtney blurted. "If I could take it back, I would."

Tess stood, snagged her books, and went out of the door after Sebastian.

Jordan turned to Courtney. "I told you something intense was going on with those two."

"His mom just died, Jordan! Tess knows what it's like to lose a parent, remember?"

"Yeah, I remember," Jordan shot back.

Sebastian was sitting on a bench in the quad. The air was chilly for the end of March, but felt good against his skin. He tried to think of anything but Nanny in an effort to stop himself from breaking down in front of his classmates.

Tess found Sebastian and sat next to him, placing her arm snugly around his waist to provide some measure of comfort.

"It seems so pointless to be here, Tess. She's gone. I'm living in an apartment the size of a shoebox. Yesterday I felt optimistic. Today I don't know what the hell I'm doing," he admitted feeling helpless. "And then those two girls…"

"You don't get over the shock in a week. I'm sorry to tell you, it's a long a painful journey," she sighed. "I should never have suggested we stay in London. We should have come back sooner to let you start adjusting."

He turned to face her and took her free hand in his. "No! Don't apologize. I needed that time with you—to be with you like that. It was the only way I was able to make it through the week," Sebastian explained. "I feel like a manic depressive. How did you deal with the ups and downs?"

"I set up a schedule for myself. It gave me consistency and a goal to work toward. It helped keep my mind busy so I didn't spend so much time thinking about my dad."

"We already have a schedule. So what you're saying is we have to keep doing what we've been doing for the past eight months?"

She smiled. "With some slight variations," she whispered in his ear, hinting at the prospect of more lovemaking.

Finally he smiled, too. He couldn't help it. He leaned down and kissed the top of her head. "I guess we should go back inside before we get in trouble. The last thing I need is detention."

Chapter 19-Never Tear Us Apart

Friday arrived at last. It had been a roller coaster week for Sebastian: he was dealing with the highs and lows of his new life. Today he was happy because Tess would be spending the night with him.

Sebastian busied himself cooking his first dinner for her. He was preparing a simple dish: penne tossed with fresh vegetables, garlic, and olive oil with a focaccia bread he'd purchased at a local bakery. The bistro table was dressed to create a romantic mood with a centerpiece of fragrant red roses and white taper candles in the center. The china, silver, and crystal all gleamed by the candle's soft glow. Sebastian amazed himself with his ability in the kitchen, thanks mainly to Alice's tutelage. He simply couldn't wait to see Tess' reaction to his efforts.

It was close to 7:00 p.m. when Tess walked into the apartment. "Hey," she greeted, placing her overnight bag on the floor. She noticed the romantic dinner table. "What's all this?" she asked, strolling into the kitchen and coming up behind him.

"It's my meager attempt at domestication and saving money. Do you approve?"

"I'll let you know after I taste it," she playfully replied, kissing him on the cheek.

Sebastian turned off the stove. Escorting Tess to the table, he pulled out a chair for her and she sat. Within moments, he placed a basket holding cut pieces of bread and a large, colorful bowl of steaming hot pasta on the table. After being sure that Tess had her Diet Coke in hand, he poured himself a glass of red wine. He sat down across from her and waited for her response.

"You made this?" she asked with surprise, looking up from the fragrant bowl in front of her after tasting the pasta.

"Yes," Sebastian replied cautiously, assuming the worst. "Is it that bad?"

"No! It's really good," she quickly complimented, digging in for another bite.

"Alice showed me how to make it."

Changing the subject, Tess asked, "Have you called Sigourney yet?"

He slowly shook his head. He was hesitant to call her: he didn't know how much Lily had told Sigourney.

"You should call her, Sebastian. Just because you choose not to have a relationship with Lily doesn't mean you can't still have one with your sister."

He sighed aloud. He knew she was right.

"Call her, then you can visit her tomorrow," Tess continued.

"But I was going to spend the day with you."

"Well, I have to spend the morning at school prepping the final proof for the yearbook, remember?"

"I forgot," he replied dejectedly. Sebastian watched as she sat back and grinned at him. He threw his arms up in the air. "Fine, you win! I'll call her after dinner."

Before he had time to deal with his nerves, Sebastian found himself in front of Sigourney's Park Avenue brownstone late in the morning on Saturday. Tess' car idled softly as he willed himself to shut off the ignition. He exited out of the car and climbed the stone stairs with trepidation, each step slower than the last, still unsure if visiting her was the right thing to do.

He eased the door open to the delicate sound of a piano concerto. Sebastian tossed Tess' keys on the antique vestibule table and walked through the heavy wooden doors into the sitting room. Sigourney stopped playing and turned toward the door. She jumped off her padded piano bench and rushed over to hug him. "What the hell did you do to make Mummy disown you?"

"It's good to see you, too," he remarked sarcastically. Sebastian ambled to the drink trolley and poured himself a glass of fifteen-year-old single malt scotch. Moving to the sofa, he sat, inhaled his scotch deeply, took a sip, crossed his legs, and then looked back up at her.

"Will you please talk to me, Sebastian?" she asked in her kindest voice. "You wouldn't tell me anything on the phone last night."

He craved a cigarette, but Tess had finally persuaded him to quit. He took another sip of scotch; it felt good going down. The cigarette craving hadn't gone away, but the scotch soothed his nerves. "Nanny died a few weeks ago."

"What? Mummy didn't say anything about that! What happened?" she demanded.

Sebastian shook his head in sadness. It still didn't make sense to *him*—how was he going to explain it to his sister? He decided to just dig in and get through it without pausing. "She passed away in her sleep. She wanted her ashes scattered in the rose garden at the castle. I took her home and Lily showed up."

Sigourney tried to process what she had just heard, but was too shocked. "You didn't tell Mummy that Nanny passed away?"

Sebastian sensed the discomfort and turned his attention to his nearly empty scotch glass. "I did tell her."

"Then why did she disown you?"

"She walked in on Tess and me. We were making love in my bedroom."

Sigourney's hand flew over her mouth. A smile crept onto Sebastian's face.

"I take it Lily left that part out when she phoned you?"

"Poor Tess," she replied. Sigourney thought for a long moment. "What were you doing having sex with Tess if you went home to bury Nanny?" she blurted loudly.

"Don't say it like that," he shot back.

"Like what?"

"Cheap and tawdry, like my only concern was shagging." He took another sip of his scotch, emptying the glass. He glanced in it forlornly and looked back up at his stunned sister. "You weren't there when I found Nanny dead. You have no idea what kind of grief it caused or how intense the experience was." Sebastian placed his glass on the nearby side table as he stood up to stretch his legs and collect his thoughts. "Tess was there for me through the whole thing. She lost her dad when she was fourteen years old. She understood the pain I was going through. It just happened. I didn't plan it," he explained.

Sigourney let a minute pass as she digested the information. "So Mummy gave you the ultimatum—the family or Tess. You chose Tess." Sigourney looked at him with amazement. "Bravo, Sebastian. You truly do love her. But what will you do now? How will you live?"

Sebastian walked toward the floor-length windows. Pushing the curtains away, he peered outside. The Chevette sat quietly, looking very out of place parked in this exclusive neighborhood. Maybe he could persuade Tess to trade it in for something a little more suitable when he got back home. "Nanny had a will and left me some money."

"Well, I'm glad you're not destitute," she stated with relief. "What about university? What about your education?"

"I'm going to NYU. There was enough money to pay for that."

Sigourney cheered up instantly. "You'll be in the city so I can see you more often!"

"Yes, but I really prefer you keep that information to yourself. I've made a clean break from Lily. This is my life, and what I do with it is none of her damned business," Sebastian warned her, sitting back down. "Can you keep your mouth shut?"

Sigourney nodded in agreement. "You know that I'd ask you to stay here, but I'd be in a heap of trouble if she found out. I'm sorry."

"No need to apologize. I'm going to be just fine. What exactly did she tell you, if you don't know any of this?" he inquired.

"She just rang me and said I wasn't to talk to you or give you any money. She said you were no longer a part of this family—full stop."

"Well, I suppose you just broke one of those rules."

"What Mummy doesn't know won't hurt her. She's in Japan. There's no chance she'll happen to pop by," Sigourney reassured him.

He leaned in and gave his sister a long hug. "Thank you. I would miss you if I couldn't see you anymore."

"Me too. You seem truly happy. Is there anything I can do to help you?"

Sebastian sat back and pondered her request. "Actually, there is. Take a walk with me down Fifth Avenue."

"What are we shopping for?"

"A ring," he simply replied.

"You're going to ask Tess to marry you?" Sigourney burst with excitement.

"I already asked her and she said yes, but it was spur-of-the-moment and I didn't have a ring."

"Sebastian, how dare you not plan and make it special for Tess," she admonished. "A proposal should be over-the-top and memorable!"

"The proposal was perfect and Tess said yes because it *wasn't* over-the-top. It was from the heart."

"I expect to hear every detail of this while I guide you through Tiffany's."

They walked down Fifth Avenue enjoying the bright sun and the gentle April breeze. Sebastian looked dapper in his navy Armani suit and silk tie. Sigourney had dressed in a brown Diane von Furstenberg wrap dress. They looked more like Wall Street employees than casual shoppers. She laced her arm through Sebastian's as they sauntered down the avenue, and he described his time spent in London with Tess and recounted the marriage proposal in full detail, much to his sister's delight.

A uniformed doorman opened the door as they approached and entered Tiffany & Company. They browsed the aisles of display cases, politely refusing numerous attempts at assistance. "What do you think?" Sigourney prodded, pointing here and there, eyeing up the beautiful diamonds sparkling under the lights.

Sebastian frowned. "I'm not sure."

"Do you have any idea what type of ring you're looking for?"

"I'll know it when I see it." He looked away from the final case and at his sister. "Let's go to Cartier."

They walked a few blocks further down Fifth Avenue until they reached their new destination. Again they perused the glass cases in search of the perfect ring. Sebastian had spied a case holding three rows of glittering engagement rings. That's where he found it—second row, third from the left. It was as if it had called to him. "I'd like to see that one," he informed the hovering saleswoman, pointing to his choice.

The clerk unlocked the case with a set of keys she withdrew from a hidden pocket in her suit jacket. She gently lifted the tray toward her so she could remove the ring. She placed it on a black velvet tray and set it down on the counter.

"That's a lovely choice," the saleswoman complimented.

Sebastian picked up the ring and examined it. It was a half-karat Asscher-cut diamond set in 18-karat gold. The diamond was square with beveled corners, secured with four gold prongs. The cut gave the illusion of a hall of mirrors as the reflection carried on into the depths of the diamond. It was simple and elegant—perfect for Tess. He turned to his sister, who nodded her approval.

Less than fifteen minutes later, Sebastian was holding a little red Cartier shopping bag and they were back on the sidewalk. They looked up and down the street for a taxi, but none were available. "Let's have lunch," Sigourney suggested instead.

"I'd like that, but you're buying, dear sister. You still have the stipend from Lily," Sebastian reminded her.

"Splendid! Let's go to the Russian Tea Room."

They turned and casually strolled along the avenue, glancing at window displays and commenting on the latest fashions and trends.

They lunched in a way that Sebastian could no longer afford, and he savored every morsel. They enjoyed Russian Osetra caviar with warm belini and vereniki— Russian ravioli. Sigourney filled Sebastian in on her upcoming recital at Juilliard. She played the role of tour guide and educated him on the hot spots in the city that he should visit once he moved to New York in the fall. He didn't have the heart to tell her he and Tess would be living in New Jersey and commuting to the university so he joined with her in her excitement. Somewhere in the back of his mind, he felt as if he had to keep a few secrets about his future plans in the event Sigourney accidentally let something slip to Lily.

After lunch, they took a yellow cab back to Sigourney's Park Avenue address. Sigourney and Sebastian hugged each other on the sidewalk and said their goodbyes. Tess had promised to make dinner for him as an enticement upon his return for making this visit to New York. He was eager to get home to his fiancée, with or without the food.

Three uneventful hours later, Sebastian was back at the apartment. The wonderful aroma of roast chicken filled his nostrils as he opened the front door. He quickly entered, softly closing the door behind him. Sebastian padded across the small room to the kitchen and then pulled Tess close. She was standing over the stove tending the meal and allowed herself to be enveloped in his arms. He kissed her softly on the neck—once, then twice, letting his lips linger.

"How was your day?" he inquired, feeling like a husband home from work.

"Good. We put the yearbook to bed and sent it off to the printers. How's Sigourney?" Tess asked, turning to face him.

"Good. It was nice to see her. Thanks for suggesting it." He smiled at her, pulling her close again.

"Are you hungry? Did you have lunch in the city?" Tess asked him after backing him away from the hot stove and tossing the tea towel she was holding onto the counter.

"Yes. We had caviar at the Russian Tea Room." Sebastian released her and took a few steps to the other side of the kitchen. He opened the noisy refrigerator door and pulled out a carafe of chilled water.

Tess scrunched up her nose at the thought of caviar. "Oh, please don't take me there."

Sebastian laughed. "Don't worry, we can't afford it anymore. Sigourney paid." He poured a glass of water and replaced the carafe in the refrigerator.

He walked out of the kitchen and put a record on the turntable. It was Bryan Ferry's *Slave to Love*. Tess followed him and she was soon swept up in his arms, dancing to the music.

"Are you enjoying this?" she helplessly inquired as she was twirled around in her jeans and sweatshirt.

"Very much so," he replied with a smile.

She nuzzled her face against his neck and whispered, "I love you."

"Okay," he replied, before dramatically dipping her as the song ended.

Tess giggled. "That sounds ridiculous."

"Believe me, I *know*."

They sat at the small bistro table eating the meal Tess had prepared. They dined on the fine china using the best silver. It seemed almost absurd to dine with such frivolity as they were eating the meal in a one-room efficiency. Sebastian had never been happier in his entire life. These moments with Tess only confirmed he'd made the right choice to ask her to marry him. They might be young, but their love was real. He was certain they could weather any obstacles that would come their way. They ate in a comfortable silence, occasionally glancing at each other and smiling.

"What?" Tess prodded, staring curiously at his toothy grin.

"I'm blissfully happy," he replied, reaching out across the table to take her hand.

"Your day in New York was that good?"

"No, it's not New York—it's you."

"I feel the same way about you." She stood up and walked around the table. He pushed his chair back and she took a seat on his lap. Sebastian took her chin in his hand and pulled her closer until their lips touched.

After a long and tender kiss, he slowly pulled away and asked, "Did you happen to make any dessert?"

Tess frowned. "All you can think about is dessert?"

"Well, maybe later," he muttered, kissing her again, running his fingers through her soft curly hair.

"Much later," Tess agreed as she settled into his embrace.

Tess lay in bed on her side, her head propped up in the palm of her hand. "So tell me what happened in New York."

"I told Sigourney about the trip to London. She promised she'd keep her mouth shut. If Lily catches wind Sigourney is talking to me, she'll disown her too."

"It's not fair," Tess sighed.

"That's just how it is. I did tell her we're getting married, though."

"And?'

"And she's very happy for us, although I did get scolded for my pathetic proposal."

"It was perfect," Tess smiled, reminiscing. "I think it was the most romantic thing you've ever done for me."

"That's exactly what I told Sigourney. And she said she won't forgive us if she isn't invited to the wedding."

"There you go with that wedding talk again."

"I'll continue talking about it until we set a date."

"What date did you have in mind?" she asked, semi-annoyed at his insistence.

Sebastian rolled over and opened the bedside table drawer. He withdrew a bound leather date book. Flipping through the pages, he pointed his finger at a date. "May twenty-seventh, 1987. Freshman year will be finished and we will have the whole summer to enjoy our wedded bliss," he beamed.

Tess shook her head. He would not let up until she committed to a date. "I can't do it. I'm sorry, Sebastian." She stood and pulled the top sheet off the bed, wrapping it around her body. She walked to the tiny window and gazed outside, staring at nothing in particular.

"Why are you afraid? You agreed to marry me the first time I asked you. Are you having second thoughts?" Sebastian was confused. He had no idea what was going on in her head. He tried not to panic.

"We're so young. College is going to change everything. What happens if we grow apart or fall out of love? I think it would be smarter to wait before we make it legal. I mean, marriage—that should be forever, right?"

"Exactly. It *will* be forever." Sebastian walked over to her and kissed her forehead. "I don't expect it will be easy, but there is nothing in this life that I'm willing to fight for more than us."

Tess turned to look at him, uncertainty filling her face.

"I meant what I said in London. Marry me and I swear I'll adore you every day."

"Let me get accustomed to living with you full-time before you ask me to start planning a wedding." Tess didn't want to hurt his feelings—she just needed him to understand how overwhelmed she felt. "I can only do one thing at a time. I need to graduate high school, move in with you away from my mom, and settle in at NYU. I need to do this methodically. It's just how I am."

Sebastian grabbed a pen and paged to the back of his agenda until he found a blank piece of paper. He jotted down her list in order then added at the end—plan our wedding. He walked over to her and placed the list in her hand. "See? It's not so difficult. I'm not delusional, Tess. I know marriage will be the hardest thing I'll ever do. Well, that is until we have children," he added.

"Yes. If marriage is hard and requires my full attention, then how am I going to get through college with a 4.0 GPA?"

"Four years from now I could be dead," he said matter-of-factly. It might have been cruel, but he hoped it would get his point across.

"Don't you ever joke about that."

"I'm not joking. Your mother is right—life's too short. None of us knows what will happen. I want to be your husband, and I won't wait four years for it to fit into your day planner, Tess," he said in a raised voice.

"Don't pressure me. I'm stressed enough!"

"An hour ago we made love. It was amazing and exciting and you cried in my arms because you were so happy." He paused and gave her the most intense gaze. "There are only two things in this life that I've been absolutely sure of: first, Nanny's unconditional love for me. Second, we are meant to be together for the rest of our lives."

"Can we compromise?"

"What do you propose?" he asked with suspicion.

"Give me until December. I'll make a decision at that time."

"Okay, I can wait until December," he agreed. "But I just want to let you know, if you agree to a May wedding, I'll do all the planning. You can concentrate on college and all you have to do is just show up in your wedding gown on May twenty-seventh."

"Sebastian, I truly love you, but please, please, no more wedding talk," Tess begged.

"Until December," he agreed, against his better judgment. Hell, he would have married her right there, right then, wrapped in bed sheets. But he also knew that to deal with Tess, he had to compromise. He desperately wanted to give her the diamond engagement ring he had bought earlier in the day, but now was not the time. Timing was everything.

Chapter 20 - Life's What You Make It

May had arrived and it would be only a few short weeks before finals and graduation. The four friends sat at the lunch table discussing the prom.

"So, are you two going?" Courtney asked, directing her question toward Sebastian and Tess.

They answered simultaneously.

Sebastian said, "Yes."

Tess said, "No."

They turned and looked at each other with surprise.

"Communicate much?" Jordan teased.

"You don't want to go?" Sebastian asked.

"No," she simply replied.

"You have to go. It's senior prom!" Courtney exclaimed.

"Why do I have to go?" Tess challenged.

"Don't be melodramatic," Jordan interrupted, and then turned to Courtney. "Who are you going with, Courtney?"

"Jack Thomas," she answered. "I guess you're going with Jeff?"

"Yep," Jordan confirmed.

Now Courtney, Jordan, and Sebastian were looking at Tess as if she were from a different planet. The bell sounded, signaling the end of the lunch period. "Saved by the bell," Tess muttered, standing up from the lunch table with a sigh of relief.

"We'll talk about this later," Sebastian announced, guiding her by the elbow to her next class.

"Yes, later," she agreed, coming to the end of the hallway. She turned left to go Advanced Placement Calculus. He turned right for his chemistry lab.

Tess drove them back to the apartment after school. The tension level was palpable in the cramped car. He could understand her hesitation in agreeing to set a wedding date, but the prom, he just did not understand.

"Will you come inside so we can talk?" he asked opening the passenger door, trying to break the mood.

She removed the key from the ignition. Tess grabbed her backpack full of books and diligently locked the car door. Silently, she followed him inside.

Sebastian took off his St. Alexander's blazer and threw it haphazardly on the bed. "Why don't you want to go to the prom, Tess?" His tie landed next to the blazer.

"Sebastian, look around you. We're in an efficiency apartment that comes with bills and responsibility. We have no jobs. The only reason you have money is thanks to Nanny Jones, who had the foresight to make some wise investments. This is our reality. Senior prom just doesn't seem that important."

"But isn't it some rite of passage? I've seen the John Hughes movies. Won't you feel as if you missed out on something monumentally important if you don't go?"

"Life isn't a John Hughes movie!" she said in exasperation. "I've worn couture to dinner at Tavern on the Green. Do you really think dry chicken and a DJ could ever live up to that? Why do you care? You don't have this antiquated function in England anyway."

He pulled her into an embrace, his annoyance abated. "God, I love it when you talk high fashion," he cooed. "Nothing could ever compare to Tavern on the Green. But tell me, if you hadn't met me, would you have gone to prom?"

"I don't know, Sebastian. Probably not. I mean, who would want to take the serious smart girl? I'm the girl everybody thinks doesn't have a life or doesn't know how to have fun," she explained.

"First, you have a wonderful life and I *know* you know how to have fun," he beamed with a mischievous grin. "You are the sexiest and smartest girl I've ever met and I would be honored if you would accompany me to the prom."

He was grinning from ear to ear, being her charming Sebastian. "Damn you. You won't let this go, will you?"

"No. I want to show off my sexy, gorgeous fiancée at the dance. Please go with me?"

Tess rolled her eyes. "Fine, you win—but only because you agreed to not talk about the wedding until December."

He leaned in to kiss her. "See? Compromise is fun."

* * *

The prom was being held at the Evergreen Country Club. They started the evening at Tess' house. Mrs. Hamilton was grinning at the two lovebirds.

Sebastian was wearing his favorite custom-made gray suit, a white shirt with shiny cuff links, and a navy paisley tie. He knew it wasn't the normal prom attire, but he didn't care. He looked ten times better than any of his fellow students would look in their rented tuxedos with pants that were too short and sleeves that were too long. His hair was parted neatly to the side and flawless.

Tess couldn't take her eyes off him. He looked so handsome. She couldn't believe he belonged to her. Tess decided to wear her Calvin Klein strapless dress, which she paired with black one-inch-heel pumps and nude stockings instead of the black silk stockings and Manolos that drove him wild. She could barely walk in the stilettos—how was she going to be able to dance in them? She didn't want to draw too much attention to herself when she walked into the room wearing couture while everyone else was wearing puffy teal gowns from the Deb Shop. Her hair was pulled up in a twist, showing off her bare neck. She wore the diamond earrings Sebastian had bought her for Christmas. Any pangs of regret she had about going to the prom were washed away when she saw the look of joy on Sebastian's face.

"You two look so incredible. My baby girl is all grown up," Mrs. Hamilton admired. Tess turned pink from embarrassment. Tess' mother grabbed the camera and took a few quick shots. "Okay you two—outside. I want to get some pictures in the sunlight."

Kate ushered them out the front door and stood them in front of the dogwood tree. Sebastian instinctively placed his arm around Tess' waist. "You look wonderful," he complimented in her ear. "Thank you for doing this for me."

Tess turned to look up at him and smiled. "You're welcome." The picture was snapped. "Mom, I wasn't even looking at the camera!"

"I know, Tess. It's called a candid shot," her mother replied with laughter. She went on to snap a series of shots as they played it up for the camera. Sebastian even acted as photographer to take a picture of Tess and her proud mother.

* * *

Half an hour later, they were seated in the Chevette, driving to the County Club. Sebastian had wanted to rent a limo to take them to the prom, but Tess had put her foot down and insisted they take the Chevette. He agreed to her frugality, if only to avoid and argument. Being in a relationship with Tess was trying at times, but there so no other person he'd rather share this journey with.

They entered the ballroom and got in line to have the obligatory photo taken under a white pergola draped in silk flowers. Tess found their table: it was round and seated three couples. Courtney and Jordan were their tablemates. Sebastian pulled out a chair so Tess could take a seat.

Jordan and Courtney looked at Tess with their mouths open in awe.

"Please wipe the look of shock off your faces," Tess mumbled, taking a seat.

"You look amazing, Tess," Courtney complimented.

"Where did you find that dress?" Jordan asked.

"New York," she replied without enthusiasm.

"It must have cost a fortune. When did you have time to go to New York when you weren't even sure you were coming to the prom a week ago?" Jordan inquired.

Sebastian was enjoying this way too much. "I bought her that dress back in November," he answered.

"Sebastian…" Tess began, but was cut off by a chaste kiss on the lips.

Courtney and Jordan raised their eyebrows in unison. Jordan held out the palm of her hand in front of Courtney's face and wiggled her fingers. "Pay up."

Courtney grabbed a five-dollar bill from her clutch and placed it in Jordan's hand.

"What the hell was that all about?" Tess asked with an irritated tone of voice.

"We had a bet on whether you and Sebastian were a couple of not."

The comment amused Sebastian and he found himself laughing. "You could have just asked," he told the girls.

"Tess would never fess up, Sebastian."

"Then you should have asked me," he countered, coyly.

"So how long have you two been together?" Jordan asked outright.

Sebastian glanced at Tess, waiting to see if she would respond. "Don't stop now, you're on a roll," Tess told him.

He looked at Jordan. "Define 'together.'"

Tess sighed aloud and stood up from the table. "I'm going to the ladies' room."

Jordan ignored Tess and continued her conversation with Sebastian. "How long have you been kissing her?"

"November."

"Wow. She never said anything. Why?"

"Because she wanted our relationship to be private. She didn't want it detracting from our education," Sebastian explained. "Look, you don't know what I had to do to get her to agree to come tonight. I wanted her to have this experience. So far she is having a miserable time—please back off a bit."

Tess arrived back at the table and sat down.

"Here comes dinner," Sebastian noticed as the waitstaff began to enter the room with trays of food.

After dinner, the curious crowd watched as Sebastian escorted Tess to the dance floor. He was used the attention—it was no different from the paparazzi in London; only no one here took pictures. There were whispers among the crowd. They couldn't believe Sebastian's date was Tess. By some miracle, Tess was no longer the dowdy, scholarly bookworm. She was now the beautiful swan in the perfectly fitting, very expensive dress. He sensed Tess' discomfort and pulled her into an embrace as the DJ put on a slow dance record.

"Everyone is staring at us," she said, nuzzling her head into his chest, trying to hide from the glances of her fellow students.

"They're just jealous," he reasoned.

"You're enjoying this," she muttered.

"Immensely."

"Enjoy it, then. We're hitting the books tomorrow to study for final exams."

"Yes, darling, but tonight you're mine." He leaned in and whispered in her ear, "You don't happen to be wearing the La Perla lingerie I bought you at Bergdorf's?" Even though he had purchased it six months before, he had yet to see her wear it.

She looked up at him with a wicked grin. "What if I am?"

"Oh, then I think we will have to leave this party a little earlier than intended."

"In that case, I can confirm I am wearing it. But you have to take off the dress to see."

He closed his eyes and let out a low moan. Taking her by the hand, he escorted her off the dance floor. In no time, they collected her purse from her chair and all but ran out ballroom to get back to his apartment. He wasn't sure if the ploy was intentional on Tess' part, but it certainly worked. Sebastian had no desire to stay until the end of the prom when he could spend a quiet, romantic evening in bed with his girl.

They spent the next week taking their final exams. Friday was their last day of high school. The graduation ceremony would occur the next Tuesday evening in the gymnasium. Sebastian and Tess didn't have time to celebrate, because he had to pack up the efficiency and Tess had a valedictorian speech to write. Sebastian understood how important this speech was to Tess, so he began the packing alone, allowing Tess time to work on her speech.

Sebastian pulled his leather overnight bag out of the closet and placed it on the bed to begin his task. He'd have to be out of the efficiency by the week's end.

Tess was sitting on the bed, bent over a notebook open on her lap, working on her speech. She scratched out what she'd written and rewrote it repeatedly. Tess refused to start the speech earlier due to the rigid study schedule for final exams. It didn't really matter what her final test scores were—it wouldn't change her NYU acceptance or that fact that she would be number one in her class. She had worked too hard and it meant too much to her. She would pour everything she had into this speech.

Sebastian opened the bag and found the corner of an envelope peeking out of the inner pocket: the letters for Nanny. He had forgotten about them. *How could I have forgotten*, he asked himself? He sat on the corner of the bed, trying not to disturb Tess, and removed them from the bag. Carefully, Sebastian opened his letter, anxious what might be inside. A small, square, black-and-white photograph fell onto his lap. Sebastian picked it up and turned it over. The man in the photo looked just like him, but it wasn't Sebastian. The date printed on the scalloped edge read *July 1965*. The man wore tennis whites. He stood in front of the main fountain at the castle, water splashing behind him. Three children sat on the ledge of the fountain wearing wide smiles. "Oh my God," Sebastian whispered as he realized what he was looking at.

Tess put down her tablet and peered over his shoulder. "What is it?"

"My father," he said, unable to take his eyes off the image.

"You look just like him," Tess observed. "Why are you so shocked?"

"This is the first picture I've ever seen of him," Sebastian explained, his breath shallow and quick.

"Really?"

"I told you Lily banished him from our lives. There were no pictures in the house. Like father, like son," he mused, staring at the image of his young father. "Growing up, no one ever talked about him. The little I do know was thanks to Nanny."

"So where did the photo come from?" Tess wondered sitting next to him.

"Nanny." Sebastian unfolded the letter and read it aloud.

My darling Sebastian,

You are well on your way to being the best person you can be. I'm so very proud of you, my son. Remember the things I taught you and use them well.

I know growing up without your father has been difficult for you. Even though I was able to explain what transpired to cause your father's departure from your life, I know you had so many more questions that I could not answer.

I promised Lady Irons I would never divulge your father's name while I was employed by her. As you read this, I am gone, and you deserve to know the truth. You are the spitting image of your father, Martin Christopher Baker.

When he disappeared from our lives, I don't know where he settled. I hope his name will be a starting point if you choose to start a search to find him.

Have a glorious life, my dear boy. I love you more than anything in the world.

Nanny

Sebastian stared at the letter and tried to catch his breath. The news was unbelievable and he was having a difficult time processing it.

"So Irons is Lily's last name? Your brothers and sisters, what name do they use?" Tess asked in confusion.

"Irons. I guess Lily had it legally changed after the divorce. Max and Victoria never talked about it. Sigourney was too young to remember."

"That seems pretty extreme. It must not have been easy to accomplish back in the sixties."

"Not that difficult when you come from a powerful family and have unlimited resources," he reminded her. Sebastian handed Tess the letter that Nanny had left for her.

Tess opened her letter. It was simple, brief, and to the point—just like Nanny's personality. She read it aloud as well.

Dearest Tess,

When Sebastian asks you to marry him, say yes.

He will love you forever.

Sincerely,
Nanny Jones

"How did she know? Did you tell her?" Tess asked.

"I didn't know I was going to ask you to marry me until the question spilled out of my mouth. It wasn't planned—you know that. I guess she just knew," Sebastian reasoned. He reached for Tess' hand and intertwined his fingers with hers. "Do you really believe there is an afterlife, a place where people you love move onto after they die?"

"Of course I do."

"Do you really believe it, or was it just engrained into your brain as a child? I was never raised with religion."

"That's why they call it faith, Sebastian."

"But this is odd, don't you agree? It's as if Nanny is talking to us from the grave."

"It's a gift. Don't question it."

"If it's such a gift, then why didn't she just tell me what to do? Why did she leave the decision to find my father to me?"

"That's called free will."

"Please stop with all the religious mumbo jumbo. I just want you to tell me what to do," he pleaded.

"It's not my decision to make." Tess thought on the matter, and then said, "But if I were you, I think you should focus on the immediate future. Let's graduate, move into the condo, and begin college. Think about your options. You'll be in America. You're going to need someone in England to do the leg work for you if you decide to pursue this. I don't know what it would cost. But if you want to find your father, I think you need to be in London. Are you willing to do that right now?"

She was right. When he couldn't think clearly, Tess could. He had gotten along without his father for the first eighteen years of his life. He could certainly wait a few more. All he desired right now was to start his life with Tess. He leaned in and kissed her on the lips. "Thank you."

Graduation took place in St. Alexander's gymnasium. Kate Hamilton beamed as her daughter delivered the valedictorian speech to the bright and eager faces of the future. Henry, Alice, and Sigourney applauded Sebastian as he walked across the stage to receive his diploma. After the ceremony, the group settled in for a late dinner at Giovanni's Italian restaurant. They sat at a large round table dressed in a red-and-white checkered tablecloth with an open bottle of wine.

"Kate, you must be very proud. Tess gave a wonderful speech," Sigourney complimented.

"I am," Kate agreed. "I'm glad Sebastian has family so close and that you were able to be here for him today."

"Are you two heading to any graduation parties tonight?" Henry asked after sipping from his wine glass.

"No, we just wanted a small celebration with our family," Tess explained. "We get possession of the condo tomorrow, so we didn't want to be out late."

When dinner was finished, Sigourney, Henry, and Alice said their goodbyes. Mrs. Hamilton hugged Sebastian and Tess in unison. "Good luck with the settlement tomorrow. I'll see you on Saturday."

Sebastian sat on his bed, happy the long day had drawn to a close. "Well, Miss Valedictorian, do you feel different?" he inquired as he unlaced his dress shoes.

"Yeah, I do."

"How so?"

"I feel like that chapter of my life is over and I'm really excited about our next step together," she explained, sitting down next to him.

"I, for one, will be very happy to never let you leave my bed again."

She playfully pushed him over. He fell back onto the bed and she moved on top of him. "I'm ready to celebrate now," she purred, kissing the corner of his mouth.

Sebastian didn't need to ask her what she meant as she reached down and felt his excitement growing. Tess put the same energy and determination into her lovemaking skills as she did any other skill she was determined to conquer and master.

"Practice makes perfect," she reminded.

"You certainly are perfect," he agreed between kisses, pulling her hair back into a ponytail to keep it from tickling his face.

In the morning, Tess accompanied Sebastian to Margo Milton's office. After a few hours of signing form after form in the presence of his attorney, Margo handed Sebastian two shiny silver keys to his new home.

He parked the Chevette in the underground garage and took the elevator to the fourth floor. Sebastian took the key out of his pocket and unlocked the door. He swept Tess up in his arms and walked over the threshold.

"What are you doing?" Tess laughed, holding onto his neck.

"I'm taking you inside our first home," he replied, stepping into the living room.

The condo was modern, with tall, exposed ceilings. Behind them was the kitchen with a breakfast bar. It had a gas range, microwave, double-door refrigerator, and dishwasher. It was very different from the old, dodgy galley kitchen in the efficiency. A spiral metal staircase extended up to a loft over the kitchen. He took her by the hand and pulled her up the stairs. "This will be perfect for your desk. A tranquil place where you can study."

Once back downstairs, they walked to the master bedroom. It had sliding glass doors that lead out to a concrete balcony which overlooked the Hudson River. There was enough room there for a small table and chairs. Sebastian planned to put their little bistro table there. The master bedroom was complete with an en-suite bathroom that had a sunken spa tub with a separate shower stall. There was a double vanity, so they wouldn't have to share or shove each other out of the way on hectic mornings. The toilet sat in a little closet for privacy. It seemed the bathroom was nearly the size of the entire efficiency apartment where they'd recently resided.

The second bedroom was smaller and was separated from the master by another bathroom. "Your mom can sleep here when she comes to visit," he announced, opening the bedroom door.

When they finished looking at all the rooms, they walked into the living room, where the focal point was a floor-to-ceiling window with a stunning view of Manhattan.

"What do you think?" he asked with anticipation, hoping she would love it as much as he did the first time he laid eyes upon it.

"I love it," she smiled. "I love you."

"Are you afraid?" he whispered.

Tess shook her head. "No, I'm excited."

"Me too," he agreed, leaning down to kiss the crown of her head.

Sebastian and Tess stood arm in arm in front of the full-length plate glass window, admiring the view of Manhattan. Today was the first day of next chapter of their life together. It would be filled with ups and downs, triumphs and tribulations, new experiences and many firsts. Whatever came their way, they would face it together. After all, life really is what you make it.

About the Author

Theresa Troutman lives in Pennsylvania with her husband and their crazy dog, Niko. She loves reading, theatre, traveling and is an active member of the SCBWI.

Other titles by Theresa Troutman:

My Secret Summer
A Special Connection
Love This Life:
Love's Great Adventure Series Book 2 will be released
Summer 2014.

Connect with Theresa:

https://www.facebook.com/theresa.troutman.author
Twitter: @theresatroutman
website: http://theresatroutman.wix.com/theresa-troutman
https://plus.google.com/u/0/11566896553962827815
5/posts
http://www.pinterest.com/theresa4503/

40306460R00217

Made in the USA
Charleston, SC
30 March 2015